KEPT SECRETS

A Whispering Pines Mystery, Book Two

Shawn McGuire

OTHER BOOKS BY SHAWN MCGUIRE

WHISPERING PINES Series
Missing & Gone (prequel novella)
Family Secrets, book 1
Kept Secrets, book 2
Original Secrets, book 3
Hidden Secrets, book 4
Rival Secrets, book 5
Veiled Secrets, book 6
Silent Secrets, book 7
Merciful Secrets, book 8
Justified Secrets, book 9
Secret of Her Own (novella)
Protected Secrets, book 10
Burning Secrets, book 11
Secret of the Season (novella)
Blind Secrets, book 12
Secret of the Yuletide Crafter (novella)
Wayward Secrets, book 13

HEARTH & CAULDRON Series
Hearth & Cauldron, book 1

GEMI KITTREDGE Series
One of Her Own, book 1
Out of Her League, book 2

THE WISH MAKERS Series
Sticks and Stones, book 1
Break My Bones, book 2
Never Hurt Me, book 3
Had a Great Fall, book 4
Back Together Again, book 5

KEPT SECRETS

A Whispering Pines Mystery, Book Two

Shawn McGuire

Brown Bag Books

Copyright © 2017 Shawn McGuire
Published by Brown Bag Books
ISBN-13: 978-1979311021
ISBN-10: 1979311021

For information visit:
www.Shawn-McGuire.com

First Edition/First Printing November 2017

For my Brunch Bunch.
Aimee, Becky, and Kristy, your unfailing support and
never-ending brilliance means the world to me.
Love you, ladies!

Chapter 1

AS THE MID-JUNE SKY TURNED from dusk to dark, I smiled, amused by the nine-foot-tall clown wandering from pine tree to pine tree, switching on the solar lanterns that hung from random limbs. A dude on stilts; that answered my question as to how they powered up the lanterns. Some that automatically turned on as the light started to fade would be more practical, but this was far more entertaining.

For nearly a month I'd heard about the Whispering Pines circus. Today, I finally got to experience it for myself, alongside my friend Tripp Bennett.

"Do you want to ride the carousel next," Tripp asked, "or get caramel corn?"

This carousel was the most amazing I'd ever seen. The double-decker beauty had two rows of animals on the bottom, one on top. Like nearly any other merry-go-round there were horses, but this one also had rabbits, reindeer, camels, lions, cats, giraffes, frogs, and goats. For those who couldn't climb up on an animal, there was a swan-shaped bench and a submarine that looked like it had come straight out of a Dr. Seuss undersea fantasy.

"No question, the carousel." I pointed to the upper deck. "I've been eyeing that zebra every time we pass by."

"Zebra it is." He pointed out the iridescent animal just behind my intended transport. "I'm going to ride that purple-blue-green seahorse-dragon thing."

While we waited for both of our preferred creatures to be free at the same time, we watched the sideshow acts scattered along the midway. No one could miss the tall woman, she had to stand at least seven feet with red hair that hung almost to her knees. She was dressed like a puppeteer, holding strings attached to a one-armed little boy who pretended to be her marionette. They were absolutely charming.

A few yards away, a man balanced on a large ball while juggling flaming torches. Wary parents maintained a wide perimeter, encouraging the juggler while holding their children back to avoid any fire mishaps.

"I can't believe he's blind," a teenage girl said as she and her family wandered past.

"The juggler?" I asked.

"The juggler," the father said. "Isn't that incredible?"

It was, but no more so than anything else around here.

Across the red-brick-paved midway from the juggler, a woman hung by one leg from a hoop that was suspended between two large pine trees. She spun so fast she was a blur, and then in a blink of an eye, she was spinning by one hand. And then by only the back of her head. She mesmerized me with all the contortions she put her body through. As her routine came to the end, her spotter lowered her to the ground where she waved and bowed to the crowd. Then her spotter approached her with a wheelchair we hadn't even noticed.

"Look at her," I said as she positioned her right leg on the footrest. "She can only use her left leg. I couldn't have done what she just did if I had four superhuman legs."

"We're up." Tripp took my hand and led me up one short staircase to the carousel platform and then to another that led to the top deck.

We rushed like excited children to our rides. A little girl pouted when she saw me mount the zebra, but seemed to forget about it when she spotted a white unicorn with a beautiful flowing mane a few spaces up.

I looked behind me to see Tripp with a grin covering his face as his seahorse-dragon went up and down, the calliope music enveloping us in happiness. As the ride slowed to a stop — I swear, our turn lasted much shorter than the others — Tripp jumped off his mount and then helped me down. I patted my zebra on the rump and thanked him for the lovely ride.

"You ready to go home?" Tripp asked once we were back on the ground.

Before I could answer, a woman came up to us. *Early thirties, dark-brown hair in a braid hanging halfway down her back, olive skin, black-brown eyes.* Dressed in khaki-green cargo pants, a gray tank top, and hiking sandals, she looked like she had just stepped out of a South American jungle.

"Sorry to interrupt," the woman said with a slight Spanish accent. "I have a couple questions for you if you don't mind. My name is Lupe Gomez. I'm a journalist, working on a series of articles about Whispering Pines. I was hoping to get your thoughts on the circus. Who are you two? Do you live here or are you tourists?"

"I'm Jayne O'Shea," I said, "he's Tripp Bennett. I guess you could say we're temporary residents. We're doing repairs to my grandparents' house and getting it ready for sale. My thoughts on the circus? What's not to love? It's a circus."

"I agree," Tripp said. "There are people of all ages here, from tiny babies to older folks. I have yet to see anyone who didn't have a smile on their face."

I looked up at him. "Someone paying you to be the circus promo guy?"

"I didn't know there was such a job. Does it really pay?"

Laughing, I turned my attention back to the reporter.

"You said your name is Lupe? Who are you writing these articles for?"

"I work for an online Wisconsin travel magazine, *Unique Wisconsin*. Tell me, what's been your favorite part?"

"My favorite," I said, "had to be the big top performance."

"Oh, yeah," Tripp agreed, "that was great."

"Are you staying for the night performance?" Lupe asked.

"I don't think we need to see it a second time," Tripp said.

"The second performance is for adults only." Lupe winked and waggled her eyebrows. "If you know what I mean."

"An X-rated performance?" My face flushed as my proximity to Tripp suddenly felt far too close.

Lupe shook her head. "It's not X-rated, but the costumes are skimpier and the performances are racier and the atmosphere, well, go see for yourself."

"I don't think we should miss that." Tripp turned to me, suddenly bright-eyed and eager to see skimpiness. "Will Meeka be okay for another hour and a half?"

Meeka, my West Highland White Terrier.

"She should be fine," I said. "She had a very busy day of standing at the end of the dock and barking at every boat, jet ski, swimmer, and fish that went past. Then she chased some invisible something-or-other around the yard. She was so tired by the time we left, I think she was passed out on her cushion before I even closed the door."

"Then let's go watch the racy sword swallowers," he begged.

I paused, wondering exactly what that would entail.

"Before you go." Lupe held up a professional-looking camera. "Could I get a picture of you two for the website?"

I propped my hand on my hip and leaned against Tripp as he draped an arm over my shoulders. Lupe snapped a few shots, promising to choose the best one. I gave her my email address, and she said she'd send me copies.

"You two are really cute together." She smiled at the images on her camera's screen and then clamped a hand over her mouth when she saw my scowl and shaking head. "Sorry. Have fun. I'm sure I'll see you around. I'm here all summer."

We walked the length of the midway, past games and rides for little kids, to the big top and entered for the second time that day. For the afternoon performance, we had underestimated the number of people who would be there. We got there too late and had to sit at the far end. Not a problem this time, either we were really early or this wasn't as big a deal as Lupe made it out to be. The bleachers were practically empty.

It was the same tent, but the atmosphere felt very different from two hours earlier. Gone was the traditional circus setup, replaced with what led me to believe we were going to see a *Cirque du Soleil*-style show. The lighting this afternoon had been bright, animated spotlights. Now those spotlights were filtered to cast a rosy, romantic glow. Long fabric curtains, that served dual-purpose as a backdrop behind the three rings and a staging area for the performers, had also been swapped out. Earlier, they had alternating stripes of vibrant primary colors—red, yellow, green, and blue. Now, the curtains were black, red, ivory, and gold. Romantic French accordion music played softly in the background. I could hardly wait to see how this performance would differ from the family-friendly one we had already seen.

Tripp placed a hand on my lower back, sending shivers through me despite the hot evening air, and guided me toward seats right across from the center ring. He sat close to me, almost too close. I sure hoped this wasn't a mistake. The entire village of Whispering Pines was already sure we were dating. At least a dozen times since we got to the grounds this afternoon, I had to explain that we were only there as friends. Although Tripp made it clear he would like to be more, I wasn't ready to take that step yet.

Claiming the need for air flow, I scooted a few inches away and let out a slightly shaky breath. Why was I so jittery? We were two friends having fun at the circus. Maybe my sudden attack of nerves had nothing to do with us. I scanned the tent, searching for anything that could signal trouble. Nothing. It had to be all that *dating* and *together* talk people kept throwing at us.

I was an ex-cop, though, and always trusted my instincts. I'd stay alert, just in case.

Chapter 2

IN ADDITION TO THE SET change, the pre-show entertainment was drastically different as well. Instead of the earlier troupe of funny clowns in bright-colored clothing, the clowns here now were more like sexy jesters. The women wore short dresses or skintight bodysuits in traditional jester stripes or block patterns of red, black, and white. The shirtless men wore striped leggings that looked painted on and left little to the imagination. The jesters greeted people as they entered the tent, flirting shamelessly with everyone. We arrived a few minutes too early. They hadn't been there yet to greet us.

Tripp held his hand over my eyes when he saw me staring. I did the same when a woman in a very short black and red cancan dress, thigh-high black fishnet stockings, and wavy honey-blonde hair passed us on her way down the bleacher stairs. She carried a large pole with bags of caramel corn clipped all over it. A slowly spinning sign at the top of the pole read *$2 Each.*

Tripp stood to get the woman's attention. "Caramel corn!"

She turned, leaving us both momentarily speechless as we took in the long, full beard and thin mustache covering her otherwise feminine face. Then we both burst out laughing.

"I'm so sorry," I said. "You took me totally by surprise."

"My dear," the woman said in a very proper tone, "if I received a quarter every time someone gave me that response, I'd have enough razors to last me three lifetimes." She stroked her beard. "Don't apologize. I'm a performer. I chose this job because it brings people joy. The perfect profession for someone who has the body of a woman and the face of a man, don't you think?"

I nodded as Tripp pulled a bill from his pocket and handed it to her. "Two bags, please."

The bearded vendor gave him a wink and a wiggle as she stuffed the five-dollar bill into her cleavage and sashayed away.

"How embarrassing," I said as I opened my snack bag.

Tripp's eyes closed as he enjoyed a mouthful of corn. "You forget where you are. Everyone here is a little different."

He meant Whispering Pines in general, not just the circus. The Northwoods Wisconsin village had less than one thousand full-time residents, most of whom were followers of the Wiccan religion. During the summer tourist season, the population on any given day easily tripled. With its part-Renaissance faire, part-Medieval England feel, the cozy village next to a pristine deep blue lake was a magnet for tourists.

As we munched on our caramel corn, I scanned the big top again, both looking for anything suspicious and simply taking in the crowd. My initial feeling, that this performance must not be very popular, could not have been more wrong. The seats were filling rapidly.

To keep us entertained before the main event began, there were a few warmup acts in addition to the sexy jesters. Straight ahead of us in the center ring, a woman the size of an eight-year-old performed with lions. Throughout her act, a man hovered nearby with a tranquilizer dart gun. That was all well and good, but if one of the animals charged or decided to chomp down as it held the tiny woman in its mouth, it would already be too late by the time he fired the dart.

To our right was the same aerial artist who had been performing outside earlier, the one who surprised everyone by getting into the wheelchair. She had changed out of her simple leotard into a red bra-top, black hot pants, and fishnet stockings. I paid attention this time, noting that she did most of her tricks using her left leg, and if she used her right leg she held her foot to ensure it wouldn't release. Still, I was amazed at how good she was and wondered why she was only a warm-up act.

"Is anyone sitting here?"

I turned to find a teenage girl with long hair that couldn't seem to decide if it wanted to be straight or curly. The teenage boy standing next to her had the brightest white teeth I'd ever seen in my life.

"Hi, Lily Grace. Hey, Oren. Haven't seen either of you around in a while."

"This is the first free night I've had since the season started," Lily Grace said.

"I have nights free," Oren said, "but I'm usually too exhausted to do anything."

"Lots of business at the marina?" Tripp asked him.

"Every boat, wakeboard, and kayak has been rented every day this week." Oren's tired eyes were rimmed with dark circles. "I think there was a canoe and one windboard left today. I've never seen it this busy."

"That's got to make your dad happy." Tripp offered his bag of caramel corn.

"That's an understatement." Oren took a handful of corn. "I don't know how he can see anything through those dollar signs in his eyes."

"How about you?" I asked Lily Grace, the village's

youngest fortuneteller. "How goes the readings?"

"Thousands of satisfied customers." She kept a straight face for about two seconds before breaking. "More like a hundred. Just feels like thousands." She picked at the hot-pink nail polish chipping off her left thumb. "It's your fault, you know. I was all ready for a summer of gazing into a crystal ball and spouting all that scripted psychic stuff." She put her hand to her mouth, her eyes wide. "Oops. Did I say that out loud?"

"I see a journey in your future." Oren held his hand to his forehead. "I see someone with an R in their name. I see money."

"But is the money coming or going?" Tripp played along.

"Yes," Oren said, and the two of them burst out laughing.

Lily Grace gave her boyfriend a blank stare and arched one eyebrow. He clamped his mouth shut and folded his hands in his lap.

The day we met, Lily Grace told me she was a fortuneteller with no ability to tell a fortune. Then she took my hands and was struck by her first ever vision. Or so she claimed. I didn't believe in a lot of the stuff the Whispering Pines' villagers claimed was real—like fortune telling and witchcraft—but the residents sure did. In thanks for turning on her granddaughter's ability, Lily Grace's grandmother sent me a basket of scones and cookies from Treat Me Sweetly, the local bakery. Whatever had happened, I couldn't take credit for it, but I was happy to accept the treats.

"Are you as skeptical as your girlfriend, Mr. Bennett?" Lily Grace asked Tripp as she expertly wove her hair into a long braid. "Geez, it's hot tonight."

"I like to keep an open mind," Tripp said. "And don't call me Mr. Bennett. I'm not that much older than you."

"You're twenty-eight, she's seventeen," I said. "You're

practically a fossil."

"Then twenty-six must make you ancient," he teased back."

"Speaking of skeptics," I said, turning my attention back to Lily Grace, "you didn't believe in the ability either until you did that reading for me."

Ignoring me, Lily Grace held her hands out to Tripp. "Should I read you?"

"Now? Right here?" Tripp asked. "No, maybe another time."

"Okay." Lily Grace gave her characteristic, nonchalant shrug. "You know where I am."

We sat and watched the bleachers continue to fill toward capacity. Lily Grace was right, it was hot tonight. And the number of bodies was raising the temperature in the tent even more. The circus crew turned on large fans around the tent, creating airflow, but I was still overheated. I'd worn a sweater, not for warmth but because my peasant-style dress had a lowcut neckline that made me a bit self-conscious. I took off the sweater and tucked it beneath my seat.

"Don't let me forget that," I said and sat up to see Tripp appreciating my now-exposed cleavage. I pointed to my face. "My eyes are up here."

"I know where your eyes are." His gaze remained in the same place, and I swatted his shoulder to break his trance.

The lights blinked once, and the warmup performers bowed and scattered. Leah, the tiny lion tamer, directed the cats back to their cages. Once the animals were gone, the man with the tranquilizer gun pushed the tall sections of fencing that had kept the animals contained within the ring out of the way for the next acts. The large fans the crew had turned on were loud, so they turned off all but the one to our right. The murmuring of the crowd died down as the lights went dark. And then came a breathy, sexy, man's voice over the speakers.

"Ladies and gentlemen, the Whispering Pines Circus is pleased to have you join us for our evening show."

A spotlight snapped on and focused on the ringmaster standing just outside the center ring. *Approximately five foot eleven, slender, light-brown complexion, late thirties.* He was the same ringmaster from earlier, but his traditional black pants and red tuxedo jacket from this afternoon were gone. He now wore red and white striped leggings tucked into knee-high black boots. His body-hugging, red satin jacket with long tails gleamed in the lights. He wore nothing underneath, revealing his toned torso.

"My name is Creed, and I am your ringmaster," he said with pride. "I'll be your guide on a journey we're sure you'll not soon forget. Now, please welcome Dallas Brickman, our knife thrower."

Creed held an arm out to the center ring, firmly tapped his crystal-encrusted walking stick two times on the ground, and then gave a low bow. The spotlight on him went out, and others turned on to highlight the ring.

Dallas was dressed like a pirate and threw knives, swords, and small cutlasses at his victim, a beautiful woman in a wench costume with a heaving bosom. Like the other men, he was shirtless, sporting a six-pack that made it difficult to concentrate on his act. It took until halfway through it for me to realize his peg leg was a real prosthesis and not a prop. How many Halloween costume contests had he won with that peg leg pirate look?

All the performances blended seamlessly from one into the next. Before we knew it, the final act of the night was starting. Berlin, an aerial artist and the star of the show, appeared through a fog near the top of the tent where she spun slowly on aerial silks. Her bodysuit was the same color as her skin, giving her the appearance of performing naked. The lights glinted off a beautiful gold gilt mask that covered the right half of her face, her blonde hair twisted into a bun. Seemingly one with the fabric, she did mid-air twists and contortions, turning and arching her body beautifully before dropping into a splits position that would have ripped me in two. Then she started to spin like a ballerina in a child's jewelry box, the fabric billowing around her. Finally, Berlin climbed all the way to the top of the tent, easily fifty feet in the air.

"The silks aren't hanging right," Lily Grace cautioned. "See how they look like they're snagged on something?"

Fortunately, Berlin realized this as well. Dangling at the top of the tent, she pointed first at her silks and then at the one running fan. One crew person darted into the shadows and made an adjustment so the fabric hung free again while another turned off the fan. Once safe again, Berlin began wrapping the silks around her waist again and again. Suddenly, she plummeted downward, spinning faster and faster before stopping just inches from colliding with the ground. While it was a spectacular move, the spell of her performance had been broken, the full impact of the blazing freefall ruined by the snagging of her silks.

When she got to the ground, a visibly angry Berlin stepped away from the fabric and dropped into a low curtsy. The other performers came back out and formed a row behind her for a final bow. The lights dimmed on them and shone again on Creed, standing front and center before the audience.

"Thank you for joining us this evening. We hope you will return soon and that you enjoy the rest of your stay in Whispering Pines."

The lights went black in the tent for a few seconds and then slowly came back up as the audience cheered and started to file out.

Tripp pointed at the fan to our right. "Looks like it blew the fabric and made it snag on something."

"Probably that animal fencing," Lily Grace said from behind me. "Gianni is going to get his butt chewed."

"Who's Gianni?" I asked.

"The guy with the tranquilizer gun," she said. "He's the veterinarian and only person still encouraging me to go to vet school rather than stay here and be a fortune teller." She shot Oren a look. He must've wanted her to stay. "Anyway, Berlin has asked him dozens of times to move that fencing further back after Leah's act. I don't know if he forgets or if he's just stubborn."

"Berlin could've been seriously hurt." I stared at the offending fencing.

"It had to be an accident," Lily Grace said, as though convincing herself. "Gianni wouldn't intentionally hurt anyone."

"It's not out of the realm of possibility that someone has a problem with Berlin, though," Oren added.

My former-cop instincts sent tingles through me. "What kind of problem?"

"I don't want to say she's a diva," Oren began.

"That's because she's not a diva," Lily Grace snapped, cutting him off. "She's a strong-willed woman who's excellent at what she does. That doesn't make her a diva."

Oren gave Tripp one of those knowing guy-to-guy looks, and my instincts tingled again. Maybe life at the circus here wasn't all bright lights and smiles like it appeared.

Chapter 3

I PULLED MY CHEROKEE TO a stop in front of the garage next to Tripp's old F-350 pickup truck. Since the first day I got here, I'd been staying in the small apartment above the boathouse. It was perfect for me and my little dog Meeka. Tripp had been helping me with house renovations, so he moved his popup trailer from the campground near the highway to the side yard. Other than using the kitchen and the basement bathroom inside the house, he lived in that popup. He'd be fine over the summer, but if we were still here when winter came to northern Wisconsin, we'd need to make different plans for him.

"Today was a lot of fun," Tripp said.

A yawn snuck up on me. "It was."

We'd been working so hard on renovations, we both were dead tired at the end of each day, Tripp especially. When I brought up the idea of a Saturday afternoon away from the work, he was all for it.

We stood in the driveway now, him looking down at me, me looking out at the lake. Despite all the teasing today, and his desire to be more than friends, Tripp told me he understood my need to keep things platonic. He made me feel safe and cared for like a big brother or best friend. But there were moments, like this one, that filled me with confusion. As we stood there, close enough that our body heat was mingling, I knew if I looked up, the expression on his face would make my breath catch and my thoughts would wander to places *friends* didn't go.

I looked up—yep, there it was—and gave him a smile. "Good night, Tripp. See you in the morning."

"Night, Jayne."

I climbed the stairs that ran along the outside of the boathouse, crossed the sundeck to the set of French doors that served as the entrance to my little apartment, and found Meeka sitting on the other side glaring at me. The second I open the door, she burst out, tore down the stairs, and raced over to her preferred pee spot near the trees.

"Sorry," I called. "I didn't plan to be gone so long."

I leaned against the rail, waiting for her to return, and stared out at the lake. Moonlight glistened off tiny ripples, and a soft breeze blew against my face. I was originally only supposed to be here for a week. My assignment was to come up, go through Gran's house, and get it ready for sale. It was a big house—seven bedrooms, seven and a half bathrooms—so unless I had hired a team of people, there was no way it would have been ready in one week. When I found that someone had broken in and trashed the place, it took about a minute for me to know I'd be staying much longer.

There was also the issue of the dead woman in the backyard. Local law enforcement showed little interest in figuring out what happened to her. Being a former detective, I couldn't accept that so conducted my own investigation.

During my first week here, I met Tripp, Lily Grace, Oren, and a score of other people who were now friends. A few, like Tripp and Morgan Barlow, quickly became more than just friends. They were almost like family, but better. The last thing I'd expected was to fall in love with Whispering Pines. Now, I didn't want to leave.

Meeka trotted up the stairs again and right on past me,

still irritated that I made her wait so long. Inside, I pulled off my dress and tossed it in the hamper, slipped on an oversized T-shirt, and gave Meeka an apologetic belly rub before climbing into bed. As had become my routine, unless rain was coming in, I left all the windows and the doors open, screens pulled to keep the mosquitoes and other critters out. That meant I could fall asleep listening not only to the soft sloshing of the water in the boat garage below, but also the amazingly soothing sound of the wind whispering through the tall pine trees that surrounded the village like sentinels.

This was where I was meant to be, I had no doubt. The problem was, I also had no job. If my parents didn't agree to the bed-and-breakfast idea Tripp and I had proposed three weeks ago, the house would be on the market as soon as we were done with the renovations. Then I'd have nowhere to live and no choice but to return to Madison. There had to be a way for me to stay.

***

"It's looking really good in here," I said while climbing onto my standard stool at the kitchen bar the next morning.

"You're just trying to motivate me to remove more wallpaper." Tripp flipped a piece of Cheddar to Meeka while putting the finishing touches on a veggie and cheese omelet for me. Before landing in Whispering Pines, he had wandered the country, working miscellaneous jobs. One of them as a cook making home-style food at a diner. So, in addition to being able to fix just about anything around the house, he had wicked good kitchen skills.

"Is it working?" I grinned. "I keep telling you I'll help."

"You still have bedrooms to pack up. And you need to call that guy to come and get the furniture that needs refinishing."

"Damn. I keep forgetting about that."

I accepted the plate from him, held it out so he could add two pieces of thick rustic toast, and then set it on my placemat while pulling my cell phone out of my back pocket. I added CALL GUY ABOUT FURNITURE to my to-do list. Keeping notes and taking pictures was about the only thing a smartphone was good for around here. There was zero cell reception.

That lack of cell phone service was the initial theory for why the house had been vandalized. The previous sheriff had guessed that a group of teenagers, bored because they were forced to be off-line and out-of-touch, had decided to have a little fun. I agreed with him until I realized that what I thought was graffiti, painted in black ink on every wall downstairs, might really be malicious messages for my family.

Morgan Barlow identified the marks as sigils or magical witch symbols. She thought it was possible that someone had placed a hex on my family, so she was doing a little investigative work for me. I didn't for one minute believe in magic or hexes, but I did think someone had an issue with my grandparents, or more likely my family in general since Gran and Gramps were both gone now. Whoever had done this was trying to scare us off. Good luck with that.

As we did every morning, Tripp and I chatted while we ate breakfast, making a plan for what to do in the house that day. For the most part, I agreed to whatever he said. He knew a hundred times more about renovation than I did, after all.

"Will you stain the floors next?" I asked. He had already stripped the hardwood floors and covered them with heavy paper to protect them from damage.

"No, we'll do that last. Accidents happen and we won't have to do touch-ups that way."

"Works for me. Let me know what I can do."

Tripp remained quiet for a few minutes, seemingly focusing on his breakfast, but I knew what was coming next.

"Have you thought about furniture at all?" he asked. "Your grandparents' antiques are great. Is that the look you want to go with?"

"You know there's no point in worrying about decorating right now. We haven't gotten the go-ahead from my parents yet."

The more I thought about our plan for a bed-and-breakfast, the more I liked the idea. While becoming a B&B caretaker had never occurred to me before, it was the perfect way for the two of us to stay in Whispering Pines.

"When do you think you'll talk to your mom again?" Tripp asked.

I let out a hard sigh. Honestly, he was getting a little pushy about this. "I sent her the business plan two weeks ago. The numbers looked good to me, but she hasn't been able to track down my dad yet." The house had belonged to his parents and his was the only name on the will, so we needed his approval for this venture. "Apparently, he's working on some dig site in Egypt. Mom says they found another mummy tomb or some ... sweater!"

"Excuse me?"

I groaned and let my head fall back. "I forgot Gran's sweater at the circus last night."

His forehead furrowed as he processed that. "What sweater?"

"The one I tucked under my seat and told you to not let me forget."

"What made you think of that?"

"I have no idea. Talking about the house and the furniture. Maybe my brain is thinking about packing up Gran's bedroom. Who knows?"

"Finish your breakfast. At this point, it's either there or it's not."

I wasn't sure if that was comforting or upsetting. I ate quickly, told him I'd be back soon, then went to get my car keys and Meeka's leash. She'd love to see the big cats.

Set deep into Whispering Pines' two thousand acres, there were two options for getting to the circus grounds. The first was to park in the public lot on the west side of the village and walk through the woods for a good half hour. A nice walk when the sun was shining and the birds singing and all that. Not the most convenient at night or when in a hurry.

I chose the second option, which was to drive around to the far side of the acreage and park in a lot that was about a five-minute walk on a groomed, compacted dirt pathway to the circus' entrance. As we got close to the grounds, I heard a commotion through the trees.

"Come on, Meeka. Something's wrong."

We jogged past the empty ticket booth and kept going straight to the big top where a crowd of carnies had gathered. Some were talking, some stood with their hands over their mouths, some were crying. I squeezed my way through to the tent entrance where Janessa, the circus' business manager, stood and prevented people from going into the tent.

Five foot five, thirty pounds overweight, medium-brown skin, close-cropped Afro, mid-forties.

The first time I met Janessa was at a village council meeting. She had a big, confident personality in a slightly damaged wrapper. Her arms extended only six or eight inches from her shoulders, both ending with elongated hands, each with three long thin fingers.

"It's a congenital birth defect called phocomelia," she'd told me, as though she'd said it a million times before, even though I hadn't asked. "It's a known side effect of the anti-nausea drug thalidomide, but was just a genetic luck of the draw in my case."

That was Janessa's way, take control of a situation before it could get away from her.

"What's going on?" I gestured at both the crowd and the big top tent. "Why is everybody so upset?"

Meeka had become agitated as well, giving me signs that she scented something coming from inside the tent.

"It's Berlin," Janessa said slowly, as though processing her words as she said them.

A pit like a lead weight formed in my gut, and my cop's instincts kicked into overdrive. "What's wrong with Berlin?"

She shook her head. "She's dead."

Chapter 4

"BERLIN?" I ASKED. "AS IN the aerial artist I saw perform last night?"

Janessa nodded, her expression grim.

Meeka strained against her leash and let out a couple of sharp barks. She was a trained K-9 officer in both narcotics and cadaver search and had worked for a short time at my station in Madison. A Westie was an unusual choice for K-9, but Meeka had a good nose, tons of energy, and could fit into tight spaces if necessary. She could perform her duties well, more so with cadavers than narcotics, but was quirky which made her undependable at times, so they retired her after only two years. She pulled even harder against her leash, looked up at me, gave one more bark, and sniffed in the direction of the tent. She scented a dead body.

"Meeka, sit." She did but was still agitated. I turned back to Janessa. "What happened?"

"Wish I knew. I haven't been inside. I've been standing here, giving Berlin a little privacy until someone comes."

"That's going to take a while." Whispering Pines didn't currently have an active law enforcement officer. "Has anyone called 9-1-1?"

She pointed down the midway. "Creed is taking care of

that."

"If you don't mind, I'd like to go inside and secure the scene until a deputy gets here."

Janessa knew my background as a detective in Madison and, for a very short time, I'd been known around the village as Deputy O'Shea. Unfortunately, I had a hard time following the then-sheriff's directive to stay out of a murder investigation, and he fired me after only three days.

"It'll ease my mind to know someone has an eye on Berlin." Janessa stepped aside to let Meeka and I pass.

The lack of law enforcement in the village had been a problem for weeks; now it had officially reached the critical point. As the newest member of the village council, I had repeatedly reminded the other members that we were in the thick of tourist season. While most of our visitors were fine, upstanding citizens, there were a few who liked to spend their time here getting drunk and rowdy and causing minor chaos. We needed to bring in a new sheriff soon. Yesterday wouldn't have been soon enough. Once I was done doing whatever I could for Berlin, I was going to call an emergency council meeting. We were going to fix this problem and decide on a new sheriff today.

Meeka continued to tug on her leash, leading me through the big top to a spot between the center and right-hand ring. I had expected to find Berlin's body lying on the ground, but Meeka was looking up. I startled to discover Berlin's limp body hanging twenty-five or thirty feet above the ground, the same spot where she had done her performance last night. Her aerial silks were wrapped around her hips, resembling a rock-climbing harness, and her left arm had become trapped against her torso beneath the fabric. Her right arm dangled freely. Another length of the silks had wrapped around her neck. From where I stood, I could just make out what looked like scratches on her neck. Almost certainly self-inflicted as she tried to ease the constriction on her throat.

As gravity pulled her downward, her body had arched, turning her into a sort of human bow with the fabric acting as the bow's string. The tightening silks could have cut off her air supply, but from the purplish hue of her face, I guessed that lack of blood flow due to her carotid arteries being squeezed was the bigger problem. People can go a surprisingly long time without oxygen. At one time or another, nearly every child participated in a *who could hold their breath the longest* contest. My sister Rosalyn, especially when in full tantrum, could beat anyone, anytime. To my knowledge, she still could. Free divers, those who swam to great depths, could go for twenty minutes or more on a held breath. But it only took as little as seven seconds for a person to pass out from pressure on the carotid.

"Appears to be death by strangulation," I said softly. The cop in me, however, was immediately skeptical and started thinking of alternate possibilities. What were the chances that an artist of Berlin's caliber would become twisted in her silks that way? Was it possible she'd been killed and strung up? Could it have been suicide? Not a guaranteed method, but people found highly creative ways to move on to whatever came next when they decided to choose their own ending. So yes, suicide was a possibility.

I directed Meeka over to the bleachers and ordered her to sit and stay. She obeyed, but crawled beneath the seats instead of sitting near them. Good enough.

"Isn't it horrible?" Creed, the ringmaster, appeared at my side.

"It is. Do you know who found her?"

"Tilda Nelson did not even an hour ago. She is absolutely inconsolable."

"Tilda was close to Berlin?"

"Very close," Creed confirmed. "They were roommates. Berlin has ... *had* been with us for nearly four years. Tilda came to the circus with her son Joss about two years ago. The women became friends on day one."

"How long had they been roommates?"

"Since shortly after they moved here. Joss was a toddler, and Tilda needed help with him. Berlin fell in love with that little guy even faster than she became friends with Tilda and within the week asked if they wanted to move into her tent with her."

"Has anyone else been in here?"

"Other than myself and Tilda," Creed said, "no one that I am aware of. Tilda came to my trailer right away. While I called the authorities, Janessa ran over here to stand guard."

"Let's make sure no one else does come in," I said. "It might take a little while before a deputy gets here. I'll stay and guard the scene until they do. We need to be sure that everyone else stays out. Can you help me with that?"

Creed bristled a little at my request. "Of course."

"I don't mean to sound cold—"

"But you can't help yourself." He gave me a small, tight smile. "I remember that you were a detective."

"Glad you understand."

If it weren't for that hint of a smile, and the fact that Creed was also on the village council with me, I'd think I had another enemy in town.

After the performance last night, Tripp and I waited for the tent to clear rather than joining the stream of people leaving. That meant we were the last people to catch a horse-drawn wagon ride back to the parking lot on the far side of the village where we had parked. While we waited for our wagon, we wandered around and came to an area full of small tents that looked like miniature versions of the big top. This was where the performers and other carnies lived.

That's also where we found Lupe Gomez standing outside one of the tents, listening to a heated argument between Tilda Nelson, the aerial artist who needed a wheelchair, and Berlin.

"From the little bit I heard," Lupe told us as though dishing up a tidbit so juicy it was dripping, "Tilda is complaining that the warm-up acts get no respect. She wants a chance at an act during one of the performances. She's good, but with someone like Berlin as the star of the show, it'll be a long time before Tilda gets a spotlight act."

Jealousy, professional or otherwise, was a common motive for murder. I started to explain all that to Creed and didn't even have to finish my statement before he told me that the roommates argued a lot.

"Only about one thing, though," he said. "As I mentioned, Berlin had been the star of our show for nearly four years. She is … was a phenomenal performer, an amazingly talented artist, and a genuinely good person." His voice broke and he stared at the ground, needing a moment to collect himself. "Unfortunately, when you are the best, you have a lot of people clawing at you to pass you by."

People clawing at you to pass you by. The visual that description produced in my brain made me cringe.

"Berlin and Tilda were like sisters," Creed continued, "and like many sisters, each wanted what the other had."

"Sounds like Tilda wanted a spot in the show. What did Berlin want that Tilda has?"

"A child." Creed made a soft, snorting sound that said, *we're never happy with what we have, are we?*

"That was a good relationship?" I asked. "The one between Berlin and Tilda's son?"

"Absolutely. Joss treated Berlin like a second mother."

"Sounds like you feel Tilda is innocent in this."

"No doubt in my mind. As I said, they were like sisters. They argued, but I can't imagine Tilda hurting Berlin."

"Is there anyone who you can imagine harming her?"

Creed tilted his face skyward, as though looking for strength there, and let out a soft, sad chuckle. "There are a few."

"Any names you'd like to share with me?"

He stared down his slender nose at me and shook his head as though coming out of a trance. "Wait. Do you think this was murder? A second murder in Whispering Pines in as many months?"

"Do you think it would be possible for Berlin to become entangled in her own silks that way?" I gestured respectfully at Berlin's body, still hanging from the rafters.

"Not really." He crossed his arms, fingers tapping on his lean biceps, and considered this for a moment. "She and Gianni Cordano didn't get along well."

"The veterinarian?" I asked, and Creed nodded. "Last night, Tripp and I were waiting in the bleachers while the big top cleared. When the tent was nearly empty, Berlin stormed out onto the performance floor over to Gianni. She demanded to know why he refused to move that fencing just five more feet as she had repeatedly asked."

"Many of us had become weary of that ongoing argument. Gianni insisted the fences were fine, and Berlin was afraid they'd interfere with her silks. It wasn't likely that the fencing would cause a problem, but on that one, I had to give the point to Berlin. There really was no reason Gianni couldn't move those fences a few feet further."

"But the fencing was in the way. I was at the performance last night, I saw her silks snag on that last section. Just like they are now."

I pointed to Berlin's silks, which were currently entangled on the same section of fencing.

Creed paled. "I was so shocked by everything else, I hadn't even noticed."

"You said no one else has been inside the tent. Last night, the fan apparently blew the fabric. Were any of the fans on when you first came in here?"

"No. And before you ask, Tilda insisted she didn't touch anything. I asked."

Then how did the fabric become snagged this time? I watched last night, it's not like the silks flew around that much. For the most part, it hung relatively straight.

"I still don't want to believe she was murdered," Creed

said. "Maybe it was a horrible accident."

He seemed anxious for that to be true. Couldn't fault him there. I'd prefer an accidental death to a murder any time. Still, I'd need to prove it one way or the other.

"We have Gianni as a possible suspect," I said. "Who else would want to harm her? You indicated that there were a few people."

"Berlin and Dallas had their moments. Again, though, it was never over anything severe enough that it would have led to murder."

"You'd be surprised what could lead to murder. You mean Dallas the knife thrower?"

"Knives, machetes, swords." Creed sighed as if in awe. "The man has excellent aim. In fact, I can't remember ever seeing him miss."

"What would they argue about?"

"I can't say as it was really an argument, but he wanted to try and put together an act with Berlin. It had a very high danger level. Definitely a closing act."

"Let me guess," I said. "Something to do with that last move of hers, when she goes to the very top of the tent and spins to the ground."

"Right you are." Absently, Creed licked his finger and marked one point on an invisible scoreboard. "Berlin called it a variation on a barrel roll. Or log roll. Or maybe that was the figure eight something-or-other. I can't remember, she had so many moves." He paused for a moment to think. "At any rate, Dallas wanted her to perform that move and when she got near the ground, he would throw knives at a target in the background. He was thinking balloons or something else that would make it obvious he had missed her and hit his target."

"And she didn't want to do it? I would have loved to see that."

"I'm sure many people would have. I even encouraged it."

"But?"

"I'm not sure what Berlin's objection was," Creed said.

"Honestly, I think she liked being the closing act and didn't want to share the spotlight."

Oren's words from last night echoed in my ears. "I heard that Berlin could be a bit of a diva."

"I wouldn't classify her that way. Berlin was demanding, a perfectionist, but she always expected more from herself than she did from anyone else." He lifted a slim shoulder. "I guess that tends to rub some people the wrong way."

"Especially coming from a woman." I thought of all the officers at the station down in Madison who didn't get promoted to detective when I did. Many of them were older, I was only twenty-five at the time, but I was the better candidate. That wasn't ego speaking, it was a simple fact. That didn't stop them from making rude remarks and spreading lies about how I got that promotion.

"Thanks for the information, Creed. Unless you have anything else, I'm going to have a look around while we're waiting for a deputy to get here. We should probably keep the tourists off the grounds for now."

"The grounds don't open until one o'clock, so no problem there. In fact, we'll shut down altogether for today."

"I was about to suggest that. The deputy will take hours investigating the tent. It would also be best if all the carnies stay here. The deputy will likely want to interview everyone."

"Will do." He gave me a salute. "And I'll keep an eye out for anything suspicious."

I couldn't help but laugh inside. Everyone was an amateur investigator. Although, when I was a cop, I received some case-breaking tips from the public. I took out my phone and opened a memo app to record the information Creed had just given me before I forgot anything. Then, I closed the app and turned on my camera. I took pictures from every angle, not only of the area directly surrounding Berlin, but of the entire tent, highlighting the numerous entrances, all of which had someone posted to keep looky-loos out.

Staying near the bleachers, so I wouldn't corrupt the crime scene, I scanned the dirt and wood chips on the ground surrounding the three performance rings. The center ring still held animal cages and fences, and, as best as I could recall, all the equipment appeared to be in the same spots as when we left last night. I focused on the length of silk wrapped around Berlin's neck. It was also tangled on the section of fencing she had complained to Gianni about last night. That presented as a little too convenient to me.

As I took a few more pictures of Berlin, I noted that she was again wearing a mask, one that covered half her face just like the ones she wore during her performances yesterday. I zoomed in on a photo and saw that this mask was plain and the same ivory shade as her skin. The others were elaborate and part of a costume. Was this some quirky artistic thing? Or had she been hiding her face for some reason? Maybe she was born with a birth defect like a cleft palate. Maybe she developed a disease, cancer perhaps, that had deformed her face. Or maybe she was the victim of violence and had been hiding scars from an attack. Physical beauty was important to people. Not having it could make someone feel like they didn't belong and want to run away to someplace like Whispering Pines. Or maybe she was hiding herself, as in hiding from someone who was looking for her.

I focused the camera to get a close-up of the length of silk entangled with the fence. The sections were made of simple chain link fencing on metal poles. Each pole had a lockable wheel at the bottom. When Gianni, the veterinarian, unlocked the wheels and pushed them aside, the sections accordioned together. This was where the fabric had snagged, in the V formed by the folded-together fence panels. Did this happen accidentally, as in the fabric had gotten blown again, or did it have human assistance? In my opinion, it would've taken a monsoon wind ripping through the tent to cause this.

Using the close-up view on the camera like a telescope, I scanned the area around the fencing. Something was lying in the wood chips between the empty animal cages and fence sections, but I couldn't tell what it was. I took large steps, attempting to leave as few footprints as possible, crossed to the center ring, and used it as a sort of balance beam walking path. Ensuring there was nothing of importance on the wooden ring I might step on, I made my way carefully around to the fencing and immediately spotted what I had seen on my screen. A tranquilizer dart?

Chapter 5

FINDING A TRANQUILIZER DART WASN'T really that surprising. It was lying near the wild animal cages; the veterinarian had probably dropped it. The clear plastic syringe had black dosage markings and was topped with what looked like orange feathers.

What kind of drug did the veterinarian load into his darts? What effect would that drug have on a person? How much medication would need to be administered to knock a person unconscious? How much to kill? How long would that take?

Had this dart been used on Berlin? If it had, it obviously hadn't stuck. In fact, it lay a good ten to fifteen yards away from her. Assuming she had been practicing at the time, I suppose it was possible that the trajectory of her twisting and spinning had sent the dart flying and it landed here. Or maybe the fabric had pulled it free. Or maybe Berlin pulled it out herself and threw it.

I glanced up at the woman, then followed the fabric back to the spot where it was snagged. Normally when investigating a scene, I could "see" the events through the victim's eyes. This time, disturbingly, I ended up in the killer's head.

Berlin is practicing her routine as I enter the tent. She's climbing, climbing, climbing to the top. Once there, she wraps her silks around first one of her legs and then the other. She does this again and again until she's so wrapped up, it looks like she's wearing a diaper. She positions herself and then drops twenty feet before jerking to an abrupt stop. Unhappy with the move, she unwraps her legs, climbs back to the top, rewraps her legs, and prepares to do the move again. Just before she does, I raise the dart gun and fire.

But then what happened? I had far more questions than answers. I sensed a research session coming when I got home and could already hear Tripp's "this isn't your problem" speech.

With my arms out to the side, walking like a tightrope walker or a gymnast on a balance beam, I retraced my steps, trying to step in the same spots I had before. I searched for any possible evidence as I returned to the bleachers and a few minutes later, Creed entered with a uniformed deputy from the County Sheriff's Department. Evan Atkins had been patrolling Whispering Pines for the past few weeks while we were between sheriffs.

"Evan," I said extending my hand, "nice to see you again. Well, maybe not nice considering the circumstance."

"Good to see you, too." He gave a little chuckle as he shook my hand. "I have to ask, are you attracted to murders or are murderers attracted to you?"

He meant the Yasmine Long investigation, the young woman I had found dead in my backyard the day I arrived in Whispering Pines.

"For my own well-being," I said, "I certainly hope it's not that last option. And I'm hoping this death was an accident."

He hadn't seen Berlin's body yet, so I pointed up and then filled him in on everything I knew at that point, including when I had gotten there, when I had last seen Berlin, and the possible suspects Creed had told me about.

"Thanks for the information," Evan said. "It's always

good to compare notes to make sure we're getting the same story. As you're well aware."

"I haven't touched anything," I said, "but did spot something on the ground over by that fencing. I walked along the center ring over to the spot to get a better look."

He laughed again, but it was strained this time. "Couldn't help yourself, hey?"

I pointed out my route, including my footsteps in the wood chips, and then showed him the picture on my phone. "It's a tranquilizer dart. That's all I know, I didn't get any closer, just wanted you to know that it was there."

"In case I missed it during my own investigation?" This time, the strain sounded more like annoyance.

I got it, my services were no longer needed. "I'll get out of your way." I called for Meeka, "Come, girl."

The little white dog crawled out from beneath the bleachers, reminding me why we had come back to the circus in the first place. I hurried over to the spot where we sat last night, grateful to find Gran's blue sweater still tucked beneath the seat where I left it.

Outside the tent, the day had already heated up, and the crowd hadn't thinned much. A chorus of questions bombarded me.

"Is it really Berlin?"

"Is she really dead?"

"How did she die?"

"Did she kill herself?"

I looked into the crowd after that last question. "Who said that?"

A large tricycle, powered by a hand crank rather than foot pedals, pulled forward, driven by a woman with no legs. As in her legs had either been amputated where they joined her hips, or she had been born without legs.

"I said it." The woman held her head with her chin raised. A challenging pose.

"Don't listen to her," someone from the crowd called out.

"She doesn't know what she's talking about."

I took a couple of steps toward her. "Do you have reason to believe that Berlin would want to kill herself?"

She didn't answer. In fact, she clamped her jaw shut and looked away.

"I'm Jayne O'Shea. I worked here with Sheriff Brighton for a while. I used to be a detective for the Madison Police Department. If you have a legitimate reason to believe that Berlin wanted to kill herself, you need to let the deputy know. If it was an accident, we don't want to tarnish a good woman's name. If Berlin was killed and there's a murderer running around Whispering Pines, you don't want to lead him down the wrong path. If you're just trying to cause trouble, I suggest you go to the back of the crowd and remain silent."

The woman glared at me but remained mute.

"I'll ask one more time," I said. "Do you have reason to believe that Berlin wanted to kill herself?"

"*Used to* work with Sheriff Brighton," the woman mocked. "*Used to* be a detective. Unless you're someone who can actually do something, I don't have to tell you anything."

Internally, I flinched. She was right, she didn't have to say anything. Externally, I maintained my detective demeanor. I hoped.

"You're right," I said. "I can't get involved with the investigation. But I can certainly let the deputies know they need to question you. What's your name?"

"Marilyn." She lifted her chin again. "My name is Marilyn Half."

Was she serious? A woman with no legs had the last name of Half? I looked to the person closest to me, who happened to be the seven-foot-tall woman with long red hair.

"It's a stage name. I'm Colette. I'm good friends with Tilda and Berlin. I watch Tilda's little boy Joss all the time. I can tell you without hesitation that there is no way Berlin killed herself."

I was about to start asking more questions when I heard not only Tripp's voice in my head but a familiar female voice as well. Morgan had joined him in my brain, and they were both telling me to stay out of this. Tripp added that I needed to come home and get back to packing up the bedrooms. Since Ms. Half had just shot holes in my authority, it was time to go anyway.

"The man inside the tent," I told the crowd, "is Deputy Evan Atkins. I'm sure he's going to want to talk to many if not all of you. I strongly encourage you to be honest with him straightaway, no embellishment. Remember that any little thing you can tell him might help. The faster he has the facts, the faster he can put this to rest and the circus can get back to normal."

"How's it going to be normal without Berlin?" someone called.

I knew it was hard for them to think about the future when this tragedy had just happened. And they certainly didn't want to hear any trite words of comfort from me. Instead, I offered a simple, empathetic smile and walked away.

Meeka and I started down the path back to the parking lot, the heat and humidity of the day making her pant and my jeans stick to my legs. I should've worn shorts. We hadn't gotten even a hundred yards when I heard somebody behind me.

"Jayne," a female voice called. "Hang on."

I turned to see Lupe Gomez running up to me. She had taken that last wagon with Tripp and me last night. As the horse clomped down the path, the wagon swaying side to side, Lupe told us about her assignment to do a series of articles on the village.

"Fortunately, this place seems to be loaded with eccentrics," she had said. "I should have plenty to write about."

"These are good people here," Tripp had responded with a warning tone.

"I can tell that." Lupe let her head drop back so she could gaze up at the star-packed sky. "Dude, don't worry. I'd never print anything negative about anyone unless they were like a serial killer or something. Then it wouldn't be negative, would it? Just be the ugly truth, and that's on them, not me."

Over the years, I'd become accustomed to forming quick opinions about people. I analyzed body language, paid attention for facial tics, and listened to what their words weren't saying as well as what they were. My initial opinion about Ms. Gomez wasn't exactly glowing. She seemed almost excited about the possibility of trouble in the village.

"Lupe, hi," I greeted now as she stepped into line with me. "You made it home safely last night?"

"Sure did. I was so worked up from the performances and everything, I stayed up half the night writing my first piece. I've been a reporter for a long time. Sometimes a travel reporter, sometimes special interest, sometimes investigative. All nonfiction stuff, you know? But I'm telling you, there's something about this place, the village in general, not just the circus, that really turns on my creativity. Last night, I had some crazy fiction thoughts running through my brain. I may have a novel drafted by the time I leave here."

Lupe spoke quickly and could cram more words into one breath than anyone I'd ever met.

"I'm on my way home." I held up the sweater in my hand. "I forgot this here last night and just stopped by to pick it up. Who knew I was going to stumble into a death?"

"I know. How sad. I got here early so I could get a feel for what the circus was like with just the carnies and no visitors. That is what they call themselves, right? Carnies? That's what I heard, but I don't want to, you know, be offensive or anything."

"Yep. Even though this isn't a carnival, they refer to themselves as carnies."

"Okay, good. Anyway, I'm working on a piece about carney life. Wasn't expecting it was going to involve death, too. That's why I wanted to catch up with you. They wouldn't let any of us into the tent. For obvious reasons, I guess, but I saw you go inside. You were in there for a long time. Why did they let you in? What's going on? What did you see?"

I stared at her for a beat. Trying, again, to get a read on this woman. She claimed to be writing light, human interest pieces, but her tone was more investigative. With a bit of wacko thrown in. I got it, she was here to do a job. A woman had died and she wanted to report on it.

"I'm sure you can appreciate that I'm not at liberty to say anything." Really, I was a civilian like her and could say anything I wanted, but the cop in me demanded I not reveal any important details. "You know that Berlin, the aerial artist, has died. I can confirm that. I really shouldn't say any more, though."

Lupe jerked a thumb over her shoulder at the circus grounds. "I just heard you tell everyone that you used to be a cop. Is that why they let you go inside?"

"Yes, that's why. Deputy Atkins is the investigator, so you should talk to him. Anything I told you would be speculation."

"Oh, come on, Jayne. You were in there for over an hour. Once a cop, always a cop. You're telling me that you didn't snoop around?"

Now, she was getting on my nerves. I said nothing, just stared at her.

"Even if you just stood there with your back to the scene," Lupe pushed, "you must have seen something when you walked in. Don't worry, I don't want to turn the circus into a horror show. I'm not looking for anything, you know, nasty." She wrinkled her nose and made a face as proof of that. "Being a circus performer is serious stuff, I respect that. Berlin put her life on the line every time she climbed her silks. The lion tamer, Leah, she's just a little spot of a thing. One of those big cats could gobble her up like a snack in thirty seconds flat. Sorry, I don't mean to be crude. Then there's the knife thrower's assistant. I mean, what if he misses? And that guy who jumps off that platform into, what, a teacup of water? If he was off by just a foot — "

"Lupe," I interrupted before she concluded that example, "I'm not going to tell you how Berlin died. When investigating a crime, the detectives need to keep key details to themselves. The manner of death, for example, is something that only the killer would know, so they don't want that made public."

Her smile faded, but the curiosity in her eyes stayed bright. "I understand that. I've covered stories about death before. I know to keep things off the record."

"Nothing is really 'off the record,' though, is it? Things *accidentally* slip by." Lupe's jaw clenched and she took a step back. "Look, I know your job is to ask questions, and clearly you're very good at that."

She gave a curt nod of thanks.

"Can I offer a suggestion?" I asked.

"Sure."

There was no way to stop Lupe from digging into her story. If she was going to do that anyway, maybe she could help.

"Go ahead and ask your questions. If someone gives you an important detail, like how Berlin died, tell Deputy Atkins. Let him know what you find out and who told you. You never know when you could end up providing him with the lead that could help him solve the case. And if you help him, you never know, he might help you."

She never broke eye contact with me while I spoke, studying me as much as she was listening to my words.

Forming her own opinion of me. Apparently, she decided I was condescending.

"That would be so, like, awesome, wouldn't it? To help solve a case? Thanks so much for your advice." Her tone was saccharine sweet and her smile placating. At least, that's how I took it. Lupe was smarter than I'd given her credit for. She tilted her head toward the circus grounds. "I'm going to head back over there now. It's hard to stay away knowing I might be able to help. You know?"

She was gone before I could tell her I understood exactly how she felt. The day I stumbled across Yasmine Long's body, I had been away from police work for nearly six months. The instant I realized Yasmine's death was not accidental, I was in cop mode again. Now, realizing that Berlin's death was also probably not accidental, I was itching to go and help Deputy Atkins investigate.

Meeka tugged on her leash as though she knew exactly what I was thinking and was trying to pull me away from the thoughts.

"I know, you're right. Let's go home and help Tripp. We need to make one quick stop on the way. Do you want to say hi to Morgan?"

Meeka wagged her tail and tugged even harder.

Chapter 6

SHOPPE MYSTIQUE WAS CRAMMED TO the rafters, literally, with just about every metaphysical, magical, New Age, or Wiccan item imaginable. To the left of the front door, two huge bookcases held a couple hundred apothecary bottles filled with dried herbs and plants. Old-fashioned tea-stained labels identified the contents of the alphabetically arranged bottles. In other areas around the cottage, tables were loaded with Morgan's handmade cosmetics and bath and body products that rivaled anything my mother carried in her day spa in Madison. Shelves held oils and incense, stones and crystals, hand-dipped candles, amulets, charms, talismans ... you name it, Morgan had it. If she didn't carry what a customer was looking for, she had something that would work even better. She also assembled personalized charm bags and witch balls for protection or bring good luck.

"Blessed be, Jayne," greeted Willow, Morgan's pale-skinned red-headed assistant, when Meeka and I walked in.

I never knew how to respond to the Wiccan greetings, worried that replying with the same phrase might be considered blasphemous from a non-Wiccan, so settled with, "Hey. Is Morgan busy?"

"I believe she's stocking freshly-charged crystals." Willow pointed kitty-corner across the store to the left.

I'd been around Morgan enough to know "freshly-charged" meant she let them sit under the moonlight in her garden last night.

Morgan, striking in a sleeveless dress that looked to be made from multiple layers of breezy black chiffon, placed her palms together and bowed her head when she saw me. I motioned that I'd be in the cozy reading room off the main shop, and she held up a finger, indicating she'd be right there. At the complimentary tea station outside the room, I prepared a cup of "Headache" blend, hoping to fight off the pain starting between my eyes, poured some water into a paper cup for Meeka, then settled into my favorite spot on the worn-velvet loveseat in the reading room. Instantly, my body relaxed.

Morgan appeared a minute or two later and lowered onto the other end of the loveseat. Before she could ask, I told her what had happened at the circus, and even though there was no one in the room with us, she spoke in a voice low enough that only I could hear her.

"Berlin is dead?" She played with the Triple Moon Goddess amulet at her throat, the rings she wore on each finger clicking together as she did. "And you don't believe it was an accident."

"I can't say for sure."

She arched an eyebrow.

"It's not like I did a thorough investigation. I was just securing the scene, keeping people away from her."

She continued to stare mutely at me.

I let my shoulders drop in surrender. "Okay, fine, yes, I looked around. Is it possible that she simply became entangled in her silks? Sure. Do I believe that's what happened? Not really."

"That makes two murders in less than two months." Morgan flipped her wavy elbow-length, raven-black hair behind her shoulders. "What's going on around here?"

"I don't think anything is going on. These two deaths don't look to me to be related. Just a nasty coincidence."

"I thought you said there are no coincidences."

The witch was persistent today. "Anyway, this isn't my job. Right? You and Tripp have told me many times to mind my own business. So that's what I'm going to do. I need to focus on the house." I took a sip from my mug, then another, and waited while the heat and herbs pushed the pain out of my head. After one more sip, I changed topics. "There is another reason I stopped in here. We have a different problem that needs to be addressed."

"What would that be?" Morgan asked and floated around the corner to prepare her own cup of tea.

"The fact that we still have no law-enforcement personnel on duty."

"Flavia reports that Martin is recovering nicely." Morgan rejoined me on the loveseat. "He'll likely be ready to return within the month."

"We can't wait a month." I took another sip of my tea and let out a long, slow breath. Instead of vanishing, the pain migrated from behind my eyes to the base of my skull. "Besides, while Martin did a good job at the administrative tasks, he's not qualified to be sheriff. He wasn't qualified to be a deputy. The village's residents and visitors deserve better."

Morgan sighed wearily as she scratched Meeka's head with her long painted-black fingernails, much to the little dog's delight. "You're right, we need to bring someone on board."

"And we need to do so now. As in today, tomorrow at the latest. What are the procedures for calling an emergency council meeting?"

"I'll take care of summoning everyone." She narrowed her kohl-lined eyes. "Why are you smirking?"

"You're a witch. I just imagined everyone being sucked

away from whatever they were doing and plopping down at the table in the conference room."

A little girl wearing a purple tutu with silver stars had walked into the reading room with her mother just as I said that. Her eyes went wide with magical admiration for Morgan, and I couldn't help but laugh.

Morgan made a face at me that said, *now look what you've done*. "I'm an herbal healer, not a teleporter."

I winked at the little girl, and she giggled behind her hand.

"I'll arrange for a meeting this evening," Morgan said. "Oh, that won't work for Creed and Janessa. They'll have performances."

I shook my head. "They closed the circus today due to what happened."

"Of course they did." She closed her eyes for a moment, presumably thinking of Berlin. "This evening it is then."

"Perfect. Thanks."

I stood to leave, Morgan rising as well, but before I could go, she took hold of my arm and turned me toward her. She placed a hand on each of my shoulders, saying nothing until I looked her in the eye.

"I feel a lot of tension coming off you, Jayne."

I shrugged. "Just found another body. Well, I didn't find the body this time, but it's still upsetting, you know?"

"I do know." Morgan's voice was soft, soothing. "This tension has nothing to do with Berlin. What's going on?"

No sense trying to hide anything from Morgan Barlow. Sometimes I swore she was part mind reader. "Tripp is working too fast on the house."

She tilted her head in confusion. "Isn't that a good thing?"

"The main level, except for the floors, will be done soon, this week maybe. Then we'll start upstairs. The bathroom renovations will take a while, but it's all cosmetic stuff in the bedrooms. Once that's done ..."

A look of understanding crossed her face. "You'll have to put the house on the market. You haven't been able to convince your parents on the bed-and-breakfast idea yet?"

"Not yet. As far as I know, Dad hasn't come out of the desert to even read the email Mom sent him." I drained the rest of the tea from my cup and sighed. "At least my headache is going away. What's in this?"

"The headache blend? One pinch each of lavender, chamomile, rosemary, and mint. Now tell me, what's the real problem?"

When Morgan wanted to help someone, she held on like an attack dog.

"The real problem is, the longer I stay here, the more I want to stay. You know that. Whispering Pines feels like home to me. Running a bed-and-breakfast isn't something I ever considered, but the more I think about it the more I like it, and if that's the only way for me to stay here, I'll do it."

Morgan lifted one shoulder in a small shrug. "Perhaps that's not the only way."

"What are you thinking?"

"I'm not thinking anything." Morgan spread her arms wide and looked skyward. "You just took the first step."

"I did? How did I do that?"

"You proclaimed your desires out loud. Now the universe knows what you want, and if you pay attention, it will show you how to get it."

Oh, geez. Morgan and her woo-woo. I had to admit, her absolute certainty in these things did comfort me.

"I need to look for signs now? Is that what you're telling me? Build it and they will come, that kind of a thing? Or will the clouds form a message in the sky?"

"You play the skeptic very well, dear Jayne."

I handed her my empty teacup. She promptly peered in at the leaves stuck to the inside and arched an eyebrow. "Hmm."

"What?" I looked into the cup as well.

"Oh nothing." She held the cup away from me. "You don't believe anyway."

I rolled my eyes and left the reading room. "I've got to get home. I'm going to pop in next door and grab a coffee. The tea soothed me too much; now I need a pick me up. I'll let Violet know about the council meeting tonight."

Morgan walked me to the shop's front door and paused next to the large wood table that served as the checkout counter. "Willow, you'll be able to close for me tonight, won't you?"

Willow shot a look at me like that was my fault. I guess, indirectly, it was. Mostly, Willow didn't seem to care for me.

"I'd be happy to," Willow replied with little evidence of happiness.

"Very good." Morgan turned back to me. "Let's plan on a six o'clock meeting. Blessed be."

The cottage directly east of Shoppe Mystique was the village coffee shop, Ye Old Bean Grinder. Like most of the other buildings in the central village area, the coffee shop was stained a shade of brown so dark it was almost black. While Shoppe Mystique embraced each customer with an aura of Wiccan magic, Ye Olde Bean Grinder was equally welcoming but in a much homier way.

Café tables, each surrounded by two or three chairs, were scattered about. For nine months out of the year, the stone fireplace in the corner roared with welcoming flames that warmed the entire shop and created an atmosphere so cozy, patrons wanted to stay all day. Warmth wasn't necessary during the summer months, so the cavity was filled with a dozen or more vanilla scented candles instead. Same welcoming effect without the heat.

"Morning, Jayne," the five-foot-tall owner called out as she slid three full paper cups across the counter to a waiting customer. Violet, one of the first people I had met when I got here, was blessed with flawless, creamy light-brown skin and gleaming long straight black hair. "Do you want your regular?"

After my first visit, she remembered my favorite beverage—an extra-large mocha with a double pump of vanilla and extra whipped cream. Normally, she started preparing the drink the second she saw me enter the building, but not today.

"You are probably the greatest barista ever," I said. "Not only do you know my favorite drink, you can tell when it needs to be tweaked."

"What would you like me to do to it?"

Violet never stopped moving. I swear, it was like a superpower. If she wasn't preparing a beverage, she was filling the bean hopper with fresh coffee beans, or putting more beans into the roaster, or restocking the covered dish on the counter with scones from Treat Me Sweetly, the local bakery, ice cream, and candy shop. And that was during the off-season. I assumed the man currently wiping down tables was her helper for the tourist season. I was glad to see him. Violet would run herself into the ground otherwise.

"Let's go crazy," I said. "Let's do the same drink, but substitute salted caramel for the vanilla and let's ice it today."

"That sounds good," Violet crooned, already preparing the beverage. "I was thinking about creating a Drink of the Day. Maybe that will be my first." While reaching for ice with one hand, she handed me a biscuit for my pup with the other. "Maybe I'll call it The Meeka."

Hearing her name, Meeka stood at attention, tail wagging, and let out a little *ruff*.

"I think she approves." I handed Meeka her biscuit.

Violet slid my drink across the counter to me, but when I grasped it, she grabbed my wrist, pulled me into her as she leaned across the counter, and whispered, "I hear there was some trouble at the circus last night."

For a place that had zero cell phone reception, I was always shocked at how fast news spread. Maybe Violet's real superpower was super hearing.

"I assume you know who Berlin is," I said solemnly. "Or I should say who Berlin was."

"Oh, no." Violet bowed her head and uncharacteristically stood perfectly still for a moment of silence.

"A deputy from the County Sheriff's Department is investigating. That's partly why I stopped in here. It took more than an hour for him to get to the scene after Creed called 9-1-1. We need to do something about a new sheriff. Morgan is letting everyone else know, but the council is going to meet tonight. Six o'clock sound good?"

"Sure, I can make that work. My brother can handle the last couple of hours alone." She waved her new helper over. "Come meet Jayne."

Six foot two, top half of his straight black hair tied into a ponytail, light-brown skin.

"Hi, Jayne. I'm Basil," he held out a hand with long, slender fingers.

I couldn't help but laugh. "Your parents named you Violet and Basil? Let me guess, one of them is a green witch?"

"You got it," Basil said. "Nice to finally meet you. Violet has told me a lot about you."

Identical yet different. Basil towered more than a foot over Violet. Where Violet's eyes brilliantly matched her name in color—and she swore she didn't wear colored contacts—his were so deep brown the pupils couldn't be distinguished. Other than shade, their eyes matched exactly, as did their skin tone and shiny hair.

"So," I joked, "you're twins?"

"We are actually," Violet said. "Born on different days, however. I arrived just before midnight, and he was born just after."

Of course, she would be the *big* sister.

"The Meeka is delicious," I said holding my drink out to her in a toast. I gestured down at the real-life Meeka. "We would be honored to have your first Drink of the Day named after her."

I thought of Tripp, toiling away on the house all alone and asked Violet for a second drink. This one I paid for. She insisted that because my grandparents were the original settlers and founders of Whispering Pines, no O'Shea would ever pay for anything in her shop. While I appreciated that gesture, I always made sure to leave a generous tip.

"Thanks. See you tonight, Violet."

It occurred to me as I left that Oren had been wrong about Berlin. Everyone seemed to like her. Everyone, that was, except for the person who killed her. The more I thought about it, the more I became convinced that Whispering Pines did just have its second murder. The first one, last month, shook up the little village. The death of one of their own just might rock the place off its foundation.

Chapter 7

WHEN MEEKA AND I FINALLY got back to the house, we found Tripp in the great room, which he appeared to have converted into a snow globe. He was scraping the walls like a madman, wallpaper bits flying everywhere. Meeka thought it was great fun to catch the floating pieces until I told her not to eat them. She snorted at me, unintentionally blowing pieces across the floor. This started a whole new game.

"Is this standard procedure," I asked, shielding my eyes from the soaring shards, "or are you taking out frustrations over something?"

Startled, he jumped and spun toward me. "I just want to get this done. I'm sure your grandma was a lovely person, but paper on every wall?"

"Guess that was the style back in the day. Since there's almost no graffiti upstairs, maybe we can try just painting over the paper there?"

We planned to paint the walls a light blue, Gran's favorite shade, but no matter how many coats of primer we put over the wallpaper, we couldn't cover whatever magical black ink the vandals had used. Removing the paper was the only option.

Tripp agreed instantly to the painting over paper idea. "It's sure worth a try. Might have to do a little scraping here and there to remove loose bits, but nothing like this. Seriously, if anyone ever says the word wallpaper to me, I may hit them."

"Here." I handed him his Drink of the Day. "Take a little break."

My cup was almost empty, but I sat with him anyway and explained why it had taken me so long to return when all I had intended was to run and get my sweater.

"Stay out of it," he warned.

For a second, I flashed to one of the many arguments I'd had with my ex-fiancé Jonah over me quitting my job with the Madison Police Department. But Tripp wasn't Jonah, and right now Tripp was just frustrated about wallpaper.

"I don't know what you're talking about," I said innocently.

"Yes, you do. I know you, you'll want to help."

"And because you know me so well, you know I won't be able to leave this alone."

"Jayne—"

"Tripp." I echoed his tone of irritation. "A woman has died, and there is no law enforcement in this village. The County Sheriff's Office will investigate, but—"

"But you feel responsible to the people of this village."

I considered that. "I don't think responsible is the right word. It feels like more of an obligation. I was a cop, after all. I made a pledge to serve and protect, and just because I'm not currently working as a cop doesn't mean I shouldn't honor that pledge."

Tripp said nothing for a minute, alternating between sipping his Meeka drink and staring at his paper cup.

"I have an idea," he said quietly. "I'm not sure you'll like it, but it would serve a purpose."

I looked over my shoulder at him. "What's your idea?"

"Why don't you hang up a PI shingle? If you're going to

be investigating anyway, you may as well make it legal."

Me? A private investigator? Not something I'd ever considered.

"It's not a *bad* idea," I responded. "Not sure how much business I'd get in Whispering Pines, though."

"Well, it seems you get at least one murder investigation a month."

Not funny. Not that he'd intended it to be.

"I understand what you're saying," I said, "but what the village needs is a law enforcement official, not a private investigator. There's an emergency council meeting tonight to talk about this. Hopefully, a want ad will be out tomorrow morning."

"There is another benefit to considering my option."

"Let me guess. If I open a private investigation firm, that would mean I had a legitimate business in the village and could stay."

"Probably wouldn't be as lucrative as a bed-and-breakfast, but you'd probably need an administrative assistant." He flashed me a toothy grin.

My heart ached for him. After ten years on the road, searching for the mother who left him with his aunt and uncle when he was thirteen, all Tripp wanted was to stay in one place. Like me, he decided Whispering Pines felt like home, but council rules stated only those who didn't fit anywhere else — the misunderstood and victimized Wiccans, fortune tellers, the physically disabled, etc. — could live in the village. Sure, he could stay at the campground or rent a guest cottage for as long as he wanted, but he needed income to make that happen. No one would give him a job because he didn't live in the village. It felt like reverse discrimination to me, although the council insisted it wasn't.

"Segregation, then," I'd say.

They'd come back with, "These are your grandmother's directives," figuring I wouldn't argue about any rule Gran had implemented.

I pushed the thoughts away and sat quietly while Tripp finished his iced coffee. Something would come together for the two of us and allow us both to stay here. Like our bed-and-breakfast dream. Like I did whenever I spent too much time in the great room, I started envisioning guests milling about. I imagined children playing in the backyard and teenagers hanging out on the dock or pulling canoes out of the boathouse. Adults would sit on the covered back patio for B&B hosted wine-and-cheese gatherings, and by the end of the night, strangers would have become friends. I didn't want to admit it to him, but Tripp's vision was becoming my vision.

Once he was ready to get back to work, I asked, "Can I help?"

He waved at Meeka who was still blowing wallpaper bits across the floor into a corner. "You could help her clean up the mess I made. I'll go grab the Shop-Vac from the garage, and you can start vacuuming."

I stood and gave him a little bow. "I am here to serve you, sir."

Still bent at the waist, I raised my head and met eyes with him. He was giving me a look that sent a shiver straight through my core.

"I said serve you. Not service you."

"A man can dream." His voice was husky and he gave me a little wink before heading for the garage.

I looked down at Meeka who turned her back as though to say, *you stepped right into that one, lady.*

She was right. And I did it a lot. I had to get control of that. The mixed signals I was unintentionally sending him wasn't fair to Tripp. I needed to figure out what I wanted, but how could I start a relationship when everything else in my life was so up-in-the-air right now?

That was an excuse, and I knew it. I simply wasn't ready. Hopefully, his patience wouldn't run out before I finally was.

Chapter 8

AFTER LEAVING HER ALONE FOR so long last night, Meeka was not about to let me head into town without her tonight. Tripp decided to hang out at the village pub, Grapes, Grains, and Grub, and I told him I'd join him there after the meeting.

At the heart of the village commons was a huge round garden about the size of a standard city block. Pea gravel pathways created a pentacle, or five-pointed star, inside the circle. Different flowers, herbs, and a few colorful vegetables filled the triangular sections of the pentacle. Benches, so people could sit and enjoy both the garden and the view of the lake, were placed between the sections.

At the very center of the pentacle was a gleaming, white marble well the villagers called a negativity well. Instead of tossing in coins and hoping that wishes would come true, you were to whisper whatever was bothering you into your hands and throw the words into the well to rid yourself of the problem. When I was little and my dad would bring me and my sister Roslyn to the well, I always envisioned the water at the bottom soaking up the words and then, like a drain in a sink, they would flow into the lake and get gobbled up by fish.

The Inn, slightly crooked and made of white plaster and wood slats stained black-brown, stood on the southeast edge of the Pentacle Garden near the lake. It was the second building built in Whispering Pines, Morgan's home being the first. The Inn was also where village council meetings were held. Morgan and two older ladies saw Meeka and me coming and waited for us outside the building as we cut through the garden instead of going around it.

"Blessed be," Morgan greeted. "Jayne, I know you know their names, but I'm not sure you've met Effie or Cybil in person yet."

"I'm Cybil," said the first woman. *Four foot ten, dark-brown skin, raspy voice, multicolored turban wrapped around her head making hair color indistinguishable.*

"Lily Grace's grandmother." I held my hand out to her. "It's a pleasure to meet you."

Cybil wore a long gypsy-style white skirt, a white T-shirt and white lace blouse tied at her waist. Six or eight necklaces, each made from a different-color bead, hung around her neck, numerous bracelets lined each arm, and large rings encircled each finger. While clenching a large cigar between her teeth, she took one of my hands in both of hers and held it tightly. She closed her eyes and a smile formed around the unlit cigar. She said nothing, even after opening her eyes again, just smiled and nodded. It seemed Cybil the fortune teller just read me.

I turned to the other woman and felt my heart warm. "You must be Effie."

Light-olive skin, five foot six, head wrapped in a colorful turban. Effie was dressed similarly to Cybil, but in head-to-toe lavender accented with bits of black and white. Where Cybil was fresh-faced, Effie wore a touch of dramatic makeup—pencil thin drawn-on arched eyebrows, eyes lined in black, and two-inch-long fingernails each painted with a different wild pattern. I couldn't help but smile at the duo.

Next thing I knew, Effie pulled me into a hug.

"Oh, my dear girl," she crooned. "My dear girl."

Even though we had never met face-to-face, she and I had a connection. Gran and Effie had called me one night about a year and a half ago. Effie hadn't been able to contact her granddaughter but had a vision she felt would lead to her whereabouts. Her vision was spot on and helped me find Jola within a few hours.

"It's so good to meet you in person," I said. "How is Jola?"

"She graduated in May. Got that nursing degree and after interviewing at a few other places, she decided to come back here."

"To Whispering Pines? That's great."

Effie brimmed with pride. "She's going to work at the healing center."

Currently, the healing center could only deal with cuts and scrapes, sunburns, and other minor issues. It would be good to have someone who could deal with more urgent situations.

"Ladies," Morgan said gently, "as much as I hate to break this up, we should probably get into the meeting now."

We crossed the lobby to the registration desk, greeted the super-friendly pock-faced Emery working there today, and went behind the desk to a door that led to the conference room. The simple room had the charming feel of the rest of The Inn with short ceilings, plaster walls, and a cozy stone fireplace tucked into the corner. In stark contrast, the sleek chrome and glass table, large enough for all thirteen of the council members, looked like it had been pulled from a boardroom in a building on Wall Street. Everyone was there, waiting for us.

The council was made up of original citizens and prominent business owners from around the village. Along with Morgan, Effie, Cybil, and me, the others included Violet from Ye Olde Bean Grinder, Mr. Powell who owned the village repair business, and Sugar, half-owner of Treat Me Sweetly. Creed and Janessa represented the circus, Maeve owned Grapes, Grains, and Grub, Laurel managed The Inn, Donovan owned Quin's clothing shop, and finally, there was Flavia Reed.

Quite honestly, I had no idea what Flavia did, other than fulfilling her duties as the village's self-appointed mayor. She didn't own a business and, as far as I knew, was on the council only because her family was among the original settlers of Whispering Pines. Rumor had it she lived off a large inheritance from her parents and the life insurance settlement she received when her husband died twenty years earlier. I barely knew the woman, but for whatever reason Flavia didn't like me, and I decided it was best that I kept my distance from her.

"Nice that the four of you could join us," Flavia said as we entered the room. Sheriff Brighton used to run the meetings, but since he was no longer with us, Flavia snatched up the responsibility.

"We sat down two minutes ago, Flavia," Violet said, pulling her feet crisscross onto the chair. "It's not like we've been waiting an hour for them."

Flavia stared down her ski-slope nose at Violet and then turned toward me. "Ms. O'Shea, I understand you called this meeting. Care to fill us in on what was so urgent?"

"Happy to. I'm sure that by now you've all heard about what happened at the circus." I turned to acknowledge Janessa and Creed. In Creed's chair sat a person who resembled the ringmaster, except this person was a woman, not a man. She smiled, presumably at the confused look on my face.

"It's me," she said in a sultry, sexy voice, "just in a different package today."

"I'm sorry?" And just that fast, I realized Creed was gender fluid and was presenting his female identity now. In profile, I saw that this woman had the same long, slender nose and narrow, softly clefted chin.

"Call me Credence, darling," she instructed and returned her attention to the rest of the group. "Yes, sadly for Jayne, she arrived at the big top this morning just in time to learn that our beloved Berlin had been killed."

Along with nodding heads, there were a couple gasps. Apparently, not everyone had heard about Berlin's passing.

"You're claiming that Berlin was killed?" Flavia asked me, not Credence. "Do we know this for certain? Could it have been an accident?"

"Questions like yours is exactly why I called the meeting," I explained. "Fortunately, Janessa stood guard to keep the public out of the tent. When I arrived, I secured the scene while we waited more than an hour for the sheriff's deputy to arrive and conduct a formal investigation."

"You just can't keep your nose out of what's none of your business, can you?" Flavia sniffed her own pointy nose in my direction.

She was trying to upset me. I wasn't going to take her bait.

"Someone needed to ensure that evidence was not compromised, or we might never be able to figure out what happened." I glanced around the table as I spoke. "The village has been without on-site law enforcement for almost three weeks, and I'm the most qualified to take charge of a situation like this. It's unacceptable any time of year to leave the sheriff's position vacant. In the middle of the tourist season, with thousands of people here, it's unthinkable. We've put this off long enough. We need a new sheriff, and we need one now."

"Are you volunteering?" Laurel, The Inn's manager, asked with a wink.

Before I could open my mouth to respond, Flavia stepped in again. "Martin is doing much better. He has every intention of returning to duty as soon as he's able."

"I like Martin," I said, "and respect his efforts, but he's

not a trained officer and not qualified to take over as sheriff."

Flavia stood from her chair, planted her hands firmly on the table, and glared at me. Beneath the table, sensing that my emotions were rising, Meeka leaned against my legs and then lay on my feet.

"Jayne's right, Flavia," Morgan said. "I'm sure none of us would have an issue with Martin returning to a deputy or assistant position, but we have a responsibility to our visitors. If we neglect that responsibility, they'll stop coming and that would mean certain death for the village."

"A number of our guests have already asked about the death at the circus," Laurel said. "We've been able to ease their fears, but permanent law enforcement would help."

"What are we proposing?" Flavia asked, her voice clipped. "Does anyone know of a candidate for sheriff?"

All eyes turned to me, probably thinking of my connections at the Madison PD.

"I know someone," Donovan said.

Flavia's attention snapped to him. "You do?"

"I do. My cousin's son. His name is Zeb Warren. I'll grant you, he's young, but I understand he's extremely dedicated to law enforcement."

"Very well," Flavia said, pleased with this option. "I vote that we bring in Zeb Warren on a trial basis and see how he does."

In other words, she wanted to be sure that Mr. Warren could adapt to Whispering Pines' expectations. Or rather, Flavia's expectations. If he could do as told, the way Sheriff Brighton apparently had, our pseudo-mayor would be happy.

"I second the vote," Donovan said.

No surprise there. Donovan, a six-foot-tall sturdily built man, was reduced to lapdog behavior whenever Flavia was around. I couldn't for the life of me understand what sort of spell she had cast on him, which was an actual possibility in this village, but there was nothing she could demand that he wouldn't do.

"Any objections?" Flavia fixed her stare on me, as though expecting me to argue.

I'd reserve my opinion until I saw Donovan's cousin's son in action.

"We need to get somebody in office," I said, "and this is the first step. If for some reason Mr. Warren doesn't work out, we'll find someone else."

All the members agreed. A unanimous vote? There was never a unanimous vote with this group.

"Unless there is any other urgent business that needs to be discussed this evening," Flavia said, "I call that we adjourn this meeting."

"Seconded," Donovan said immediately.

"We are adjourned," Flavia said.

Credence looked at me as we stood from our chairs and rolled her eyes. "There really is no reason for us to be that formal."

"Makes her feel powerful," I said. "By the way, sorry about my reaction earlier."

"Don't give it another thought." Credence dismissed it with an elegant flick of her fingers. "Honestly, if you had walked in dressed as a dude, I would've given you the same reaction."

We left the conference room together, passed through The Inn's lobby, and out onto the front porch.

"How's everything at the circus?" I asked.

"The initial shock has worn off." Credence bent to scratch Meeka's ears and then confided, "They're scared. Me too. We're afraid there's a killer on the loose. I'm so glad you called this meeting. Three weeks is two weeks and six days too long to go without law enforcement."

"Deputy Atkins talked to everyone? He did a thorough investigation?"

"Like you said he would be, he was there for hours, so

I'll say yes. He did talk to nearly everyone. Gave me his card, said to call if anything else came up, and promised to swing through as often as possible."

"That's as much as we can ask. Hopefully, our new guy, Mr. Warren, will get here fast."

Credence gave a little shrug. "We've always got you. Thanks for stepping in this morning. I'm not quite sure how I would've handled everything without you there."

"Happy to help, but I'm sure you would have done fine."

"*I* probably could have," Credence placed a hand over her heart and winked, "but Creed tends to be a wimp."

She gave me a finger wave and walked off.

Morgan appeared at my side then. "Are you headed home now?"

"No, I told Tripp I'd meet him over at Triple G." The smell of greasy bar food wafted over from the pub about fifty yards away and my stomach rumbled.

"I'll walk with you." She hooked her arm through mine. "You know, there's a much easier solution to this whole sheriff situation."

A voice behind us asked, "Is that who I think it is?"

We turned to see Cybil and Effie, then turned back to determine who Cybil was pointing out. I assumed she meant the woman who had just exited Grapes, Grains, and Grub. She seemed familiar even from this distance.

Approximately five foot six, strawberry-blonde hair in a pixie cut, five or ten pounds overweight.

"Oh my Goddess," Morgan said and slowed for Cybil and Effie to catch up. "If you think that's Reeva, you're right."

"Sheriff Brighton's wife?" I asked. Also, Flavia Reed's sister. No wonder she looked familiar.

"That's her." Effie called Reeva's name and hustled over to her, Cybil hot on her heels.

As excited as Morgan, Effie, and Cybil were to see that

Reeva had returned, Reeva didn't seem at all interested in standing in the center of the village commons to catch up with her old village mates. All she would say was that she'd come to pack up Karl's house. Since she was his only remaining relative, sorting through his estate was left to her.

"Sounds like my situation," I said.

She turned to me, her intense blue eyes and long, slender nose just like her sister's. Reeva was an inch or so taller than Flavia and her less-than-warm disposition seemed rooted more in sorrow than in nastiness.

"Who are you?" Reeva asked.

I held out my hand, which she accepted. "Jayne O'Shea."

"Lucy and Keven's granddaughter." Reeva immediately recognized my name. "I heard that your grandmother had recently passed. I'm very sorry." She froze as a thought seemed to occur to her. "You found Yasmine."

"I did," I said simply, hoping my sympathies for her were conveyed in my tone and expression.

Her lips tightened, an expression much like Flavia's, and she studied me a little closer. Yes, I was the one who had pushed the investigation into her daughter's death. Her eyes remained locked on me a moment longer, then she turned and walked away, leaving Effie and Cybil speechless.

"Give her a little time," Effie told Cybil. "She probably just got into town. We'll stop by and see how she's doing tomorrow or the next day."

"I wonder if she'll sell the house," Morgan said after the fortune tellers left. "I can't remember the last time a house was sold in Whispering Pines. They usually just pass on through the families."

"Maybe she'll want to stay."

"That," Morgan said, "would be either the best thing that's happened to Whispering Pines in a long time or the worst."

"What do you mean?"

"First tell me, did Flavia seem strange to you at the meeting?"

"Flavia always seem strange to me. But if you mean was she acting differently, no."

"That means she doesn't realize her sister is back. You know there's bad blood between them."

"Yes, but I heard that Reeva is very forgiving. Maybe she's let it go."

"It would actually be better for everyone concerned if there was still some tension between them. The last thing we want is for them to team up."

"Why?"

"Because Reeva is quite a strong kitchen witch."

I closed my eyes and let out a sigh. How many kinds of witches were there? "What exactly does a kitchen witch do?"

"She protects hearth and home," Morgan said. "They also tend to be excellent cooks."

"Oh, so Sugar and Honey are kitchen witches." Sugar made the best scones on the planet, Honey the best ice cream.

Morgan smiled at my understanding and then turned serious again. "Bad blood between sister witches could be very bad indeed."

"What are you saying? Dueling wands at midnight beneath a full moon? A cook-off for the golden cauldron? The loser has to wear the ugly robes at the next coven gathering?"

Thankfully, Morgan and I had become good friends; I might be in danger of having a hex cast on me otherwise. Instead, she simply shook her head.

"Sounds to me like you're talking about negative intent," I said. "You've told me many times that the first rule of Wicca is to do no harm."

"You've heard the saying 'Hell hath no fury like a woman scorned,' right?" Morgan asked, and I nodded. "You don't want to be around when the fury of a scorned witch lets loose. Especially fury that's had twenty years to simmer."

Chapter 9

FOR THE NEXT THREE DAYS, neither Tripp nor I left the ten-acre thumb of land that jutted into the lake and comprised my grandparents' private piece of Whispering Pines. The walls in the great room were almost free of wallpaper, and the closer we got to finishing that awful task, the more determined we were to get it done. Tripp worked late into the night until every wall had been stripped of paper and cleared of glue. Now and then I'd vacuum, but mostly I continued packing up the seven bedrooms. The largest, fullest, and one that would take the most time was Gran's. It would also take a lot of emotional energy. I planned to do it last.

The second to last room I emptied had been my father's when he was a boy. It was large with a beautiful alcove that overlooked the lake. The longer I spent in there, the more easily I could picture long ago piles of dirty laundry on the floor and the sheets in a twisted heap on the unmade bed. Gran hadn't done much to it since he moved out after high school. She'd tidied it and packed away things like his clothing and school items, but left out the models of the pyramids he had built and his books on ancient Egyptian curses. It had a frozen-in-time feel to it and obviously hadn't been used in a very long time. Seventeen years, to be precise. Poor Gran. Their feud devastated her.

Whatever had happened to cause the rift had also hardened Dad's heart against everything related to Whispering Pines. He was determined to get rid of the house and its contents, even stating that he had no interest in any of his childhood possessions and instructing me to toss them all in a dumpster. I had a feeling he would regret that later, so carefully packed up everything in the room, except for the furniture, and planned to have it all shipped to my parents' house in Madison.

I had just finished the room when Tripp appeared in the doorway.

"I'm beat," he said. "Ready to call it a day?"

"Your timing is perfect. I'm done in here and was just thinking that I'm ready for dinner. Since you're covered in paint, how about I go start grilling burgers?"

"Yum. I'll clean up and meet you on the sundeck."

Half an hour later, we were sitting with Sprecher Black Bavarian Lagers in hand and quarter-pound cheeseburgers, tangy coleslaw, and mustardy potato salad on our plates.

"You've been kind of quiet the last couple of days," I said while loading my fork with slaw. "Something wrong?"

I figured it was the whole bed-and-breakfast issue.

"Do you really think Lily Grace could tell me something about my mom?"

I offered an empathetic smile. "I'm sure she'll tell you something. I guess there's only one way to find out if it'll help. Let Lily Grace do a reading. We can go see her tomorrow if you want. It's up to you what you do with the information she gives you."

He nodded. "I think I want to try."

Most nights after dinner, Tripp and I would sit on the deck and talk, enjoying the cooler night air and breathing in the fragrance of the lake water. The shadowy shapes of the pine trees swayed against the darkening sky, their branches and needles brushing together and making the whispering sounds that gave the village its name. Tonight, Tripp wasn't in the mood for any of it. When we were done eating, he said good night and headed for his trailer. Unsure of what to do by myself, I considered a quick kayak ride. It wasn't dark yet, but it would be soon, so that was out.

Instead, I found a tennis ball in the boathouse garage and played fetch with Meeka, something we hadn't done in a long time. After I tossed the ball out onto the water, she would race down the dock and launch herself into the lake to retrieve it. The only downside to that game, other than a sore throwing arm for me, was that Meeka then smelled like wet dog and fish. After giving her a bath, I crawled into bed with a sci-fi book I'd been wanting to read. I was worried about Tripp, though. I wasn't used to seeing him so down. Not only couldn't I concentrate on the book, I didn't sleep well.

***

"What's going on over there?" Tripp pointed at the large gathering outside the sheriff's station.

We had just picked up paint and a few other supplies at Sundry, the general store on the far east side of the village, and were on our way to see Lily Grace.

"I have no idea." I pulled the Cherokee into the small parking lot behind the sheriff's station." Let's go see."

We found Morgan on the edge of the crowd.

"Our new sheriff has arrived," she explained as though he'd just been delivered via FedEx. "You didn't know?"

"We've been working on the house," Tripp said. "We haven't been into the village for a few days."

"Has anyone met him yet?" I asked.

"Donovan has, of course," Morgan said. "And Flavia, I believe. They spread the word that we should all gather here to meet him. And his mother."

"His mother?" I asked.

Morgan held my gaze for a couple seconds and then looked away. "You'll see."

I was about to push her for more information when Flavia appeared in front of the crowd, standing on a stepladder so everyone could see her. "Thank you all for coming," she said. "It's been many weeks since our beloved Sheriff Brighton left us, and the council realized it was time, for the good of the village and our welcome visitors, to fill his vacancy."

The council realized? Please. If I hadn't said something, we would have gone on without a sheriff for … I don't even want to think about it. No big deal, I didn't need credit for bringing law and order back to Whispering Pines.

"You didn't come to hear me speak, though," Flavia continued. "I'd like to introduce our new sheriff. Please give a warm welcome to Zeb Warren."

As the crowd applauded, Flavia stepped down and a young man in jeans and a black uniform shirt climbed the stepladder. Honestly, it took me a few seconds to realize that this was our new sheriff. Donovan said he was young, but he didn't mention he still slept with a blankie.

"He's not really our new guy, is he?" I asked Morgan and Tripp.

Morgan said nothing.

"He looks like he just graduated high school."

"Give him a chance," Tripp said. "Remember, plenty of the officers in Madison felt you were too young to be a detective."

"I was twenty-five years old and had been a patrol officer for four years. I earned my advancement." I flung a hand at the person standing before us and whispered, "Look at him. He's still got pimples. He's a Boy Scout, not a sheriff."

"Thank you so much." Sheriff Zeb's voice cracked. "I can't tell you how proud and excited I am to be serving the people of Whispering Pines, Wisconsin. I understand I've got some awfully impressive boots to fill. Uncle Donovan and Ms. Flavia have told me a lot about Karl Brighton. I plan to get straight to work, but I'll be looking to you all to help me out while I find my bearings here."

"He means he'll need us to fill in for him during nap time," I whispered.

"Stop," Tripp scolded.

"Remember your karma, Jayne." Morgan gave me a cautionary look. "You receive what you put out in the world."

"There's someone I'd like you all to meet," Sheriff Zeb said. "Come on up here, Mom."

A woman with a huge grin climbed up next to him on the stepladder while Donovan held onto it, ensuring it wouldn't topple over. She looked like an aged hippie in her long skirt and Birkenstocks.

"I'd like everyone to welcome my mother, Vera Warren," Sheriff Zeb called out. "Mom will be helping me out around the station."

"Oh, no," I muttered to myself. "Please don't say it."

"Say what?" Tripp asked.

"I guess," Sheriff Zeb announced with a shrug, "that she'll be like my deputy."

"That." I spun to face Tripp and Morgan. "Is he serious?"

Honestly, if this guy showed up at my station in Madison looking for a job, they'd send him to the mail room and give him a cart, not a badge and a gun.

"Let's go for a walk." Morgan looped her arm through mine and led me down the Fairy Path toward the yoga studio and healing center. When we were out of earshot of everyone else, we stopped walking and she asked in a disappointed mother's voice, "Why are you being so contrary?"

I inhaled and counted to three. Meeka leaned against

my leg, her way of trying to calm me down.

"Sorry for being contrary," I said, "but do you have any idea how old Mr. Warren is?"

Morgan gave me an awkward smile. "I believe Donovan said he's twenty-one."

That was a year or two older than he looked.

"Maybe he knows more than I'm giving him credit for," I said, "but twenty-one is the minimum age to be appointed as a *deputy*. This means he has little or no experience. Just because Whispering Pines is small, that doesn't mean we don't deserve quality people running it. I was a member of the Madison Police Department for five years. When I think of everything I didn't know on day one versus everything I had learned over those five years, it's truly mind-blowing."

Why did the Whispering Pines village council refuse to take law enforcement seriously? Zeb needed supervision and lots more training. I suppose I could try to help him.

"I agree with you." Tripp's voice was low and soothing. "Look, we know how by-the-book you are. How about we give him a chance, though. Your captain is putting together a list, right?"

"He is." I sent my former captain in Madison a request for potential candidates the day of the council meeting, and he promised to send me some names.

"Remember what we said about Pine time?" Tripp asked.

A few weeks earlier, when I was concerned that Sheriff Brighton and Deputy Reed didn't seem very concerned about investigating Yasmine Long's death, I complained about it to Tripp. He told me I was too used to things working at a big-city pace. Whispering Pines, he said, worked at its own speed. He called it Pine time.

I tapped a pinecone on the ground in front of me with my toe then kicked it off the path. "You're right. I need to give this guy a chance."

The thing was, Berlin had died four days ago. The more

I thought about how she died, the more I was sure she'd been murdered. Deputy Atkins had thoroughly investigated, but the County's resources were already tapped. He wouldn't likely do more with this case unless the autopsy results came back indicating a suspicious death.

"What are you thinking?" Tripp asked.

"I'm thinking about Berlin's death and how I hope it doesn't get ignored or forgotten with everything else going on."

"Is there any way to stop you from digging into this?" Morgan asked.

"Sure. If our new sheriff pays proper attention to it, I promise to leave it alone."

"But you don't think he will," Tripp said. "Do you?"

Staring back down the Fairy Path, I could still see the crowd gathered there, the new sheriff still talking. I was basing my opinion on his appearance alone. Discriminating against him based on his age. Like so many had done to me.

"I told you, I'll give him a chance."

But I had what I felt were legitimate concerns and I'd stay alert to them. If there was a killer running around Whispering Pines, and I believed there was, I couldn't in all good conscience leave the safety of the villagers and tourists in the hands of a newbie sheriff and his mother.

Chapter 10

AS THE CROWD BY THE sheriff's station dispersed, Tripp and I returned to the Cherokee, Morgan to Shoppe Mystique. I had just put Meeka in her crate when I spotted Creed walking around to the back of the station.

"Give me a minute," I told Tripp and jogged over to Creed. "Haven't talked to you in a few days. How are things going?"

"A little better," he said. "We're operating on our normal schedule again, but the big top performances don't feel right."

"What are you doing for a closing act?"

"First, we shine a spotlight on the chandelier Berlin used in some acts and have a minute of silence for her. Then Dallas and Abilene close the show."

"That sounds very touching."

He shrugged. "It's working, for now. Honestly, though, things are tense. The carnies want answers. *I* want answers."

"It's eating *me* up. I can only imagine what you all are feeling. Would you do something for me?" He arched his eyebrows in question. "Let me know when the new sheriff makes an appearance up there."

Creed gave me a knowing smile. "Sticking your nose in

again?"

"A death is a priority. A death due to murder, is a whole other ballgame. I want to know he can do the job. If he's not going to work out, we need to make that decision right away."

Creed nodded toward the station. "After the sheriff finished talking with the crowd, I told him I was happy to speak with him about Berlin when he was ready. He thanked me, but I felt brushed off."

Zeb had better not ignore this. Everything in me was screaming that I should just go up to the grounds right now and talk to people. To Gianni who clearly had issues with Berlin. To Dallas who'd also had disagreements with her. To anyone else who knew anything about her. I'd be stepping on the new guy's territory, though. Not to mention, I had no jurisdiction in Whispering Pines. Or anywhere, for that matter.

"Promise you'll keep me informed?" I begged Creed. "Keep your eyes open for anything odd." Then I laughed because what wasn't odd around here? "Let me know if I can do anything."

"I will." Relief was evident on his face. "I know that maybe you shouldn't be digging around in this—I heard about the trouble you got into over Yasmine Long—but I cared a lot about Berlin. If someone murdered her, I want that person brought to justice. If no one else will do it, I'm happy to let you snoop around."

I returned to the car, feeling a little more at ease but ready to get a lecture about staying out of it from Tripp. Creed and I had only been a few feet away; he must've heard our conversation. He said nothing, though, as I moved the Cherokee from the little parking lot behind the sheriff's station to the one closer to the Fortune Tellers' Triangle—an area framed by the creek, the two-lane highway that bisected the village, and the road that led to my house. He was either upset with me or nervous about what Lily Grace would tell him.

***

At the parking lot on the west end of the village, we took a flight of stairs to a tunnel that crossed beneath the highway. Meeka and I led the way, Tripp following a few feet behind. Our footsteps released the smell of moss and damp, loamy soil, and after fifty yards or so, we came to a literal doorframe covered in climbing vines in the middle of the woods. A long thick row of tall bushes, pine trees, and deciduous trees acted like a hedge along either side of it.

Through this dramatic entrance, we could see the fortune tellers' area, my favorite place in the entire village when I was a child. Except for Gran and Gramps' house, of course. Gypsy wagons with spoked wooden wheels were scattered randomly about the one-acre area. Hand-painted signs on the sides of each wagon advertised the teller's name and specialty — palmistry, tarot, crystal balls. The bright jewel-tone shades of the wagons — pink, turquoise, purple, and orange — made them pop against the earthy browns and greens of the surrounding forest. Beyond them was another four or five acres that held the cottages where the tellers lived.

Since most of the residents had gone to the station to meet Sheriff Warren, the Triangle was almost empty except for a handful of tellers and tourists waiting to have their fortunes told. While we waited for Lily Grace to return, Meeka met a friendly schnauzer to play with and Tripp and I chatted with some tourists. Well, I chatted. Tripp was too nervous to do anything but smile and nod, and only if I prodded him to do so with a nudge of my elbow. Within a few minutes, Lily Grace was back.

"You ready for me to do a reading, Tripp?" The slight eye roll said she still wasn't comfortable with her gift.

He grunted that he was, and she led us to a small clearing behind the wagons. Instead of a wagon like the others, she had a tent of sorts made of large, multicolored scarves tied together at the corners and flung over ropes tied to the branches of surrounding pine trees. Beneath the scarf tent was a simple wooden platform covered with numerous handwoven rugs and large pillows that served as seats. At the very center was a two-foot-tall round table covered with still more scarves. Very bohemian.

"This is temporary," she said. "I have to decide if I'm staying here or going to veterinary school after I graduate in the spring. If I stay, I'll get a wagon too."

She held out a hand, inviting Tripp and me in.

"Do want me to stay or leave?" I asked him.

"You can stay," Tripp said with a shrug. "I don't care."

His tone said he wanted me to stay, so I chose a large cushion in a corner of the tent and sat crisscross. Meeka climbed into my lap and snuggled in for a nap. Lily Grace sat on a thick round cushion on one side of the table, tucking her legs inside her floor-length skirt—a crazy patchwork of browns, tans, and turquoise fabrics. Tripp sat across from her on a large square cushion.

"The only way I can make this work," Lily Grace began, "is to hold your hands. I don't have a clue how tarot works, and the only thing I see in a crystal ball is my own face."

She reached her hands across the table, palms up, and nodded for Tripp to place his hands palms down on top of them. From where I sat, I could see her face but not Tripp's.

Lily Grace inhaled deeply and closed her eyes for a few seconds. When she opened them again, a subtle change from teenage girl to fortune teller had occurred.

"I understand you're searching for an answer," she said. "What's the question?"

Tripp fidgeted on his cushion, hands still on Lily Grace's. "My mom took off when I was thirteen. I was fifteen the last time I heard from her, and I started looking for her when I was eighteen. I just want to know if she's okay." So softly I almost didn't hear, he added, "It's fine if she doesn't want me in her life."

Lily Grace closed her eyes again. "Tell me about her. What does she look like?"

"She's beautiful." His voice quivered the tiniest bit. "Sandy blonde hair halfway down her back. Eyes like mine. Average height, five-five maybe, and tiny."

With her eyes still closed, she pressed her palms to his. Her head and shoulders started to sway slightly side-to-side.

"I see a woman and a little boy," she reported, her voice breathy and with little inflection. "They're at a playground. He's laughing as she pushes him on the swings."

"She used to take me to the playground every night after dinner," Tripp explained, "unless it was raining. Then we'd go home and after my bath, she'd read me a bedtime story."

The pain in his voice was so raw, I had to blink back tears.

Lily Grace began to sway again and after another few seconds, her brow furrowed. More swaying, more frowning. She said nothing for almost a full minute, then she opened her eyes and pulled her hands away from Tripp's.

I could barely hear Tripp's voice as he asked, "What did you see?"

She hesitated before saying, "There's no guarantee that what I see is accurate." She rocked back-and-forth on her cushion, a motion that seemed to be more self-soothing than vision inducing. "Remember that, okay?"

He nodded and with more grit repeated, "What did you see?"

"Two things. First, the outline of the state of Missouri. Then, a headstone. I didn't see a name but there was a date. About two years ago."

Tripp looked down, cleared his throat, and nodded slowly. "Thanks. What do I owe you?"

"I don't charge friends," Lily Grace said.

"What do I owe you?" he repeated, his voice a growl

now.

Without waiting for her answer, he stood and set two twenties on the table. He turned to leave the tent, wouldn't or couldn't look at me as he did, and then headed in the direction of the parking lot. Meeka leapt from my lap and chased after him.

"It's not my fault if people get bad news," Lily Grace said, clearly upset.

"No, it's not," I assured. "He'll be okay. Not knowing what happened to his mom has been eating him up for almost fifteen years. I'm more concerned about how he'll react to the fact that she might have been alive up until two years ago and never contacted him."

"This sucks so bad." Lily Grace flapped her arms at her side as though they'd fallen asleep and she was trying to wake them up. "I hate it when I have to tell people bad stuff."

Random cop memories flashed in my mind. Having to show up at parents' doorways to let them know their son or daughter had been in a car accident. Letting a spouse know that her husband had died because he'd been in the wrong place at the wrong time. Informing someone that the trail had run cold on their missing loved one and there was nothing more we could do to find them.

"I understand completely," I said. "Helping people and making their lives better is the good part. Delivering bad news makes for a bad day all around."

"How do I deal with that?" she asked desperately. "It happens a lot more than I expected."

"You tell yourself that you provided an answer, and that's a good thing. As far as I'm concerned, knowing is always better than not knowing."

She stared at me, her gorgeous light-turquoise eyes glistening. I pulled her into a hug and after about two seconds, she pushed away from me. At first, I thought she was just uncomfortable with the physical contact, but the look on her face said it was something more.

"What's the matter?" I asked.

She let out a fed-up groan. "I saw something."

"For me? What did you see?"

Lily Grace made a face. "Body parts. Miscellaneous bloody arms and legs. What the hell was that?"

Thoroughly disgusted, she turned and walked into the woods without another word.

Chapter 11

TRIPP MADE IT PERFECTLY CLEAR he didn't want to talk about what Lily Grace had seen. So, we worked in separate areas of the house. I started on the bathrooms upstairs. By late that afternoon, I had finished packing up five of the six, plus the hallway linen closet. The only thing left for me to do on the second floor was to pack up Gran's bedroom and bathroom. That was it. I couldn't avoid her stuff any longer.

It was quitting time for the day, though. I'd start on those last two rooms first thing in the morning.

Downstairs, I found that Tripp had completed all the edging in the great room. No small task, considering all the corners, baseboards, and windows he had to paint around. Looked like he'd be putting paint on the walls tomorrow. That would be a big day. It had taken a month to get to this point.

I couldn't find him anywhere in the house so went out to his trailer in the front yard.

"Tripp? I'm going to start dinner. Did you want to eat with me?"

There was no response, and I assumed he wasn't in the popup either. As I started to walk away, he said, "I'm good. See you tomorrow."

"You're sure?"

"Good night, Jayne."

What was the right thing to do when a normally upbeat person became depressed? Since I'd met him, the closest Tripp had come to a bad mood was when he felt I was endangering myself by getting involved with the Yasmine Long investigation. That was different, though. Now, he was down about his own life. We couldn't know for sure that Lily Grace's vision was accurate, but as far as Tripp seemed concerned, his mother was dead. With few options, all I could do was give him space.

A search of the house refrigerator rewarded me with leftover barbecued ribs and mashed potatoes that I warmed up and ate on the back patio. I sat there for so long, lost in thought and entranced with watching boats and jet skiers gliding past on the lake, the next thing I knew, the sun was hanging low in the sky and fish were snapping at bugs on the lake's surface.

Fireflies blinked in the weeds along the tree line. Confused by the little lights that kept turning off and on, and looking at me like I was doing it, Meeka wore herself out trying to catch them. When the mosquitoes got so thick the bug zapper couldn't keep up, I whistled for her and we went in for the night.

As we sat in my cozy little apartment, watching a Brewers game on the small TV and then switching over to Netflix when it was obvious the Brew Crew had the game wrapped up, a feeling of intense loneliness came over me. Meeka had crawled up on the loveseat next to me and fell asleep. I placed my hand on her chest, letting her body heat and steady breathing comfort and ground me.

"Thank god for you and Tripp. I don't know what I'd do without either of you."

This need to be with people was new for me. Until coming to Whispering Pines, I never had a problem being home alone at the end of my shift. That was probably because, as a cop, I spent my entire workday with people from all walks of life. When I got home, I was usually so exhausted it didn't matter if Jonah was there or not. I would pretty much do what I was doing now, sit and watch TV with my dog before going to bed.

Now, I'd become used to having company every night—sitting on the sundeck with Tripp or going into the village and having dinner with whoever was at The Inn or Grapes, Grains, and Grub—it was like I'd forgotten how to be alone. I was probably just upset for Tripp. And there was Berlin's death, too.

Bored with the movie, I turned off the television and stood on the sundeck, breathing in the clear night air while Meeka did her doggie duty one last time. A gentle breeze blew the tall pines back and forth, their needles making that whispering sound as they rubbed together. It was almost like they were trying to soothe me with their rocking motion and *shushing* sound. I laughed when I realized I was swaying along with them, but I wasn't soothed. Time to just go to bed.

The next morning, I woke to fluffy white clouds dotting the sky. It was windy too, causing sunlight and shadows to switch places as the clouds slid by. Today was the day I had to pack up Gran's room. I couldn't put it off any longer. I started to psych myself up before even getting out of bed, continued psyching as I pulled on jeans and a T-shirt, and as I walked across the yard.

I grabbed the knob on one of the French doors at the back of the house, twisted, and ran smack into the door. Tripp was normally in the kitchen by this time making breakfast for us. I peered through one of the small windowpanes to see if maybe he was in there and simply forgot to unlock the door, but there were no lights on inside. I ran back to the apartment, grabbed my set of house keys, and let myself in.

"Tripp? Are you here?"

Nothing but silence answered me. He must be moving slowly today. I went out the front door and over to his trailer to see if he wanted breakfast. That's when I noticed his rusty old F-350 was gone. Maybe he went to pick up something from Sundry. I made coffee and poured myself a bowl of cereal. Tripp still hadn't returned by the time I was done eating.

I stood next to his trailer, gazing up the driveway as though expecting him to appear, but he didn't. I stared out at the lake. Over at the boathouse. What to do? My motivation to tackle Gran's room was now gone, but my need to be busy and do something productive was strong. Creed said he'd let me snoop around. A little thrill rushed through me.

"Let's head on over to the circus and see if we can be helpful."

I looked down to find Meeka giving me a disapproving look.

"I'll get to Gran's room. This is more important."

Meeka didn't budge. Just sat there, judging me with her black doggie eyes.

"Working." I gave the command that always put her into K-9 mode. She hesitated before standing at attention, silently expressing her disappointment with me. By the time I had finished cleaning up my breakfast dishes, though, she was waiting by the Cherokee, tail wagging, ready to assist me.

As I crept along the two-lane highway that cut through the village, I thought for the hundredth time that there needed to be fences that would force tourists to use the bridge to cross the highway instead of darting across like thrill-seeking rabbits. I had to stomp on the brakes five times in a quarter mile.

Finally, I made it to the lot closest to the circus grounds. As we neared the entrance, I saw Colette, the tall woman, and Creed standing near the ticket booth.

"We were just talking about you," Creed said.

"About me?" I asked.

"Indirectly," Colette corrected, her voice deep, which seemed to fit with her oversized body. "We were talking about getting someone else to do an investigation if the new sheriff didn't show up. Creed said you'd do it."

"That's kind of why I'm here." I turned to Creed. "Can I talk to you?"

"Sure, I've got a few minutes."

He directed me to a cluster of picnic tables near a food vendor hut. We sat across from each other while Meeka busied herself with investigating the plethora of smells, both food and animal related.

"I have an idea of what might have happened," I explained. "If I'm right, Berlin's death is definitely suspicious. Problem is, the medical examiner can only go off what her body tells him. A good investigation would uncover other important details."

"You're worried about something," Creed noted. "What is it?"

I nodded my agreement. "If the autopsy comes back as a natural death or is ruled an accident, that will most likely be the end of it. The county doesn't have the resources to dig further."

"And our new sheriff?"

I fixed a pointed look on him. He already knew my feelings on that.

"I don't think this was an accident." I took out my phone and opened the picture of the tranquilizer dart I found on the ground in the big top. "I assume you've seen these before."

Creed took about two seconds to study the picture. "Of course, that's one of the darts Gianni uses on the animals. At least it looks like the same kind he uses. I can't say for sure that that's one of his."

"I found this one on the ground in the big top while I was waiting for Deputy Atkins."

I waited for Creed to fill in the blanks.

KEPT SECRETS | 89

"That's surprising," he said. "Gianni is usually obsessively cautious with them."

"How often does he have a dart with him?"

"If he's near an animal, which he almost always is, he has darts and a dart gun with him. During performances, he uses a longer rifle-style. He claims the bigger gun instills more confidence in the audience. Any other time, he uses a gun that looks like a pistol that he carries in a holster on his hip."

"You told me earlier that there was some bad blood between Berlin and Gianni."

"Hang on, Jayne." Creed held up a hand. "I know what you're insinuating. I have a hard time believing that one of the carnies would have killed her."

"When I asked you the other day who Berlin had issues with, you only mentioned carnies. If one of them isn't the killer, that would mean another villager or a tourist is."

He considered this for a minute, tapping a long slender finger on his narrow chin. "I can't speak with any sort of certainty. Perhaps you should speak with Gianni."

I gave him a thankful smile. "I know how hard it is to discover that someone you thought you knew well turns out to be someone different." For me, that person was Jonah. After seven years together, I couldn't believe how unsupportive he had become of my career. "Do you know where I can find Gianni?"

"He should be over at the animal enclosures. Go all the way down the midway to the big top and take a left. There's an obvious trail back there that will lead you straight to them."

I thanked him and whistled for Meeka, who grudgingly turned away from the little green grass snake she was playing with and trotted over to my side. Yes, I was pulling her away from something fun, but wait until she saw the lions, wolves, and bears.

Chapter 12

AS DIRECTED, WE TOOK A left when we got to the big top. Creed was right, the pathway behind the tent was instantly visible. It was actually two dirt strips with a band of grass between them, presumably caused by the wheels of the vehicle Gianni used to transport the animals from their pens to the big top and back. The enclosures were set far enough away from the main grounds that tourists wouldn't treat the enclosures like a zoo and wander over, but close enough that it was easy to get the animals to the performances.

The area looked like a maze or obstacle course. A ten-foot-tall wooden walkway, erected on top of a six-foot-tall berm, ran between the spacious animal enclosures. Twelve feet of fencing surrounded each enclosure and ensured that the animals — lions, tigers, bears, and wolves — stayed where they were intended.

"Impressive, is it not?"

I turned to see a man standing behind me. *Late sixties, thinning curly hair that was mostly gray streaked with medium-brown, graying goatee, bright-blue eyes.*

"Are you Gianni Cordano?"

"The one and only. Around here, at least." Gianni's Italian accent with its happy lilt made me smile. "How can I help you?"

He bent and offered Meeka the back of his hand. Surprisingly, she stepped behind my legs without looking up for permission to interact with him. This told me she was uneasy about the man. Of course, there were dozens of strange smells wafting around her, and surely from Gianni as well. She had to be overwhelmed. Still, I kept this in mind as I spoke with the veterinarian.

"I'm Jayne O'Shea. My family —"

He chuckled as he stood upright. "I'm aware of the O'Shea name. Your family owns all of the land here."

"At some point, the fact that people know who I am will stop surprising me."

"I am happy to say," Gianni said, "that I was one of the first carnies to come here. Since I was a boy, my passion has been to help animals. As I got older, I started rescuing circus animals that were being mistreated or had no place to go when their circus shut down. Many years ago, I met Morgan Barlow's grandmother. Dulcie suggested this might be a place for me and my animals. I came to visit, met your grandmother, and a couple of weeks later after setting up the pens, we all had a new home." He gestured toward the wolf enclosure. "Not too long after that, we heard that someone had been shooting wolves prowling too close to his home. Those that he shot but didn't kill joined us as well."

"Another successful Whispering Pines story," I said. "I'm glad for both you and the animals. Listen, if you have a minute, I wanted to ask you about something, Mr. Cordano."

"Please, call me Gianni. I have time if you'd like to follow me. It's feeding time. The animals would not be happy to miss their lunch."

"Is it all right for Meeka to come with us?"

He looked down at the Westie and smiled. "That's fine, but be sure to keep her on a tight leash. There's little chance that an animal could ever escape from its cage, but she could easily squeeze in. I wouldn't want her to become overexcited and try to get a closer look."

I wouldn't want that either. I adjusted the retractable leash to keep Meeka close and took a firm grip on it. We followed along the walkway as Gianni pushed a large wheelbarrow filled with buckets of food. As we got to the first enclosure, the lions, Gianni pulled two large chunks of raw meat from one of the buckets. He leaned on the sturdy railing running along the walkway as he tossed the meat into the enclosure, one hunk at each end. The lions rushed up to claim their prize, protectively snarling and growling at each other as they did.

"Is this why you installed the walkway?"

"It is. It took me many years to figure out a way to make feeding time easier. I initially chose this location because of the berm." He waved a hand at the tall pines that were here and everywhere throughout the two-thousand-acre property. "We cut down the trees one hundred yards on either side of the hill and it became the perfect spot for the enclosures. Placing the animals between the hill and the trees provides good protection from inclement weather. If you're curious, all the wood has been used throughout the village for structures, walkways, and firewood."

"Nice," I said. "People around here are very inventive."

"Anyway, it occurred to me one day that if I could raise myself above the enclosure fences, I could simply toss the food in instead of having to go inside with the animals. This is much faster and safer."

"I see that you're carrying a tranquilizer gun." I motioned at the holster on his hip. "Do you always have that with you?"

"I exercise extreme caution around my animals." Gianni tossed a few large fish in for the bears. "I never forget that they are wild creatures. If I am going to be around them, I always have a way to sedate them should something bad happen."

I held my camera out to him. "Does this look like one of your darts?"

He peered through the half-moon frame of his eyeglasses at the picture, the dart's orange feathers standing out like neon in the wood chips. "Yes, that looks to be one of mine. You have questions about darts?"

"I have questions about this particular dart." I explained to him where I had found it, and he paled.

"You think I shot that dart at Berlin."

"It's common knowledge that the two of you didn't get along well."

"We had our disagreements, yes, but you're wrong with what you're implying. I did not tranquilize Berlin."

"I don't have any proof yet that she was tranquilized."

Gianni's accent grew heavier as he became obviously upset. "Perhaps you should obtain proof before you start making accusations, no?"

He was right. I needed more proof than a dart on the ground. I made a mental note to send Dr. Bundy an email as soon as I got home and ask if he found a puncture wound.

"I'm not making accusations, Gianni. I'm simply asking questions. Is it possible that you dropped that dart during the performance?"

He stood back to study me for a moment, then shook his head insistently. "There is no way I would have dropped a dart and not known it. I keep one dart loaded in the gun at the ready in case of need. I always keep others with me as well."

From a pouch attached to his belt, he removed a black leather case. He lifted a flap on the case to reveal five darts, each with different colored feathers on top, each secure in its own slot. He held the case upside down and shook it, showing me that the darts could not fall out. They needed to be pulled.

"Why are there different colored feathers?"

"They're called stabilizers," Gianni explained, his accent

softening again. "They help with accuracy. They are different colors because I pre-fill the darts so they are ready for use. The drugs are administered by weight. Since each of my animals are different, each species requires its own dosage. A dog, for example, would die if I used a tiger's dart on it." He glanced down at Meeka. "For the record, I have never used a dart on any of our dogs."

I held up my phone with the picture again. "What animal is the orange dart for?"

"Orange is for the tigers. Yellow for the lions, blue for horses, red for bears, and pink for the wolves."

"How do you decide which dart to keep pre-loaded in the gun?"

"I prepare for the worst-case scenario and keep orange loaded. The tigers weigh the most. A red dart for a two hundred forty pound black bear will not adequately sedate a six hundred pound tiger."

I stared at the picture a little longer. "You said this one looks like the kind you use. Can you tell if is one of yours?"

"There's no way for me to know." Gianni huffed, offended again. "It looks like the brand I purchase, but anyone can buy a dart. The medication, however, is difficult to obtain. It's impossible to tell from this picture if that dart has medication in it."

"What kind of drug do you use?" Dr. Bundy would need to know specifically what to look for in a toxicology test.

"Ketamine. It is a commonly used veterinary sedative. It is effective but not fast-acting. After administration, it can take as long as three to four minutes for an animal to be rendered sedate, but the effects will last for about an hour, leaving plenty of time to perform whatever task is necessary."

"Ketamine. Is that the same drug that goes by the street name Special K?"

Gianni nodded. "Sadly, it is. The effects are long-lasting

and cause hallucinations, which is why those addicted like it so much. It is also highly lethal for humans if too much is administered." He held up a hand, stopping me from asking my next question. "I keep all of my medications under triple lock. Most who work here at the circus are good, decent people. Like the rest of us, they are just looking for a place to live and earn a living. Every now and then, as with anywhere, someone with troubles ends up here. I know how addictive and desirable Ketamine is. I keep the vials in a heavy-duty lockbox. I keep that lockbox locked in a safe. The safe is locked in my office." He jingled the keys attached to his waist with one of those retractable keychains. "The keys are always with me. While I suppose it would not be impossible, it would be very difficult for someone to get at my supply."

"It would be. That's a lot of security You realize, don't you, this also means that if Berlin does have Ketamine in her system, you will be at the top of the suspect list?"

He held my gaze for a few seconds and then looked away. "I do realize that, yes. I understand what you're saying, but I'm telling you, on the lives of all of my beloved animals and every carney in this circus, I did not shoot Berlin with a tranquilizer dart, either mine or anyone else's."

That was a rather specific statement. He didn't shoot her with a tranquilizer dart. Did he shoot her with something else?

As if reading my thoughts, he added, "I did not harm Berlin. I did not wish harm to come to Berlin. We argued sometimes, yes, but as a professional, I respected her greatly. I'm deeply saddened that she's gone."

"Is there anyone else who has access to your drugs or your darts? Any of the animal trainers, for example?"

"The other reason I keep the Ketamine locked up, Ms. O'Shea, is that it is highly regulated. I must account for all dosages and would not want anyone else involved with that."

"I don't think you answered my question."

"None of the trainers have access. Neither do any of the performers."

I held his gaze for a few beats. To his credit, he didn't look away.

"I don't believe that, Gianni. A 'highly regulated' drug like Ketamine? There can't possibly be only one person with the keys to the kingdom, so to speak. You can't be with all the animals all the time. When you're standing by the cage during the performance, who's keeping an eye on the animals not in the ring? Someone else in the circus must know how to get at the Ketamine."

Gianni looked down at the ground, hands in his pockets. "If you have nothing else, Ms. O'Shea, I need to attend to my animals."

I watched while Gianni walked along the platform, tossing food into the enclosures. Apparently, I stood there for too long because Meeka butted her head against my leg. I crouched down and scratched her ears.

"He's lying. I believed him right up until the end. Someone else around here has to have access to those drugs."

Chapter 13

AS MEEKA AND I WALKED back down the midway toward the entrance, I noticed more of the attractions. Along the midway itself, there were the standard carnival games, such as throwing a dart at a balloon to win the prize listed behind it or choosing a duck floating around in a pool and winning the prize associated with the number on the bottom. There were also the standard circus "freak show" acts—the bearded lady sang like an angel and Marilyn Half, the woman with no legs, could "walk" on her hands indefinitely. With a flex here and a twist there, the tattooed man used his ink like the pictures in a book while he told stories to an eager audience.

About fifty yards to the right of the midway were the rides. The Ferris wheel, the Zipper, pony rides for small kids, and that amazing double-decker carousel. Fifty yards to the left of the midway was a row of six animal cages that looked like circus wagons. Right now, they were all empty, the animals safely in their enclosures being fed. The timing didn't escape me. Feed them before the performances so they don't snack on the spectators.

Everywhere I looked, there was something going on. Right now, everyone was getting ready for the gates to open in about an hour.

"Did you find Gianni?" Colette asked from the ticket stand where she was organizing the cash box.

"I did, thank you. He was very helpful."

She gestured toward the food tent. "I was about to go grab some lunch. Want to join me?"

I'd burned through that bowl of cereal I had for breakfast half an hour ago. "Sure. What's good?"

"Just about anything. We employ an actual chef." She pushed her shoulders back importantly. "Only the best for the Whispering Pines carnies. If you're looking for a recommendation, you can't go wrong with a chili-and-cheese stuffed potato."

My stomach growled loudly at that moment. "I think we have a winner. A chili potato it is."

The wonderful aroma of grilling food hit me fifteen yards from the tent. I was drooling by the time the buffet line worker handed me a potato. It was the size of a small loaf of bread and covered in a heaping ladle of chili. She pointed to the side.

"Cheese, onions, sour cream, and so are on the table. Let me know if there's something you want that's not there."

I topped my potato with everything I could find and then grabbed a large iced tea and a bag of dog biscuits for Meeka. I loved how anywhere I went in this village, they had dog treats. Maybe cat treats too, but I hadn't seen anyone walking a cat. Yet.

I joined Colette at a picnic table set away from the crowd. She leaned in close and spoke quietly.

"Did you learn anything new from Gianni? About Berlin's death, I mean."

"Not directly." I held a biscuit out to Meeka. "I mostly had questions related to his animals."

"And about why he and Berlin used to argue all the time?" Colette asked.

I had to smile at her direct manner. "The topic came up.

I got the impression that despite their bickering, Gianni had a great deal of respect for Berlin." I loaded my fork with potato. "What about you? What can you tell me about Berlin?"

Colette poked at her own potato and shrugged. "She was kind of ...complex, I guess you'd say. She was a diva onstage, but offstage, she was really generous with her time."

"With her time? You mean she helped other performers?"

"She did help the others. That's not what I meant, though. There are a couple of young up-and-comers here who do fine with their sideshow acts along the midway, but they're not ready for the big top. Berlin would help them with moves and choreography, stuff like that."

"She helped Tilda?"

Colette sat up, a smile on her face. "She worked with Tilda a lot. Berlin told me all the time, 'Tilda will be a star, mark my words.'" Her smile faded to a frown. "Not sure what we're going to do about Berlin's spots in the performances. Tilda will be a star someday, but she's not a closing act yet." Colette looked over her shoulder as though she'd just gotten busted leaking a big secret. "Don't tell her I said that. She'd be furious."

I mimicked locking my mouth. "You said Berlin was generous with her time, but not just in helping the performers. What else did you mean?"

"Some of the people here, you can tell they're only passing through. Berlin was here for the long haul and treated it like her home. If someone needed help with something not related to the circus, she was there. Like taking in Tilda and her son, for example. They weren't just roommates, they were a little family."

"I haven't met Tilda yet," I said. "I saw her perform the other day. Considering her disability, she is amazing."

"She's amazing either way," Colette corrected with a

scolding tone.

I placed my hands palms together in apology. I'd never done that before in my life …been hanging around Morgan too much, I guess. "Of course, she is. Sorry, I didn't mean any disrespect."

We sat in slightly uncomfortable silence for a couple minutes, eating our potatoes.

Finally, I said, "I understand Tilda has a little boy."

Colette's smile couldn't have been bigger. "Joss. He's my little buddy. Whenever Tilda and Berlin perform or practice, I get to watch him. Best part of my day."

"Creed told me they were in an accident."

Her head bobbed up and down in agreement. "Joss was only two at the time. That's when Tilda lost the use of that leg. They had to amputate Joss's left arm just above the elbow. He doesn't let it stop him, though." She laughed out loud, a hearty belly laugh. "He and I have been working on an act that we do along the midway. Since I'm so tall and he's just a little squirt, we've been trying out a puppeteer and marionette act."

"I saw you two when I came for the performance the other night. The act is adorable."

"Thanks." She beamed. It was obvious she adored the boy. "He's a natural."

"Is Tilda here? I'd like to meet her."

Colette's sunny disposition changed instantly. "You want to ask her questions about Berlin's death, don't you?" Before I could respond she warned, "She's devastated by the loss. I don't think she's been able to talk to anyone about it yet."

She gave me the impression of being a smothering mother, and I couldn't help but think of my own.

"How can you be so heartless," my mom had accused one time. "You're rubbing salt into open wounds. Couldn't you give the poor woman even an hour to come to terms?"

This barrage had come after I had to tell one of Mom's

friends that her daughter had been sexually assaulted at a party. Mom felt the fact that the underage girl "had attended a party with drinking, drugs, and degenerates" was a big enough blow for the woman to deal with.

"The right thing," Mom continued, "would have been to wait until the initial shock had worn off before telling her about the assault."

So, I should knock people back down after they started picking themselves up? That didn't seem like the better option to me.

"I understand that Tilda's upset," I told Colette. "Remember, I was a cop for many years. I can't tell you how many times I've spoken with people on their worst day. I know how to do it with empathy."

A fact my mother couldn't seem to grasp. Colette either, if her non-response was any indication.

"It appears very likely," I said, "that Berlin was killed."

"Accidents happen," Colette objected.

"They do, but you have to admit, at Berlin's level of expertise, the chances of that kind of an accident happening are very slim."

She stabbed violently at her potato. "Or her odds ran out."

Her physical reaction and the comment were so out of left field, I couldn't decide if it was a response brought on by grief or a disguised admission of knowledge.

"That is possible," I admitted, "but I'm proceeding with the assumption that she was murdered. If the killer is still wandering around Whispering Pines, for everyone's safety we need to find them."

Colette narrowed her eyes at me. "Didn't realize you'd been assigned to the case."

She was right. I had to dial back the cop attitude. "I wasn't, but no one else is digging into this. You want the truth to come out, don't you?"

She was quiet for a minute. "Tilda isn't here. She's

making arrangements for Berlin's cremation."

Cremation? Dr. Bundy would have drawn some of Berlin's blood as part of the autopsy. I needed to make sure he knew to test for Ketamine before her body was cremated in case he needed to take more samples.

"No big deal," I said as nonchalantly as I could while my heart raced. The clock was officially ticking. "I'm not going anywhere. I can meet her later." I swallowed a few more bites of potato and finished my iced tea. "Thank you for the company, Colette. And for the potato recommendation. You're right, it was great. I hope I didn't upset you with anything I said. That wasn't my intent."

Her shoulders slumped. "I know. Didn't mean to snap. Emotions are running high around here right now."

"Understandable. At the risk of upsetting you again, I heard that Berlin and Dallas would get into some fights now and then."

"I don't think they were really fighting. She just didn't want to perform with him and he wasn't happy about it, is all." She waggled a finger for me to lean in. "You could talk to Abilene."

"Abilene is Dallas's assistant, right?" I asked, matching her covert tone.

"That's her. Very territorial. If you really want to dig into this, you should talk to her."

"Thanks. I'll do that."

I stood, nearly colliding with a woman dressed like a harlequin ballerina walking past us. Her short tutu dress was patterned with the traditional harlequin triangles except it was baby pink-and-white instead of the standard black-and-white or multicolored. I immediately thought of the dolls Donovan made. Along with running Quin's clothing shop, Donovan was also a skilled sculptor. The problem was, he made only harlequin's and each had a deformity of some kind—only nostrils instead of a nose, a missing arm, no eyes. Creepiest little things ever.

"As you can see," Colette indicated the ballerina, "everyone is getting ready for the afternoon performances now. Putting on makeup and getting into costume. For some, that can take a long time. You might want to come back to ask Dallas and Abilene your questions."

I needed to get home anyway and send that email to Dr. Bundy.

"I certainly don't want to interfere with the preparation of someone who throws knives at another person."

Colette laughed at that. I gave her a little wave and hurried off to the parking lot.

Chapter 14

COLETTE'S REVELATION, THAT TILDA WAS arranging the cremation of Berlin's body, meant I had to act fast. If the body was taken and Dr. Bundy didn't have enough blood, or whatever he needed to run the right tests, we'd never know for sure if there was Ketamine in her system. Of course, the sheer number of tourists, both in vehicles and those darting across the highway, meant I had to drive through the village at a crawl on my way home, causing that already ticking clock to sound like a jackhammer in my ears. When I pulled into my driveway, not even ten minutes after leaving the circus, I thought of rush hour traffic in Madison and other big cities and laughed at my impatience. Funny how quickly new became normal.

As soon as the garage came into view, I noted that Tripp's truck was still gone.

"Where do you suppose he is?" I asked as I let Meeka out of the back. She ignored me, tearing off to run laps around the house. Not that I had really expected her to answer.

I raced upstairs to my apartment and went straight to my laptop. While there was no cell phone connection in Whispering Pines, my internet was good, not that it made much of a difference with my ancient laptop. I really needed to get a new computer. I had driven home from the circus in less time than it was taking my email program to open. By the time it finally did, I'd decided email wouldn't be fast enough. When my browser opened, approximately one year later, I tracked down Dr. Bundy's office number.

"Jayne O'Shea." He didn't sound surprised to hear from me. "Let me take a guess at why you're calling."

"You did the autopsy for Berlin, right?"

"You didn't let me guess. Yes, I did the autopsy."

"You need to run a toxicology panel before they cremate her. You do still have the body, don't you? You know that's the plan? To cremate her remains?"

"So many questions. Let's see, yes, I am aware that cremation was ordered. They're coming for her this afternoon, so yes, she's still here with me. I already ran a toxicology panel, that's standard procedure for me now."

"But you need to look for something specific."

He groaned softly, and I could almost hear him thinking, *here we go again.* I'd made the same request last month for the Yasmine Long case.

"What am I looking for this time?" he asked.

"Ketamine."

"Ketamine? That's rough stuff. I thought the streets of Whispering Pines were tame."

"Far as I know, it's not a problem with the villagers, but the circus keeps a supply on hand for the animals."

"And you think Berlin was dipping into the veterinarian's supply?"

"No, I think someone shot her with a tranquilizer dart."

I explained everything I had observed in the big top the day Berlin died as well as what I had learned while talking with Gianni and the other carnies today.

"Did you notice a puncture wound on the body while you were examining her?"

At the other end of the line, Dr. Bundy made humming

noises, probably trying to decide what to say.

"Have you been reinstated as a deputy, Jayne?"

"No, sir."

"Just can't help yourself, hey?"

I closed my eyes and laid my forehead on the table, phone still to my ear. "Opinion seems to be unanimous on that point."

"I understand you replaced Sheriff Brighton with a young man named ..." Papers shuffled in the background. "Zeb Warren. Why am I not talking to him?"

"I heard that Deputy Atkins had concluded his investigation. Unless your autopsy results come back suspicious, I don't think our new sheriff is going to dig any further." I paused, taking a moment to calm my rising irritation. I didn't understand how Warren could ignore this. "Look, I'm not trying to be nosy or cause trouble. It's just that I've heard some things and am trying to make sure that if this was murder, the killer is caught. So, did you find a puncture wound?"

The doctor hesitated before answering. "Jayne, you know I can't discuss details with you. I do fully appreciate you following your gut, though. Tell you what, I'll take another look at the body. Finding a puncture wound would give me a reason to suspect drug use. Therefore, running a couple extra tests would be understandable."

My whole body slumped with relief. "Would a test for Ketamine be a reasonable one to run?"

He hummed again. "My instinct tells me yes. If I consider all the possible drugs at a circus, specifically those requiring an injection and therefore leaving a puncture wound, testing for Ketamine would be reasonable."

I liked the way his mind worked. Very methodical.

"Thanks, Doc. You know I'm just trying to get at the truth."

"Yes, ma'am, I do know that. Your biggest flaw is that you want to do the right thing. Shame that that's such a rarity these days."

I said goodbye and pulled the phone away from my ear just as Dr. Bundy said something else.

"Sorry, I missed that. What did you say?"

"I said, if you'd just get yourself back on the sheriff's payroll up there, I could freely discuss these things with you."

I smiled. "I'll keep that in mind. Bye, Doc."

After placing the phone back in its cradle, I sat there a minute, trying to decide what to do next. There was nothing more I could do about Berlin's death right now, everyone at the circus was performing so I couldn't talk to them anymore today. I could read, take out my watercolors and try painting, or take out the kayak. Or I could do what I'd been avoiding.

Meeka was giving me a knowing look. As usual, she seemed to be reading my mind.

"Fine, let's go to the house."

It was time for me to quit stalling and start packing up my grandmother's belongings. Meeka followed me all the way up to the second floor, but when we got to Gran's bedroom, she kept going, trotting off down the hall to explore somewhere else, leaving me alone to deal with my personal ghosts.

I stood in the middle of the room and slowly spun in place, taking in everything. All the furniture was antique, some acquired from local artisans, other pieces shipped back from one of the many overseas trips she and Gramps used to go on. At over eight feet tall and twelve-inches in diameter, the posts at each corner of Gran's bed nearly touched the ceiling. The bed appeared to be massive, but it only held a full-sized mattress. Gran always said that a husband and wife slept together, as in close to each other. The thought of bringing in a queen or, heaven forbid, a king-sized mattress was unthinkable.

"You'll see, one of the benefits of having a man in your

bed is that he keeps you warm on cold winter nights. Why would I want a mattress that would put so much real estate between us?"

I laughed at the memory. She was feisty and sassy, my grandma.

What was I supposed to do with that bed? I couldn't imagine anyone else sleeping in it, and couldn't imagine it being in any bedroom other than this one.

I grabbed a stack of boxes and a roll of packing tape from the hallway. After assembling three of the boxes, I lined them up next to the dresser and then stood at the closet doorway. The other night, when I was looking for a coverup to take with me to the circus, I strode into Gran's closet with no other thought than borrowing a sweater. No big deal. I hadn't been prepared for the fact that her clothes, all these months later, still smelled like her. A combination of fresh lake air and lavender, that was Gran's scent.

Now, I couldn't step back inside. I still wasn't ready.

"Meeka," I called loudly from the hallway.

After a minute and no dog, I called again. Finally, she poked her head around the corner of a doorway at the end of the hall. Wherever she had been, she found spider webs. They covered her face, draped between her pointy ears, and stuck to her whiskers and tail. Despite being emotional a minute ago, I burst out laughing.

"You're a mess. Let's get you cleaned up."

We left through the front door, so I could see if Tripp had come back yet. My Cherokee was still the only vehicle in the driveway. Where could he be? And was he okay? And by okay, I meant both physically and mentally. He'd been a wreck since Lily Grace did that reading. He didn't have a cell phone, so I couldn't call him. If he didn't show up soon, I'd have to ask Sheriff Warren to put out a BOLO, a "be on the lookout," for him.

There were enough spider webs and grime on Meeka that I decided to just give her a full bath. Where had she been exploring that she got so filthy? She raced around the yard to dry off afterwards, and by then, it was getting close to dinner time. The last thing I wanted was to eat by myself tonight. I changed into shorts and a clean shirt, one of the pretty tunics I bought at Quin's clothing shop. With my car keys in hand and credit card in my pocket, Meeka and I headed for Grapes, Grains, and Grub. Bar food and a tall frosty mug of a citrusy summer ale were just what I wanted.

***

Meeka loved being around all the people in the village. Some of the shops allowed animals to come in as long as they weren't too large and remained under control. Bringing them anywhere near food wasn't permitted, but Maeve at Grapes, Grains, and Grub had set up a fenced-in area behind the pub for pets to hang out in while their people ate.

We followed the path from the parking lot and as soon as we got a clear view of the commons area, I knew getting my favorite table in the corner at Triple G, the one where I had an unobstructed view of the Brewers game, wasn't likely to happen tonight. I'd never seen the village so crowded. The line to get into the restaurant stretched nearly thirty yards. The lines were equally long outside The Inn and even Treat Me Sweetly.

Not sure what to do, we wandered around the Pentacle Garden and came to a group of ten or twelve people gathered between Ye Olde Bean Grinder and Shoppe Mystique. Sheriff Warren stood in the middle of them.

"What's going on?" I asked a twenty-something woman in short white shorts and a royal blue bikini top.

"Freaking lawman," she slurred, a drink or two past sober. She flung her hand toward the twenty-something man currently getting a lecture from Sheriff Zeb. "He picked a flower." She flung her other hand at the Pentacle Garden. "One flower. There has to be like a million of them in that garden. He picked one. It's my birthday."

I debated pointing out the numerous, *Please Don't Pick the Flowers* posted all around the garden, but instead said, "Happy birthday." She gave me a wobbly little curtsy. "So, your friend picked a flower for you. What's happening now?"

"The sheriff is writing him a ticket for vandalism." She spun toward me, swaying slightly. "Can you believe that?"

I could. Zeb Warren had Karl Brighton's legacy shadowing him. He was trying to prove he was just as good a lawman, but having a sheriff that ticketed tourists for minor infractions wasn't the reputation a tourist town wanted.

"Jayne."

I turned to see Morgan descending the wooden staircase of Shoppe Mystique and walked over to her.

"Blessed be." She placed her hands palms together and inclined her head slightly.

"I came for dinner, but it's crazy busy tonight. What's going on? Why are there so many people?"

"You don't know?"

I could tell by the tone of her voice she was going to teach me about something Wiccan. "I don't know a lot of things. What in particular don't I know now?"

"Today is Midsummer's Eve."

Having no idea what that meant, I gave her a blank stare.

"Tomorrow is *Litha* or Midsummer. You may know it by its more common term, summer solstice or simply the official first day of summer. Whatever label you attached to it, tomorrow will be both the longest and shortest day of the year."

"How can that be?"

"It depends on which hemisphere you're in, of course." Morgan linked her arm with mine as we walked. "Here in the Northern Hemisphere, it's the longest day with the sun shining on us for the longest possible amount of time. Our sisters and brothers in the Southern Hemisphere are celebrating winter solstice and experiencing the shortest amount of daylight."

As with anything associated with her religion, Morgan looked delighted by this. Her voice softened and her face glowed with reverence.

"I thought you worshipped the moon," I said.

"I do, but there must be balance. My garden, other plants, and even we humans need sunlight to grow, but just as important is moonlight for rest."

I gestured toward the crowds. "That's why they're all here? To celebrate the solstice?"

"Many of them. Some of our tourists come here simply for the beauty of the lake and the surrounding area and are not at all interested in the solstice aspect. A healthy percentage treat Whispering Pines as a sort of Stonehenge in America. Those people, myself and my mother included, will stay awake all night, celebrating nature and its offerings and rejoicing as the sun rises tomorrow morning. Well, Mom may not make it all night; she tires easily since having the stroke. I'll be sure to wake her in time for sunrise."

I had no religious affiliation. If anything, my parents raised me agnostic. I had no issues with other people's beliefs, though, as long as they didn't hurt anyone in the name of it. Listening to Morgan talk about her beliefs filled me with a sense of peace. Or maybe it was just Morgan, she was a very calm person.

"Where are we going?" I asked when I realized she was leading me away from the commons and toward the bridge that crossed over the highway.

"To my house," she said as though that should be obvious. "You'll be waiting hours to get into one of the restaurants. There's no reason for that; my mother has been preparing food all day. You can celebrate Litha with us."

"This isn't going to be one of those things where we put

on robes and dance around a fire, is it?"

"There will be a bonfire at the Meditation Circle tonight. We'll likely be able to see the glow from my garden. You're welcome to go if you'd like, but Mom and I prefer a quieter celebration. Instead of a bonfire, we've had a candle burning for the last two days. It's less about the size of the fire than the representation of the sun."

"Two days straight? Even when you're sleeping?"

She held up a hand, stopping my objection. "We keep it in the kitchen sink or the bathtub when we're not near it."

"During this celebration, no one will be getting naked, will they?" She told me once that being nude was a personal preference thing, but I wasn't comfortable being around naked people. Probably came from dealing with too many drunk UW Madison students who thought streaking around campus was a good idea.

Morgan laughed. "I promise, neither my mother nor I will remove any clothing this evening.

"Count me in, then."

A quick fifteen minutes later, we were coming up on Morgan's cottage. The two-story house with its multiple sharply-peaked rooflines was set thirty or so yards from the creek that wound around and through the village. A simple dirt pathway, wide enough for residents who lived next to the creek to drive on, separated the cottage from the rushing water.

The Barlow property took up almost two full acres. The cottage and lawn took up about a tenth of an acre; the rest was her garden. A five-foot-tall fence made from tree branches surrounded the garden along with thick berry bushes and tall fruit trees, creating a beautiful privacy border.

"I finally get to see your plants," I said.

"That's right, the last time you were here it was nearly midnight." Morgan unlatched a swinging gate and held it open, directing Meeka and me to follow the stone pathway to the cottage's front door.

"And there was no moon that night," I added. "All I saw were shadows."

"Well, we have plenty of sunlight remaining, so you can investigate. The Goddess has been very kind this year; all our plants are flourishing. Mama can hardly keep up."

I smiled at the endearment. Morgan didn't talk about her mom often, but it was usually sweet when she did.

"She loves it, though. Winters are brutal up here; she spends all day outside as soon as she's safe from frostbite."

Once inside the sparsely furnished and decorated house, Morgan asked me to give her a minute to change clothes. When she reemerged, gone was the head-to-toe black, replaced with cutoff denim shorts, flipflops, and a black T-shirt with a silver pentacle and the phrase "Trust me, I'm a witch."

I chuckled as we continued through the house to a conservatory. Morgan kept walking, heading for a side door that led to a small patio, but I stopped in my tracks.

"Hang on."

Shelves lined the bottom half of two of the walls. One set was loaded with empty ceramic and terra cotta pots, bags of potting soil, and other gardening supplies. The other was full of bottles and jars of dried plants similar to those in Shoppe Mystique. Racks and tables filled with potted plants were pushed up against the other two walls, while big planters filled with flowering trees or large plants sat on the floor scattered about the room. The upper half of each wall and the ceiling were all windows.

"Isn't it glorious?" Morgan smiled. "We keep tender plants in here, those that can't tolerate the whims of Mother Nature. This is also where Mom spends all her winter days. Can't keep a green witch away from her plants."

We continued out onto the equally amazing patio. The floor was made up of large flagstone pavers. A pergola formed from tree trunks and branches shaded the area and supported heavy wisteria vines. A round dining table and two chairs sat at the center. Two inviting wicker chairs were tucked into a shaded corner. That's where we found Briar Barlow, weaving grapevines into pentacle-shaped wreaths and humming softly to herself.

Late fifties, bobbed salt-and-pepper hair with more salt than pepper, tiny but not frail.

"Mama," Morgan said as she strode across the patio, "we're going to have company for the celebration tonight. This is Jayne."

The older woman looked up at me with shockingly blue eyes. I immediately saw where Morgan's strong jawline and squared-off chin came from. A smile covered her face and she stood to greet me.

"No, please, don't get up," I said.

"My stroke," Ms. Barlow said slowly and with a slight slur, "only permanently affected my speech. My body and mind are strong. I am very glad to finally meet you, Jayne. Morgan has told me a lot about you."

She met me at the center of the patio and took one of my hands in both of hers.

"It's a pleasure to meet you too, Ms. Barlow."

"Bah. Call me Briar."

"You sound like an old woman when you say 'bah,' Mama," Morgan teased while inspecting the new grapevine wreaths.

"Gets my point across with one word," Briar said.

After only two minutes, I could tell I was in for an entertaining evening. "It's very nice to meet you, Briar. Morgan tells me you take care of this huge garden by yourself."

"For a green witch," Briar began dreamily, "to be able to spend all day in a garden is a true blessing. That stroke actually improved my life. Now I don't have to go to Shoppe Mystique every day."

"I didn't realize you used to work there." I wasn't really

surprised to hear it.

"Oh yes," Briar said, "my mother opened the shop, passed it on to me, and now it's Morgan's turn."

"Were you able to prepare anything for dinner, Mama?" Morgan asked. "Or did the plants and garden fairies distract you again?"

My gaze darted to a cluster of nearby plants. I half expected to see tiny fairy faces peeking at us from around the leaves.

"I cooked." Briar pointed toward the kitchen. "I've got a feast ready for us in there. I'll let you two bring everything out."

Something in the garden caught Meeka's attention and she tugged hard on the leash, desperate to search out whatever it was.

"Is it okay if I let her run?" I asked Morgan.

"Of course. She probably spotted Pitch. He's wandering around out there digging for insects and fertilizing my plants."

Pitch was Morgan's all-black rooster. Everything about him, from his feathers to the comb on top of his head to his beady little eyes to his beak, was entirely black. My understanding was that he was all black inside as well, but I had no intention of butchering Morgan's pet to find out if that was true.

I knelt and released Meeka's leash but kept hold of her collar.

"Behave," I commanded. "No chasing the rooster. Understand?"

Reluctantly, Meeka let out a soft bark. I knew she wouldn't harm the bird, but the little Westie surely had more stamina than twenty-some-year-old Pitch. I let go of her collar and she trotted off, disappearing into the dense foliage.

In the kitchen, Morgan and I did indeed find a feast. Homemade potato salad, coleslaw, cornbread, baked beans, and Jell-O salad. A bowl filled with chunks of cut-up watermelon and cantaloupe. Corn on the cob and chicken leg quarters were seasoned and ready for the grill.

"Doesn't it offend Pitch when you have chicken?" I teased while adding a pitcher of raspberry lemonade to a tray loaded with plates, flatware, and glasses.

"It might, if he realized he was a bird," Morgan said as she grabbed the grill-ables. "Not sure what he thinks he is, but he's never had an issue with us eating his relatives."

She grinned and held the door open for me as I carried out the tray.

"Did you invite someone else over?" I asked Briar. "That's an awful lot of food."

"There are many hours between now and sunrise," Briar said slowly. "We'll nibble until we're full and pack up what's left for the rest of the week. Of course, you can take some home for you and your friend."

She winked, and a warm flush spread over me as I realized she meant Tripp.

"Tell me you made it," Morgan said seriously.

"Of course, I made it. What would our Litha celebration be without it?"

I leaned in and asked conspiratorially, "What are we talking about?"

"Mama makes the best sunrise gelato you will ever taste. Layers of lemon, lime, orange, and strawberry look like a sunrise in your bowl and taste like heaven on your tongue."

After Morgan had grilled up the corn and chicken, and I had carried out the remaining food as well as a third chair from the kitchenette inside, the three of us gathered at the table and feasted. The elder witch must have put a spell on either me or the food because I ate three platefuls and could have polished off at least one more. I decided to stop though and leave room for that gelato. If it was half as good as Morgan professed, I'd have many servings of that, too.

"You have questions," Briar said later as Morgan and I gathered the dishes together.

I looked to Morgan and then pointed at myself. "Me? You think I have questions?"

"Regarding your grandmother," Briar confirmed with a nod, "and how she died."

Chapter 15

MORGAN TOOK THE DIRTY DISHES from my hands and nodded at the chair I had been sitting in. "Sit and talk to Mama."

Before I could respond, Morgan turned and walked away with the tray. I sat, slightly uncomfortable now, and organized the remaining dishes into stacks while waiting for Briar to say more. When more than a minute had passed and she hadn't said anything, I sat back with my hands in my lap and cleared my throat.

"What did you mean by how she died? We were told that she slipped, hit her head on the edge of her bathtub, and fell into the filled tub. The letter Sheriff Brighton sent us listed accidental drowning as the cause of death."

"That's what we were told as well," Briar confirmed. "You know there's something more going on in this village. I won't go so far as to say that Lucy was murdered ..."

What? I pulled my chair closer to her. "But you think it's a possibility?"

Morgan came back outside for another load of dishes, gave us a knowing look as she reloaded the tray, and then left again without saying a word.

"I think," Briar said, "there are people in Whispering

Pines who have ambitions that do not fit with your grandmother's original intent for the village."

No sense being shy. We were talking about the possible murder of my grandmother. "Like Flavia and Donovan? Do you think they were involved with Gran's death?"

Briar was tiring, her speech slowed and slurred a little more with each minute. When Morgan came outside again after dropping off the last load of dishes, she noticed it, too.

"Tell you what." Morgan guided her mother over to one of the wicker chairs tucked into the corner of the patio. "Why don't you rest for a while? I promise to wake you up in time for the sunrise."

"I will rest if you promise to wake me up in an hour. We have company. I can sleep tomorrow."

They faced off with each other, Morgan's dark-brown eyes boring into her mother's bright-blue ones. As if choreographed, they raised their chins in unison and gave simultaneous crisp nods of understanding. Morgan propped her mom's feet onto a footrest and covered her with a summer-weight blanket. Then she came over to me and hooked her arm with mine, as she tended to do when she wanted to walk and talk with me.

She guided me along the pea gravel pathway that wound throughout their amazing garden, pointed out various plants, and told me about the benefits they held both medicinally and in a more spiritual sense.

"You can help me harvest tonight," Morgan said.

"Harvest what?"

"Herbs collected on Midsummer's Eve are extra potent. Those for love spells and charms are especially so."

As we walked along, she paused now and then to indicate the plants and herbs that we would gather later. First was a three-foot-tall, silvery-green plant with feathery leaves.

"Wormwood or *Artemisia* is used to make the alcoholic drink absinthe. The liqueur is highly addictive and hallucinogenic, so I don't make that, but the plant itself works nicely in a love charm."

"Love can be addictive," I quipped.

She smiled. "Right you are."

Next, we stopped at a grouping of flowers, each one had five rounded white inner petals surrounded by five purple, pink, blue, or yellow larger pointed outer petals. "Columbine seeds can be used in perfume or pulverized and rubbed into the hands and body to attract love."

"The outer petals almost form a pentacle."

Morgan's eyebrows arched. "I never looked at it that way. Perhaps that's why these flowers are so appealing to me."

A little farther down the path, we came to an eight-foot-tall shrub with dark-green leaves and hot-pink flowers. "Oleander, while highly poisonous if ingested, is potent in love spells.

"Well, we are often attracted to that which is bad for us."

"You're full of observations tonight." She grinned, pleased with my comparisons.

We came to a cozy little bench tucked beneath a cherry tree. The sun was starting to hang low in the horizon, and the branches of the tree protected us from the intense late-day rays.

"Mama thinks your grandmother was murdered, doesn't she?" Morgan asked.

"She didn't say that outright, but that's what she was hinting at. Do you think she's right?"

"Before last month and the shocking circumstances surrounding Yasmine's death, I would have said no. I would've told you that your grandmother slipped on a puddle on her bathroom floor and tragically drowned in her bathtub."

"But now you agree, you think murder is a possibility." It wasn't a question. "Were you able to learn anything more about the graffiti ... about the sigils painted around my house?"

"It's only been a few weeks, Jayne. I told you, I need to be very careful asking about this and wait for the right moment. I can't just bring up a topic like that. You've been here for a month already. In that short time, you've learned that the villagers are very devoted to each other. If I make accusations or even ask questions to the wrong person, it will damage the harmony here."

"Harmony?" I coughed out a laugh. "Are you kidding me? At one point, there may have been nothing but harmony here. But a young woman was murdered last month, my grandmother may have been murdered four months ago, and it looks like another woman was murdered last week. What kind of harmony is that?"

"Please tell me you're not getting involved with Berlin's death."

"I talked to Dr. Bundy earlier today."

"Oh, Jayne."

I reminded her about the tranquilizer dart and the possibility that someone may have shot Berlin with it.

"I talked to Gianni at the circus. He confirmed that the dart I found is the same kind he uses. He insisted he didn't kill Berlin, but I called Dr. Bundy and suggested he look for a puncture wound on Berlin's body." Morgan leveled a judgmental eye on me. "Look, if he finds nothing, I promise you I will leave this alone."

Morgan studied me a moment longer and then slumped back against the bench. "That's as much as I can hope for."

I wanted to ask her more questions about my grandmother, but Briar seemed to be the bigger source of knowledge for that. I could wait. The truth had been safely hidden for this long, it wasn't going anywhere. In the meantime, I brought up another topic that had been eating at me.

"Do you know that Sheriff Zeb ticketed someone for

vandalism for picking a flower in the Pentacle Garden?"

Morgan's head dropped forward and she let out a disappointed little sigh. "I hate to say it, but I have heard some complaints around the village already. Although, I can't say that he's necessarily wrong."

"Technically, no, he's not wrong, but it is extreme. The last thing Whispering Pines needs is a sheriff who tickets people for enjoying themselves a little too much while on vacation. Seriously, he could have issued a warning. There was no reason to cite the guy for vandalism."

"You're becoming upset."

"Are you going to tell me we should just ignore these things?"

"He's very young." Before I could object, she added, "Not that that's an excuse. I'm sure our new sheriff feels overwhelmed and intimidated. I don't know anyone here who didn't like Sheriff Brighton."

"Donovan?"

Morgan conceded that point. "True, but there are very few people who Donovan likes. I think we need to be a little patient with Zeb."

"The council approved him on a trial basis. We can give him a little time, but if he's not going to work out, there's no sense waiting for him to do damage before we let him go."

"I agree. For now, we're done talking about Mr. Warren and murder and sigils. This is a night for celebrating the sun and passing the torch, so to speak, from the Oak King to the Holly King."

"The what and the who?"

She told me about some of the traditional Litha celebration rituals associated with the first day of summer. Nothing unusual, mostly lots of prayers for a successful growing season and, like we had done on the night of the new moon, contemplation about goals and what we'd like to see happen over the next six months until Yule, or the winter solstice, in December.

I had to admit, I liked that Wicca was all about continual new beginnings. There was always another chance to start over and get things right.

We laughed as Meeka and Pitch played together. My little all-white dog chased after Morgan's all-black rooster until Pitch had enough and turned to chase Meeka in return.

"Instant friends." Morgan playfully bumped her shoulder against mine.

"I feel like there's an underlying message about getting along with someone so different from you. If a dog and a rooster can be friends, why is it so hard for people?"

"Sadly, it's how we're taught. If our parents teach us to accept, then we accept. If our parents teach us to hate, well, the world is a sadder place. It's a vicious circle."

The night seemed to pass in a flash as Morgan, Briar, and I chatted and gathered herbs. I could hardly believe it when I saw the hint of light on the horizon. Morgan presented us each with a bowl of sunrise gelato and sprinkled drops of dew collected from her flowers on top.

"What's that for?" I asked.

"Dew gathered on Midsummer morning bestows good health on she who drinks it."

I was all in favor of good health, but I couldn't help but note that the ritual didn't prevent Briar's stroke. Unless, of course, like Gran's fall, Briar's stroke had help. Was it possible to bring on a stroke? Or maybe someone cast a spell of negative intent against her. That made it sound like I believed in the woo-woo. I didn't. No, what it came down to was that some things were beyond our control.

The three of us went to a small east-facing balcony off a second-floor bedroom in the cottage. We stood there together as the sun crested the horizon, Morgan and Briar literally shoulder-to-shoulder, bowls of sunrise gelato in hand. I had to admit, a feeling of jealousy crept through me. My mother and I had never shared anything like this. Come to think of it, I'm not sure we had any common interests.

After we finished our gelato and the sun had fully risen, we returned to the garden where I called for Meeka. She emerged, sleepily, from a cluster of happy-looking daisies. After a night of playing in the garden, she needed another bath.

"You're not leaving." Briar gave me a pointed look. "We haven't finished our talk."

"Don't worry, I'll come back for that. Thank you so much for letting me be a part of your celebration." I may not believe the same way they did, but the sense of community I felt when I was with Morgan at times like this almost made me wish that I did. "I have a task that I've been putting off for too long."

"What do you need to do?" Briar asked.

"I have to pack up my grandmother's bedroom today. I don't know what's going to happen with the house, I really hope I'll be able to convince my parents to let me turn it into a bed-and-breakfast."

"That would be lovely." Briar placed her hands over her heart. "Not only is it a beautiful house, the location is breathtaking. You'll be full all the time."

"That's what Tripp and I think," I said. "In the meantime, we're renovating all the bedrooms and bathrooms; Gran wasn't much for keeping up with the latest trends."

Briar laughed, her shoulders shaking. "You're so right. Lucy never bothered with things like that." She looked down at her hands. "I sure do miss her."

"I do too," I said. "That's why it's so hard for me to do her room. I almost feel like if I don't pack up her things, she's not really gone."

Morgan gave me a look full of pity. I hated it when people pitied me.

"Stay right here," Morgan said. "I'll be right back."

I filled Briar's teacup with Morgan's solstice blend—peppermint, raspberry leaf, sunflower petals, rose petals, and lavender—and she told me about some of the trouble she and Gran used to get into.

"Skinny-dipping?" I demanded. "Tell me you're joking."

"It was the night of a supermoon," Briar recalled wistfully. "Lucy claimed that the extra-large full moon was charging the lake and if we swam, naked, in the moonbeams it would charge us as well."

I eyed Briar for a moment. "How many glasses of Chardonnay had you both had when she convinced you of that one?"

Briar was giggling like a schoolgirl when Morgan returned with a small, blood-red muslin bag. It looked suspiciously like the purple muslin bag she had given me a month earlier. That first one had been filled with herbs, a few stone chips, and a small pentacle charm. She claimed it would protect me from whoever had trashed my house and left sigils all over.

"What's that one going to do?" I asked of the little red bag.

Morgan placed it in my hands and then wrapped her own hands around mine. She nodded to Briar who placed her hands over Morgan's.

"The red of the bag is for courage," Morgan explained in her comforting way. "Inside is blue moonstone for clarity as well as garnet to stimulate your confidence. Sage cleanses and heals. For strength, galangal root. Morning glory blossoms for peace."

A sense of love and friendship like I'd never felt before surrounded me. I became so emotional, I couldn't speak.

"Keep this with you while you go through your grandmother's things," Morgan said. "It will help during what will surely be a difficult task."

Chapter 16

BEFORE HEADING HOME, MEEKA AND I made a loop through the village. While nowhere near as crowded as it was last night, the village commons was still far busier than it usually was this early in the morning. The crowd was more subdued as well; they all looked exhausted, probably from staying up all night to celebrate the sunrise. My gaze traveled across the Pentacle Garden and down to the lake where a cluster of people had jumped into the water. Problem was, the public beach was half a mile east.

A voice right behind me said, "The Sheriff just headed down that way."

Startled, I jumped and turned to see Lupe Gomez. Dark circles rimmed her eyes and her normally tidy braid was disheveled.

"You been up all night?" I asked.

"Of course. How can anyone be in Whispering Pines on Midsummer's Eve and not take part in the festivities?" She held up her reporter's notebook and wiggled it at me. "I would have missed out on one hell of a story if I would've given in to the call of my pillow."

"So if I add 'one hell of a story' to 'the sheriff is headed down that way,' do I end up with there was trouble last night?"

"Only if you consider swimming to mean trouble." She gestured at the group splashing around in the lake. "It's not like anyone got naked or anything. They were in the moment, having a good time watching the sunrise, and a few of them jumped in. Said something about needing to wash away all negativity in preparation for the new cycle. It was pretty fun actually."

"Did you jump in the lake, too?"

"On the grounds that I might incriminate myself in the apparently illegal activity of swimming in a non-public area, I won't answer that. Off the record? Hell yeah, I jumped in the lake."

I held a hand over my eyes as a sunshield and squinted down toward the water. "Is he seriously ticketing them?"

"I'm sure he is. He's been writing tickets all night. I've got to say, people aren't happy with the new lawman."

Neither was I. I added this to the already growing list of reasons to not keep Zeb Warren as village sheriff.

"How's your first article on Whispering Pines coming along?"

"Really well," Lupe said with a big smile. "I sent the piece to my editor about an hour ago. Shouldn't take him long to send me his corrections and suggestions. Once I make those, I'll post the full piece to the magazine's site and put up a few teasers on all of our social media locations."

"What's a teaser?"

"It's like an advertisement," Lupe explained as she flipped the cover of her cell phone-sized notebook open and closed, open and closed. "It encourages readers to click on the link and read my article. I need to come up with a couple of enticing lines about the article and attach a few intriguing pictures. I got some great shots at the circus."

I nodded at her hands, still playing with the notebook. "You seem a little nervous."

She followed my gaze and then shoved the notebook in

the cargo pocket on her right thigh. "This first piece is an important one. If I can lure readers in with it, they'll want to keep reading more about Whispering Pines. And I'll get to stay and write a summer's worth of articles. Fortunately, there's been a lot going on around here this week."

I narrowed my eyes. "Are you saying that murder is good for business?"

She stared, open-mouthed. "I didn't say that. I meant everything around here, including the Midsummer celebration. That's awful. What would make you think that?"

"No offense." I held my hands up in surrender. "It's the cop in me. Everyone is a suspect until they're ruled out."

"You suspected *me*?"

"Like I said, I suspect everyone."

Her actions that first night I met her put her on my radar. Her giddiness over Tilda and Berlin arguing in their tent after the performance hadn't sat well with me. She seemed to pop up everywhere questionable activity was happening, eager to use it for her own benefit. Of course, that could simply be a characteristic of a good reporter. Her reaction just now, one of immediate indignation, eased my concerns.

"Now that would be a great story, wouldn't it?" I asked. "Reporter comes to town, hoping to make a name for herself, and ends up a suspect in a murder because of a piece she wrote?"

This time, her expression went blank, and I couldn't help but laugh out loud.

"Wow," Lupe said. "Glad you don't have the authority to arrest anyone. I'd be a little worried." A roar of displeasure rose from the crowd down by the lake. "I'm going to wander down there and see what's going on. See ya."

"Good luck with the article. Stay neutral. Wouldn't want the sheriff to cite you for libel."

Lupe gave me a crisp salute and jogged toward the lake, cutting through the Pentacle Garden to get there.

I glanced at Ye Olde Bean Grinder and debated about stopping in for a mocha. I was still buzzing from Morgan's solstice tea, though, and didn't really need more stimulation. "I could try a decaf," I said to myself. Meeka let out a little whine in response and stood on my foot with her two front paws. "Okay, I get it, you're hungry. Let's go home. I've been avoiding this long enough anyway."

Twenty minutes later, Meeka was contently munching her kibble while I changed into work clothes and then started across the yard to the house. Normally, Meeka raced around after breakfast, chasing whatever insect or small animal she could find. Today, she ran to the far side of the yard, did her duty, and then herded me toward the doors at the back of the house, ensuring I couldn't find any other ways to delay starting this job. She followed me through the house and up the stairs. When I stood in the doorway of Gran's bedroom for too long, she pushed on the back of my legs with her head.

"Okay. I'm going to do this." I held the little red charm bag Morgan gave me and asked whoever was listening to help me with this task. Since the sweatpants I'd chosen had no pockets, I shoved the bag into my bra over my heart and stepped into the room.

Where should I start? The closet was crammed full of clothes. There was also the six-drawer dresser and her nightstand. I chose the nightstand since it was smaller and I'd be able to check something off my list faster. All was fine until I sniffed the hand lotion I found in the top drawer. The lavender aroma brought forth a flood of memories that made my heart clench and caused tears to sting my eyes. As sad as I was that Gran had died, my real problem was realizing all the missed opportunities. I had promised her so many times that I would come for a visit and never did. Emails and phone calls were wonderful, but they weren't the same as seeing her face-to-face, to be able to give and get her hugs. I screwed up. I should've visited her. Now it was too late. Yet another entry on the long list of bad decisions I'd made in the past year or so.

I sat cross-legged on the floor in the middle of the bedroom and pressed the heels of my hands into my eyelids until I saw stars. An overwhelming sense of loss enveloped me. As always when I was upset, Meeka was suddenly there leaning against me. I grabbed her and held her in a tight hug until she started to squirm. When I released her, she stood with her front paws on my legs and licked my face.

Once she was sure I was better, the little Westie jumped up into the bay window that overlooked the lake and burrowed into the mountain of pillows there. After wiping my eyes, I took a deep breath and stared at the dresser. This was stupid. The clothes in the drawers weren't Gran. The scent that would waft around me in a moment wasn't her. This house wasn't her no matter how much I felt her here.

I yanked opened the top left-hand dresser drawer, froze, and burst out laughing. It was full of socks. Same dresser drawer I kept my socks in. Something so simple, so silly, but I instantly felt connected to my grandmother again. After that, everything was easier.

Everything from the top four drawers—socks, undergarments, and pajamas—went into a giveaway box, but the bottom two held four beautiful crushed-velvet robes Gran wore during Wiccan rituals. One was a deep forest green. Another, raven black. The final two were blue, one a rich purply midnight color and the other a lighter blue the same shade as the lake outside. The lighter blue robe was the one Gran had been wearing when Rosalyn and I walked in on her in the middle of a ritual sixteen years ago. We left the next morning after Rosalyn told Mom about it. That was the last time we'd been here as a family.

It didn't seem right to stuff those robes into a giveaway box. I'd asked Morgan what to do with them. Maybe there was a witch with a need.

With the nightstand and dresser empty, it was time for lunch. The last thing I'd eaten was the sunrise gelato hours earlier.

"Let's go get lunch, Meeka."

She sprang to life from a dead sleep, raced downstairs, and waited by the back patio doors. I let her out then made the lunch Gran always made for me and Rosalyn — tomato soup, a grilled cheese sandwich, and a glass of milk. I added a peanut butter oatmeal chocolate chip cookie from Treat Me Sweetly and sat on the patio to eat and watch the boaters and jet skiers zip past on the lake, enviously contemplating jumping in. The official first day of summer had turned warm and humid with only a puff of a breeze blowing in off the lake. That little puff felt wonderful, though. The pine trees also seemed to enjoy it, waving back and forth, cooling their needles. The branches rubbed together, *wooshing and shushing* as though whispering to each other. Or me. What were they trying to tell me?

Once I finished my lunch, I felt ready to go back in and finish the job. I picked up my tray, went inside the house, and screamed.

Chapter 17

A MAN WAS STANDING NEXT to the basement door. Startled by each other, we both jumped, and I almost dropped the tray holding my lunch dishes.

"Tripp?"

I hadn't recognized him at first, mostly because he was wearing only a towel. He must've just come up from using the basement bathroom. Did he always wander through the house wearing just a towel after a shower?

"When did you get back?" I asked as he said, "Sorry, didn't realize you were here."

We both laughed. Was I staring?

With one hand securely clutching the towel at his waist, he motioned toward his trailer with the other hand. "I'll go get dressed. Be right back."

By the time my dishes were in the dishwasher and the frying pan washed, Tripp returned wearing his paint-spattered cargo pants and T-shirt.

"Sorry," he apologized again. "I should've realized you were here when I smelled the grilled cheese."

"Would you like one? I'm happy to make one for you."

I didn't wait for him to answer. He had that famished look of someone needing sustenance, so I got right to work on a twin of the lunch I just ate. He sat across from me on one of the barstools, apologized for disappearing without a word, and thanked me for cooking for him. Once the soup was warming and the sandwich grilling, I focused my attention on him.

"I was worried about you. Where have you been? Are you okay?"

"I'm really sorry," he apologized for the third time. "I should've left a note. I'd been gone for about two hours and realized I don't know your phone number."

"Huh. I guess you wouldn't, would you? There's never been a reason for you to call me."

"No. I'd much rather just cross the yard and see your face."

Feeling a flush rising in my cheeks, I turned to flip his sandwich.

"I didn't mean to worry you. I honestly didn't think I'd be gone that long, but after Lily Grace's reading, I needed to get my head on straight, you know? I headed south and after a while realized I didn't even have proof that my mother had died. Just the words of a teenage fortune teller. By that time, I was a hundred miles or so from Missouri."

"What did you do?" I placed his bowl of soup and a glass of milk in front of him then took his sandwich off the frying pan and cut it on the diagonal.

"Thanks," he said of the soup and swallowed a few spoonsful. "I crossed the border, went to a public library, and asked a librarian for help. I was hoping she could help me track down a phone number to call. Like Social Security or whatever state agency could tell me about deaths. Instead, she set me up on a computer and gave me a refresher course on doing internet searches." He blushed. "It's been a while since I used a computer."

While he dipped one corner of his sandwich into his soup, I asked, "Were you able to find anything?"

He nodded as he chewed. "We can let Lily Grace know

she was right. My mother died from a drug overdose two years ago in Kansas City." He shook his head. "One of probably two states between here and California that I hadn't gone through. I lost her trail in South Dakota and never once thought to find out if she was still alive. She wasn't that old, you know? I just figured she didn't want the hassle of being a mom."

I said nothing more as he finished his lunch. He moved slowly, almost as though in physical pain. A crease had formed on his forehead. His eyes, which usually sparkled were dull and tired, his skin ashy. I always thought knowing something like that was better than not knowing. Maybe I was wrong.

After he had used the last bite of his sandwich to sop up the last drops of his soup, I presented him with a cookie on a plate. For whatever reason, the gesture made him laugh. It started out as surprise — *oh, look a cookie* — and turned into a fit of giggles. I laughed along with him until I realized that the giggles had become sobs.

"Oh, Tripp." I rushed around to his side of the kitchen bar and wrapped him in a hug. After a few seconds, his sobbing reduced in intensity, but tears still fell.

"My mother died on the floor of a grimy bathroom in some sleazy bar in the middle of nowhere Missouri. I can't believe that's how her life ended. I can't believe she never bothered to contact me." I was about to comment, but he silenced me with a wave. "Maybe she tried. Maybe she was looking for me while I was on the road looking for her. That possibility has been eating me up since Lily Grace told me what she saw. I should've stayed in California with my aunt and uncle."

"If she had been looking for you," I reasoned, "she would have called her sister, right? If she had done that, your aunt would've told you. You said you stayed in regular contact with them."

Just that fast, his tears stopped. "I did. You're right. I

call them all the time. I think the longest I've ever gone is two weeks between calls."

His agony switched to anger and again I wondered if knowing wasn't necessarily better.

I placed my hand on his back. "I'm really sorry this happened to her and you. It's heartbreaking when someone's life takes that kind of a turn." We sat in comfortable but sad silence for a minute. "Are you feeling a little better?"

He shrugged and then nodded. "The shower and lunch helped. Thanks."

"Something is still bothering you. What is it?"

He hesitated before saying, "I don't know. I guess I feel lost. I have no parent. Maybe my father is still out there somewhere, but I have no idea where he is or who he is. And after what my mom used to tell me, that he was a complete loser, I have no desire to find him. Or maybe she was lying and he's a great guy." He rubbed his hands over his face. "God, I don't know what to think anymore. Yes, I still have family, but I have no home other than that popup out front. I have a temporary job, but once we're done with the house, then what? No one else in the village will give me a job. I don't know where I fit." He looked at me, desperation heavy in his eyes. "Where do I fit?"

I grabbed his hand and blurted, "Right here. You belong right here with me no matter what the council says about you being able to stay in the village."

After a few long and awkward seconds, I realized he'd misinterpreted another of my comments. I didn't mean *with* me, not the way he was thinking. I released his hand, mumbled something about needing to go change clothes, and rushed out the patio doors. It wasn't a lie, it was far too warm and humid for sweatpants today, but mostly I just needed to break the tension I'd just created between us.

I ran up to my apartment and splashed cold water on my face. As I pulled the towel away, I found my reflection looking at me.

"Why did you say that?" the Jayne in the mirror scolded. "You know what he wants. You need to think before you speak."

Mirror Jayne was right. I hung up the towel, pulled off my T-shirt, and noticed there was a message waiting for me on the apartment phone. How long ago had it been left? Like most people, I was so used to getting messages on my cell phone, I didn't even think to look for the blinking light on the landline. I pushed the button and continued changing clothes.

"Jayne, this is the medical examiner's office." I recognized Dr. Bundy's voice immediately. He paused for a few seconds then cleared his throat. "I wanted to let you know that I did find a puncture wound on the victim. I tested for Ketamine and got a positive result. There was more than enough of the drug in her system to kill her. Three times the amount necessary to kill a woman her size. Ketamine is slow acting, so even that much wouldn't have killed her instantly. The cause of death is strangulation. My assumption is that when she was shot with a dart it startled her, broke her concentration, and she became entangled in the fabric.

"That's all I can tell you, so don't call with more questions and please don't repeat this to anyone. I'll let your new sheriff know what I found, and word will spread soon enough. I'd appreciate it if you'd delete this message now."

I listened to the message once more then did as he asked and hit delete.

After pulling on a tank top, I walked out into the living area of my little apartment and began taping together pieces of printer paper. I made three strips with four pieces of paper in each strip and then taped the strips together. Once I had a single large sheet, I taped it to the wall above the table and chairs in my kitchenette. With marker in hand, I jotted thoughts on my makeshift suspect board.

KEPT SECRETS | 137

At the top in the center, I wrote *Berlin* and below her name *Strangulation*. On the righthand side, I wrote *Suspects*. Below that, *Gianni Cordano, Dallas Brickman,* and after a moment's hesitation, *Abilene?* All three of them had means; they saw each other every day. They all had motive. Next to Gianni's name, I wrote *regularly argued about equipment placement.* I wrote *wanted closing act recognition* next to Dallas' name, which felt weak, but it was still a motive. Next to Abilene's, I wrote *jealous lover?*

"What about method?" I mumbled. "Berlin had enough Ketamine in her system to take down a tiger, and that would have killed her if she hadn't strangled to death first. How did the drug get into her system?"

For Gianni, it was obvious: *Ketamine via tranquilizer dart gun.* What about the other two? It wasn't likely that either Dallas or Abilene got a hold of Gianni's dart guns, but they could have purchased their own equipment. Gianni did say that anyone could buy darts and a gun.

But what about the Ketamine? I shook my head, clearing the thought.

"Focus on the method first. If that holds together, then figure out how they got the drug."

I stood back and analyzed what I had written so far. Next to Gianni, I added *veterinarian.* Next to Dallas, I added *knife thrower.* Knife thrower. Was it possible for Dallas to throw a tranquilizer dart that far? My gut told me he probably could. Time to go back to the circus and asked a few more questions.

Chapter 18

MEEKA PULLED HARD ON THE leash as soon as she realized the path we were on led to the circus grounds. She loved scavenging for scraps of food people had dropped and being around the different kinds of animals. And all the wonderful smells! Being at the circus was like a little bit of doggie utopia for her.

"Let me guess," Colette said as we got close to the ticket booth, "you're not here to see a performance."

"Good guess," I said. "I'm here to talk to Dallas. I didn't get a chance to do that last time."

"It's after lunchtime. I told you before, everyone gets ready for the performance after lunch."

I stuck my hand in my pocket and pulled out a twenty. "One ticket, please."

She scowled at me. "Guess I can't stop you from going in, but I recommend not upsetting the knife thrower just before he goes on stage. I'm sure Abilene would agree."

"What time is the performance?"

"Afternoon show starts at four o'clock. That's only an hour from now."

"No problem. I'm sure I can find something here to entertain me."

Most of the crowd had made their way down to the end of the midway, everyone anxious to get good seats in the big top, I'm sure. The sideshow acts were in full swing— jugglers, sword swallowers, magicians. A tightrope walker mesmerized me as she zigzagged her way down the midway, walking along on a rope tied to poles starting at the ticket booth and ending at a platform above the big top's entrance.

Meeka and I ended up by the rides, pausing by the carousel. She seemed to know that there were animals on the ride but was confused by the fact that they kept spinning in circles.

"Doggie!"

I turned to see a little boy with only one arm jumping up and down next to a woman in a wheelchair.

"Can I play with your doggie?" he begged.

The woman in the chair looked a little different out of costume and with her long blonde hair hanging loose instead of tied up in a bun, but she had to be Tilda.

"Is it okay?" I asked her.

She shrugged. "Fine by me."

I showed the boy how to approach Meeka by offering her the back of his hand. When he did so, Meeka sniffed and looked up at me, her tail wagging.

"That wagging tail means she likes you." I looked to Meeka and assured, "Friend."

I let the leash extend and the two hit the ground immediately, rolling around together.

"Cute dog," the woman said.

"Cute kid. You're Tilda Nelson, right?"

She looked at me with narrowed eyes. "Who's asking?"

"I'm Jayne O'Shea. I live in the big house over near the campground."

"I heard the name before. How come you know me?"

"I was here the morning Berlin died. I kept an eye on the area while we were waiting for someone from the county to arrive. I'm sorry, I heard that you and Berlin were close."

She sighed, obviously exhausted. People meant well, but words of condolence could wear a person down after a while. I didn't want to harass her, but I needed to ask some questions.

"You a cop? How come you 'kept an eye on the area'?"

"I used to be a detective in Madison. While I waited for the deputy that day, I did my own mini-investigation."

I told her how I felt that Berlin's death seemed suspicious.

"Suspicious?" Tilda asked, shocked. "Berlin didn't have any family. We were close enough that she listed me as her sole beneficiary. I've been working with lawyers to settle her estate and stuff. I even got in touch with the mortician to arrange for her to be cremated. Point is, I've been talking to a lot of people about her. No one said anything about her death being suspicious."

I couldn't tell if she was more surprised or upset about this.

"I know the medical examiner who's doing Berlin's autopsy and—" What was I doing? I almost blurted out what Dr. Bundy had specifically asked me to keep secret. "I told him I felt it was odd that Berlin ended up tangled the way she did."

Smooth. Real smooth, Jayne.

Tilda raised her chin to look me in the eye. "Now I know why your name is familiar. You figured out what happened to that girl who died last month."

"That's me. Now I'm trying to figure out what really happened to Berlin. I'm sure you've answered this question already, along with a million others, but is there anyone you can think of who would want to see Berlin dead?"

"Gianni," she said instantly and with hatred in her voice. "I mean, what's the matter with that man? What's so damn hard about pushing that fence five more feet?"

"I spoke with Gianni the other day," I said. "I'll be

honest with you, at this point, I have no reason to believe he did anything. Is there anyone else you can think of who could've done this? Anyone at all?"

"I'm telling you, it was Gianni. He's a horrible, stubborn man. Janessa saw her body. She told me that Berlin's silks snagged on that damn cage again, and she strangled to death." A sob escaped her; she needed a minute to compose herself. "How horrible is that? I just can't imagine what she went through. You want to know who did this? I'm telling you, it was that greasy little Gianni."

Tilda's chest heaved with anger. Just then, Joss let out a giggle as Meeka covered him with kisses. Tilda's expression immediately turned to one of love for her little boy, all discussion about Berlin and Gianni faded away.

"He loves animals. Don't you, Jossy?"

"Yep." He tried to fight off Meeka and get more kisses from her at the same time. "I miss my kitty."

"You don't have a kitty." Tilda looked up at me, shaking her head. "I don't know where he gets this from."

"At the house with daddy," Joss said. "How come you don't remember my kitty?"

Sounded like a divorce situation.

Tilda frowned. "His daddy died the day of the car accident." She laid her hand on her paralyzed leg. "Funny how his little mind remembers things."

"I'm sorry to hear of your husband's death." I recalled my conversation with Colette at lunch the other day. "Colette told me about your accident. I hope that was all right."

She shrugged. "Not like it's a secret."

"I don't remember her mentioning that your husband had died."

Tilda turned away. "That's one thing that I don't talk about. The loss of a limb is one thing. The loss of a loved one, well ..."

She wouldn't look at me anymore. Apparently, I had

wandered into forbidden territory.

"Meeka, come." I tugged gently on her leash, and she came right over to me. "I'm sorry if I upset you, Tilda. That wasn't my intent. I just want the truth about what happened to Berlin to come out. As I'm sure you do."

Tilda was sidetracked, brushing dirt off Joss' knees and butt. "Hmm? Yes, of course, I do."

"If you think of anything else, would you let me know?"

She continued brushing Joss' dirty knees. "Sure. I can do that."

With her attention on her son now, Tilda was clearly done talking to me. No problem, I didn't want to upset her any further.

It was just after four o'clock. I wouldn't be able to talk with Dallas for another hour or so, but I could go and watch the big top performance again. I bought a ticket after all.

Meeka and I wandered into the tent where I showed my ticket to the clown at the entrance. He waved me through, offering me a flower that turned into a colorful chiffon scarf when I reached for it. He put his hands on his belly and laughed silently as though this was the best trick ever.

"Very good," I said. "You got me."

He gave a low, flourishing bow and let us enter.

I didn't want to disrupt the spectators by finding a seat in the stands halfway through the show, so I stood next to the bleachers. The family-friendly atmosphere, compared to the evening adult show, was immediately obvious. Clowns wandered all around, up and down the bleachers, making balloon animals or hats, playing little tricks like the flower into a scarf gag, and tossing small pieces of candy into the audience. The costumes were bright and colorful. The spotlights swirled around the floor, ceiling, and audience in between acts, ensuring that there was never a pause in the action.

Finally, Dallas and Abilene entered the ring closest to me, the one right of center. Instead of the sexy, shirtless, one-legged pirate he dressed as during the night show, Dallas was now a child-friendly, fully-clothed, goofball one-legged pirate. Instead of the barely clothed, bosom heaving wench, Abilene—*five foot seven, long copper-brown hair, slender but curvy*—was now a pure and innocent maiden who had somehow become tied to a wall where the pirate was now throwing knives at her. It was a silly performance, but the audience loved it.

Despite the comical, stumbling character he was now portraying, Dallas' skills were still spot on. He could spin on a dime, balance on his peg leg, and throw a knife precisely, which meant mere inches from Abilene's head. After throwing ten more knives in rapid succession, resulting in an outline of Abilene's body, he "rescued" her from one wall and then tied her to another that was covered with colorful balloons.

Tripp and I had seen the afternoon show, but I'd forgotten about this part of their act. They hadn't performed it during the adults-only show. In a swarthy pirate's voice, Dallas told the audience about a trek he had made through South America. How he came across a native tribe living deep in the jungle.

"That's where I lost me leg," he proclaimed. "A monster alligator chomped it right off me body while I took a bath in the river one afternoon. Fortunately, this tribe had the best medicine man you'd ever have the pleasure to meet. He couldn't save me leg, but he did save me life. I lived with that tribe for two years. Not only did they teach me to live with one leg, they taught their ways, including how to hunt."

This time, instead of throwing knives at Abilene, Dallas blew tiny little spears at her from a long hollow stick.

"That's a blowgun," I said.

"It is," a little boy sitting in the stand next to me agreed. "Isn't it cool?"

Chapter 19

THE ONLY DIFFERENCE BETWEEN A blowgun and a dart gun was that a blowgun was human powered and a dart gun used a CO_2 cartridge to propel the dart. And a blowgun shot tinier darts. I stood there, fascinated, while one-by-one, in rapid succession Dallas hit every balloon surrounding Abilene. He didn't take a break. He didn't need to line up. He simply stuck the tiny spears into the end of the tube and blew.

If he could be this accurate while spinning and playing to the crowd, there was no reason Dallas couldn't have hit Berlin from thirty yards while standing still and aiming. The question was, could he have blown the dart I found on the ground in the tent through a blowgun? Not the one he was currently using, the little spears were much smaller than the dart, but maybe he rigged up a bigger one. It was a question worth asking.

Dallas and Abilene were the final act. After they were done, all the performers came back out to take a final bow. While they did that, Meeka and I slipped out and rushed around to where the performers exited the tent.

"Dallas," I called out as soon as I saw him emerge.

He turned my direction, a smile plastered on his made-up face. He probably thought I wanted an autograph or to have my picture taken with him.

"Jayne O'Shea," I said and held my hand out to him. "I'd like to ask you some questions if you have a couple of minutes."

"If you want to come with us," he indicated himself and Abilene, "I'll be happy to answer questions. Are you thinking about becoming a knife thrower?"

He chuckled as though the thought was cute, but he wouldn't be laughing for long.

"I'm just curious about … the science, I guess, behind this. I'm blown away by the precision. How far can you throw accurately?"

"Depends on what I'm throwing." He chuckled again. "I imagine it's different for everyone, but for me, the larger and smaller items are harder. I'm most comfortable throwing knives."

"What about darts?" I didn't take my eyes off him, watching his body language for any twitch that might indicate he was hiding something.

"Darts? As in dartboard darts?" He looked at Abilene and winked. "Hanging out with friends, playing darts in pool halls and bars was how I got into this. I was in the service, Army. Three weeks into my one and only tour and I step on a landmine. Hard to be a soldier with just one leg, so once I learned how to get around again, I went back to the only other thing I knew how to do. Gotta say, everything worked out okay for me."

"Wow," I said. "Your attitude is pretty great. What's the farthest you can throw a dart?"

My repeat of the question made him pause. He looked at me, confused amusement crinkling the corners of his eyes. Abilene had ducked into his tent as he was telling me about his service record. She came out now with a more traditional prosthetic leg, the kind designed for athletes with the curved foot that allowed for more stability if they chose to run or do something more adventurous. She handed the leg to Dallas and then smiled down at Meeka who waved her tail once or twice and then lay down, not interested in checking out Abilene.

Dallas popped off the peg leg, swapped it out for the athletic one, and instantly looked more comfortable.

"Standard throwing distance to a dartboard is around seven-and-a-half or eight feet, depending on whether you're throwing soft- or steel-tipped darts. My record hitting the bull's-eye is nineteen feet. I've never been able to duplicate that, so I'll say I'm consistent at eighteen feet."

"That's throwing a dart by hand, right?"

My now serious tone, as opposed to my earlier giddy fangirl one, surprised him. He nodded that yes, that was throwing a dart by hand.

"How accurate are you with your blowgun?"

He shifted in his seat. "Sorry, I've forgotten your name. Who are you again?"

"Jayne O'Shea."

I could've explained further, but understanding dawned on his face and he supplied, "Ex-cop. Ex-deputy. Are you investigating me, Jayne O'Shea?"

"Not necessarily."

"I heard we have a new sheriff. Did he hire you as his deputy?"

Answering to Zeb Warren would be a demotion I'd never accept.

"No, he didn't. I'm just a curious citizen, Mr. Brickman. So, what about your blowgun accuracy?"

He sat back, propping his prosthetic leg on his opposite knee and smiled. "It's further than by hand, but not necessarily more consistent. My record bull's-eye is twenty-nine yards, consistent at just under twenty-six. Does that help with your curiosity?"

Twenty-six yards was … seventy-eight feet. I had estimated that Berlin's body was twenty-five or thirty feet in the air. Outside of Dallas' dart throwing record, but well within his range with a blowgun. And to inject Berlin with Ketamine, he certainly didn't have to hit a bull's-eye, just connect somewhere on her body.

"I can tell that you're analyzing details," Dallas said. "I didn't kill Berlin, Ms. O'Shea."

But he knew she was the reason I was asking the questions. "Do you have an alibi?"

His gaze instantly went to Abilene, who blushed and looked away. "I do, in fact. The lovely Abilene and I were together at The Inn at that time. We got there shortly after the performance the evening before Berlin died and stayed until nearly lunchtime on the day in question."

The blush on Abilene's cheeks intensified, and she became very interested in her fingernails with this revelation.

"Can anyone at The Inn verify this?"

"They sure can," Dallas said. "Check with Laurel."

"I'll do that," I said while adding notes to a memo app in my phone. "Do you happen to know if anyone else around here can throw darts? Or use a blowgun? Or a tranquilizer dart gun?"

I had his full attention now and he sat up straight. "Are you telling me that Berlin was shot with a dart? As in a tranquilizer dart?"

"I have reason to believe she was."

His confident demeanor sagged a little. "Ms. O'Shea, I liked Berlin. We had a good relationship. We'd been talking about putting together a final act." He smiled sadly. "It would've been a true showstopper."

It was fast, barely more than a flash, but I saw the glare Abilene shot at him at the mention of this show-stopping act.

"In answer to your question," Dallas continued, "I overheard a quiet conversation between a couple of the carnies one time. They were talking about how one of our performers had spot-on accuracy with shooting. It sounded like they meant regular guns, not a dart gun. I don't know who they were talking about and honestly don't remember who said it. I never heard it mentioned again so dismissed it as people just trying to get at me. Taunting me, for whatever reason. If you know what I mean."

"I think I do," I said. "I'm not sure if this has been helpful, but it's certainly been informative. I have one final question for you, Mr. Brickman. Do you have any idea who might have killed Berlin?"

He blinked twice, and then once more. Instinct told me he truly had cared for Berlin.

"No, unfortunately, I don't know, but if I had to guess, I'd say Gianni. The man has an ego on him that's out of control. Berlin was concerned about the location of the fencing. I can't, no matter how hard I try, come up with a reason for why he wouldn't move that section farther. If you do end up nailing him for this, send the sonofabitch away for a long time. Okay?" He took a second to get his emotions under control. "Sorry. If there's nothing else, I need to relax a little before preparing for tonight's show."

I believed he was being honest. Still, a visit to The Inn to verify his claim that he and Abilene had been there was now on my to-do list.

"I don't have any more questions," I said. "At least not for now. Thanks for talking with me."

As Meeka and I walked away from the "residential" area of the circus grounds, I wondered where the performers lived in the winter. Certainly not in canvas tents in the Northwoods. Then, I spotted Gianni over by the animal wagons just off the midway.

"Let's go see the animals," I told Meeka. Her wagging tail said she agreed.

"Jayne," Gianni greeted with a smile as we got close. "You are a frequent visitor to the circus, no?"

"I wish I was just here as a visitor."

"Uh-oh. You have on your serious investigator face."
Gianni went from wagon to wagon, verifying that the
latches were secure and padlocked. He looked over his
shoulder with a smile. "We certainly wouldn't want a tiger
to get loose. Why don't you ask me what you came here to
ask, Detective?"

The use of my old title caught me off guard. Especially
because he had used it as a sign of respect.

"I have to be honest, Gianni. Everyone I've spoken to
feels you are the prime suspect in Berlin's death."

"And I have told you that I did not harm her." Satisfied
with the latch on the bear's wagon, he turned to me. "I
admit, I should've moved the fence. I did not, however,
leave it there with the hopes that Berlin would be harmed."

"That's the point of great confusion. Why didn't you
just move it? It seemed like a simple, not to mention
reasonable, request."

He lifted his shoulders and tossed his hands out to the
side. "Foolish pride? Ego? I don't know how to answer that
sufficiently. I can't remember why I didn't do it the first time
she asked. There was a reason, I had something urgent to
attend to or some such. I do remember that the next time she
was rude. Or at least that's how I interpreted it. Perhaps I
was having a bad day and not feeling cooperative."

"And it turned into a battle of wills?"

He stared, forlornly, at the lion in his wagon.
"Something small and silly that I assure you I now regret."

A small group of people, led by Tilda and Joss, arrived
to see the animals then. She was answering questions.

"Tilda educates visitors about the animals?" I asked
once we had stepped ten or so yards away.

He laughed. "Tilda helps, but Joss is the real expert.
He's very smart and curious about the animals. Tilda brings
him over to the enclosures during feeding time, and he
always has so many questions. He likes to play tour guide
and bring groups over to the wagons so he can show off his

knowledge." Gianni smiled fondly at the boy. "I'm happy to let them do this. They always ask if they don't know an answer."

I pulled him even further away from the small group, not wanting anyone to overhear our conversation.

"You appear concerned, Jayne."

"Like I said, everyone is pointing at you." Part of me wanted to reveal Dr. Bundy's findings to him so I could get more of a reaction out of him.

Gianni remained stone-faced, except for the slight bobbing of his Adam's apple. "You still believe I shot her with that dart you found even though I have already told you I did no such thing."

"An autopsy has been done. They'll test Berlin's blood for drugs. If they find Ketamine, I can almost assure you that you'll be arrested for her death."

That was enough. If I said any more, I might reveal what Dr. Bundy asked me to keep quiet.

I glanced toward the animal cages and noticed that Tilda was taking great interest in our conversation. When she saw me looking, she excused herself from the group and rolled toward us.

"I will tell you one more time," Gianni said in a low, intense tone, "I did not kill Berlin."

"Then help me out here." I didn't want him to be the killer; I liked Gianni. "If you didn't do it, who did?"

His eyes darted to the rapidly approaching Tilda and he spoke in a low, rushed voice. "Talk to Dallas. He and Berlin argued as often as she and I did."

I held up a hand to Tilda, indicating she should stay back while we talked. She tilted her head, confused, but stopped rolling.

"Actually," I told Gianni, "I just came from talking with Dallas. He told me that he was with Abilene at the time."

Gianni shook his head and waved a hand as if dismissing this. "Yes, yes. Everyone knows that they practice together all the time. I'm not talking about practice time. We don't know the exact time of Berlin's death. She could have been killed in the middle of the night. Where was Dallas in the middle of the night?"

"That's what I'm saying. Dallas and Abilene claim they were together at The Inn from just after the performance that night until long after Berlin had been found dead."

The veterinarian appeared to almost visibly deflate with this revelation. "At The Inn? Together? How can that be?"

"You don't think that's where they were? Do you have proof? Because Dallas claims The Inn will vouch for them."

As if in shock, Gianni shook his head. "No, I have no proof, but I don't understand. Abilene and I, we've been seeing each other for months."

He walked away without another word, my mouth dropped open with surprise, and Tilda closed the gap between us. Joss came running over as well. I let out Meeka's leash and instructed her to go to the boy so I could talk privately with his mother.

"Is Gianni okay?" Tilda asked, curious but not overly concerned.

"Not really. I just inadvertently told him his girlfriend was cheating on him." I hated it when things came to light that way.

Tilda frowned. "Looked like you two were having a pretty intense conversation. Did it have something to do with Berlin?"

"I didn't know you had such an interest in the animals," I said, sidestepping her question. I didn't want to upset her again, especially because I had no facts, only speculation.

"Well, you know, I like them as much as any person. Joss is the real fanatic." She motioned at him and Meeka and smiled. "Look at them. This is how he's always been with animals. When we got here and he found out that there were lions, tigers, and bears—"

"Oh my," I said, unable to stop myself from completing

The Wizard of Oz line.

Tilda relaxed then, if the slumping of her shoulders meant anything. "I'd do just about anything for that little guy. If he wants to learn everything there is to learn about big cats, I'm happy to teach him. Or find someone like Gianni who can. Nothing wrong with expanding my own mind in the process, though, hey?"

"I couldn't agree more. You're a good mom, Tilda."

"Thanks." She stared at the small group still clustered around the animal wagons. "You were confronting Gianni about Berlin's death, weren't you? Does it look like he did it?"

"It's not up to me to say."

"But you must have an opinion."

"The medical examiner hasn't officially closed the case yet, so I really shouldn't say anything."

"I thought you said he ruled it a strangulation."

It had been more than a week; she just wanted an answer. I understood that. Unfortunately, I couldn't provide a conclusive one at this point. "That was the preliminary result. It can take weeks and sometimes months to get final autopsy results."

"Months? I certainly hope we're not waiting that long to make an arrest. Whoever did this to her, I want them put away."

"I assure you, I'm doing what I can to make that happen. Not that I can do much more than pass my feelings and findings onto Deputy Atkins and our new sheriff."

The color drained from Tilda's face. "From what I've heard, if we wait for the new guy, Joss will be graduating high school before anything more happens."

Another satisfied endorsement of our new lawman. Honestly, there was very little I could do directly regarding Berlin's death, other than be nosy and ask questions. But as a council member, I could do something about the other issue that was bothering me. I could help ensure we had the right person wearing the badge for the village.

As if on cue, I spotted Sheriff Warren standing halfway down the midway.

Chapter 20

THE CLOSER I GOT TO THE sheriff, I realized he was talking to a visibly unhappy Lupe Gomez. In fact, from the intense red flush on her cheeks and the way she flung her arms out to the side as she spoke, I'd say she was flat-out furious. I didn't have to get much closer before I could hear their words.

"It's called freedom of the press," Lupe said. "Ever heard of it?"

"You need to watch yourself, ma'am," Sheriff Warren said. "Not sure you know who you're talking to."

"I know who you are. I'm not doing anything wrong. I was sent here to do a job and that's what I'm doing."

"The articles you're writing are upsetting people," he said.

"What's upsetting them? The fact that I mentioned there was a death?"

Zeb hitched his thumbs into his service belt. "It sheds an unfavorable light on the village. People come here because they believe it to be a safe, family-friendly place."

Lupe stared at him with her mouth hanging open and eyes narrowed in confusion. "People don't die in safe, family-friendly places?"

"There was no reason for you to write about that situation. Like I said, talking about unpleasant things upsets our tourists."

"You know what upsets the tourists?" Lupe took a step closer.

"What's going on here?" I asked, breaking up something I feared might end with Lupe spending the night in the pokey.

"Ms. O'Shea." Sheriff Warren pushed his shoulders back. "Speaking of upsetting the tourists."

Me? "What did I do?"

"You started this whole kerfuffle."

I looked at Lupe. "Did he just say kerfuffle?"

"I think so," she fought off a small smile. "Never heard anyone actually use that word before."

I turned to the sheriff. "And how did I start a *kerfuffle*?"

He tugged at his collar, which told me he was becoming heated or upset. "You've been wandering all around the village asking questions."

"That's what I did," Lupe said. "And I wrote down their answers."

"Ah," I said. "Obtaining knowledge, and then sharing that knowledge. Dangerous stuff."

"Ladies, I will not be disrespected. The two of you are asking questions about a murder and getting people upset. We don't want the tourists to think that a murder took place in Whispering Pines."

"Even if it's the truth?" I asked.

He leveled a glare at me and then returned to Lupe. "Why don't you focus on the positive things? Talk about the beauty of the area. The entertainment at the circus. The water sports or the incredible food. There so many wonderful things."

"Basically," I said, "you want Ms. Gomez to paint a Norman Rockwell picture of Whispering Pines with her words."

"Glad you understand," Sheriff Warren said. "My own focus has been to keep anything negative off the streets. People yearn for a place where their children can run around outside without worrying that they'll get snatched up by kidnappers. They want to know that they can go to the beach and not have to watch a bunch of drunken fools causing a scene and using language they don't want to hear."

He was talking like we'd agreed to join him in this fantasy crusade of his. Then Lupe set him straight.

"Sounds to me like you're censoring freedom of expression." Her lips pursed as she scribbled something in her notebook.

"I expect the two of you to do as I've asked," he hissed, softly enough that no one else could hear him. "Ms. Berlin's death, as tragic and upsetting as it was, has been ruled an accident. There is no need to talk about it any longer."

"Ruled an accident?" I asked. "When did that happen? The official autopsy results aren't in yet."

The sheriff cleared his throat. "Once I took over here, the County Sheriff passed this case along to me. They sent me all the files, and I had a nice long talk with the investigating deputy. I reviewed the files and found no reason to believe that this was anything other than an unfortunate accident."

"So, you closed the case," I said, "even though the medical examiner's final report has not been issued yet and you haven't spoken to even one person at the circus?"

Unbelievable.

"Ms. O'Shea, I know that you were a detective in Madison. Keyword being 'were.' Now, as a civilian with law enforcement knowledge, I hope that you'll respect the badge."

I pushed my shoulders back and lowered my voice. "Don't misunderstand me, Sheriff. I have great respect for the *badge*."

Meeka leaned against my leg, sensing my aggravation, and Lupe stepped in this time. Apparently to keep me out of the pokey.

The sheriff repeated his directive, for us to focus on only the positive, and walked away.

"We need to talk," Lupe said.

"I was thinking the same thing." I stormed away from the circus grounds and led her east down the path toward the parking lot. "Have you been talking to people about Berlin's death?"

"Not the death itself," Lupe answered. "I've been talking to them about Berlin the woman, though. Don't listen to the sheriff. I'm not writing about negative stuff. I'm trying to put together a memorial piece."

"That's a great idea. I'm sure everyone here will appreciate that."

I wanted to talk to Lupe about Flavia and Donovan and how they were likely behind Zeb's positivity campaign, but I didn't want to reveal too much too soon about village politics. Especially because I didn't really know her or how much I could trust her. Morgan warned that the wrong thing said to the wrong person could cause more harm than help. She meant whoever was behind the sigils on my walls, but it was true in this situation, too. Best that Lupe and I focused on what was right in front of us.

"The sheriff is right about one thing," I said. "I'm no longer in law enforcement. Everything I've been doing has been because, like you, it's important to me that the truth comes out. I don't want to tell you how I know because I don't want to get my source in trouble, but I have a very strong reason to believe that Berlin's death was not an accident."

"We need to work together on this," Lupe said. "I was sent here to write happy vacation pieces about a quirky little village, but there's nothing stopping me from writing a darker, more in-depth piece if I come across one. I have lots of contacts that would be interested in a story like that. If we can bust this open, I want in on it."

I couldn't help but smile at how hungry she was.

Sheriff Warren just admitted he considered the case closed and wasn't going to look for Berlin's killer. Had Dr. Bundy already told him about the puncture wound and the drugs in her system? If so, did the sheriff close the case before or after he received that information? Either way, I wasn't okay with this. Berlin's death was not an accident.

I took a deep breath and prayed I was doing the right thing. "Working together sounds like a good idea."

As we continued down the path, I told her about the dart and how Gianni used Ketamine on the animals, and she told me what she had learned. While she had gathered great insight to the carnies individually, she didn't have anything new for me regarding Berlin's death.

"Right now," I said, "everyone is pointing at the veterinarian, Gianni Cordano. He's my prime suspect. Despite his insistence of innocence, he had motive in that he and Berlin had a fiery relationship. He has means in that he has a tranquilizer gun, darts, and the Ketamine. And considering Berlin died while everyone else was likely sleeping, he had opportunity."

"That's how you think he killed her?" Lupe asked. "He shot her with a tranquilizer dart?"

"She was shot with a dart, but the drug works so slowly, that's not what killed her."

"But it could have," Lupe said. "You said that dart was loaded with enough sedative to take down a tiger. If the fabric hadn't gotten wrapped around her neck, the drug would have eventually killed her."

"Good deductive reasoning. If you ever get tired of journalism, you might have a future as a detective."

"No thanks. This is way more fun. So, Gianni Cordano is our top suspect."

I released a heavy sigh. "My gut says he didn't do it.

The evidence says otherwise, and we have to follow the evidence. Gianni swears he keeps the Ketamine locked up and that no one else has access to it, but I don't believe him. That's our lead. If we can figure out that piece, we might be able to prove him innocent."

"No offense," Lupe said, "but the carnies see you as a cop, and their defenses go up when you come around. They're used to me asking questions now. I'll keep poking around and see what I can find out about Gianni and his stash of drugs."

We talked a little longer, going over the information we both had, then Lupe returned to the circus to ask more questions, and I continued to my car. My brain wouldn't let this rest. Yes, all the evidence led to Gianni, but he was so adamant that he hadn't done it. Who had then? Did he know? He was lying about the Ketamine. Any responsible veterinarian or animal trainer would be sure that both the animals and the people around them were safe. Someone else in the village could get at that drug; I'd stake my life on it. Who was Gianni protecting and why?

Chapter 21

WHEN I GOT HOME, I found Tripp's truck still in the driveway, right where it belonged. As much as I wanted to see the progress he was making inside, I wanted to learn more about Gianni, which meant research.

Once again, it took forever for my internet browser to open. When it finally did, I plugged the name "Gianni Cordano" into my search engine and ended up with thousands of hits. When I added "circus animal rescue," our Gianni popped right up. There weren't a lot of articles on him, but almost all that there were talked about the good he did for animals. A short biography mentioned the small town in Italy where he grew up and how even as a little boy he took care of animals there—walking dogs and brushing cats and feeding chickens and goats. I always envied people who knew as children what they were meant to do as adults.

Only one article discussed anything even remotely negative. It was very short and explained that he had been arrested for assault. He'd been in his late twenties at the time, and it happened a day or two after his mother had died in a car accident. Someone at a local pub had made nasty remarks about her. He was only held overnight and no charges were filed. Really, it was a case of a young man defending his mother's honor, but it did show that Gianni had a temper. Or at least he had in his late twenties.

I searched for information about some of the other performers as well. Dallas Brickman's story checked out just as he said. He had been in the Army nearly fifteen years earlier and had lost his leg when he stepped on an IED. Nothing came up on Abilene, but I didn't know her last name. And Abilene could be a stage name.

A couple of hits on Berlin, she went by only the one name, told me that she had been the star of the show almost from the start. She went through a time where she did sideshow acts, much like what Tilda was doing now, warming up the audience for *Cirque du Soleil* performances in different locales. When she finally won a spot in one of the *Cirque* shows, a jealous co-performer who had been there for nearly two years longer than Berlin became enraged. Just before Berlin took the stage on her opening night, the woman threw a cup of acid in her face. Numerous reconstructive procedures helped, but they never could repair all the scars.

"How awful," I mumbled. "That's why she always wore a mask."

"Jayne? Are you up here?"

I looked toward the sundeck just as Tripp came into view.

"Hey," he said, "where have you been?"

When I didn't answer right away, he let his head drop forward. That was the other reason why I snuck up to my apartment without going into the house. I didn't want to get the "leave it alone" lecture. Unlike Jonah, however, I knew Tripp wasn't really lecturing me. He was just concerned for my safety. Still, I didn't need to be told what to do.

"You're digging into the Berlin situation, aren't you?"

"You make it sound like some sort of case of international espionage. That might actually be fun." I lowered my voice and said conspiratorially, "The Berlin

Situation."

He made an unamused face. "Not fun. Dangerous." He pointed at my computer. "I assume you're doing research?"

I started talking nonstop. A good listener from the day we met, Tripp let me ramble while he lit the grill outside. While I told him everything I had learned from and about the carnies, he said nothing, just tended to dinner.

"Sorry," I said, "but I'm so close. I feel like I just need one more piece of evidence and I'll be able to unequivocally name or dismiss Gianni as Berlin's killer."

"Except ..."

"I know. It's not my job." I sounded like a petulant teenager and immediately regretted the tone, but my "Sorry" came across just as sulky.

Ignoring my attitude, Tripp handed me a thick slice of pizza topped with peppers, olives, onions, mushrooms, a few different meats, and double cheese.

"You grilled this?" I asked. "I was so busy talking, I didn't even pay attention. Did you make this yourself, too?"

He nodded and smiled as I took a big bite and promptly slumped with happiness into my chair.

"This is so good. I've never had a pizza on the grill before."

"I'll have to make it more often."

Innocent comments like that tended to turn into more comments about him liking to cook for me and us being together for a long time. I couldn't deal with that, not right now. So, I preemptively blurted, "Lupe is going to help me with the investigation." Followed quickly by, "Did I tell you that Sheriff Warren was trying to silence her? She argued First Amendment rights."

Tripp leaned back, eyes on his slice of pizza, and didn't acknowledge that I'd even spoken.

"Okay, I get it. I won't talk about the case anymore. Tell me what you got done on the house today."

"Finish eating and I'll show you."

We did so, enjoying the slightly cooler and less humid evening air, and then Tripp led me across the yard and through the house to the dining room.

"Wow," I said, amazed at the difference a coat of paint could make. "This looks fantastic."

While we planned to use a soft, lake-blue shade on all the other walls downstairs, we thought something different in the dining room might be fun. We went with a pale gray that had just a dash of green in it. What I hadn't expected was that the color would absorb the forest green from the pine trees outside. The resulting sage-green shade was very inviting.

"It looks a little different depending on the light outside," Tripp informed.

As happened with every improvement we made, I imagined bed-and-breakfast guests around me. They'd gather in this room around the table for Tripp's omelets and rustic French toast.

"I'm going to put on one more coat in here tomorrow," Tripp said. "Then I'll start on the sitting room and hallway. I was thinking, based on this gray and the blue we'll use everywhere else, dark blue or purple accents would look good. What do you think?"

He was putting serious thought into this house. I really hoped we wouldn't have to hand it over to a buyer when it was all done. "I love it. Really."

A huge yawn snuck up on him then. He stretched his arms out to the side and yawned again. "It's been a couple days since I slept in my own bed. I'm kind of beat. Think I'll call it a night."

"Good night, Tripp. Glad you're home."

Not quite ready to head to bed myself, I moved up to the sundeck. The sun had finally set on the first day of summer, but a thin band of light still highlighted the horizon. Meeka climbed up onto the lounge chair with me and snuggled in against my legs. As with every other night sitting out here, I became perfectly at ease. Being anywhere else or doing anything other than sitting right here, watching the trees mingling against the purple-blue sky and listening to the goose bump-inducing cry of the loons, was unthinkable.

I was trying to be patient with Mom, I knew she had to track down my dad in the middle of the desert, but it had been over a month since I presented the B&B idea. I'd call her tomorrow and push harder for a yes.

First thing the next morning, I was woken by the sound of a car horn softly beeping outside my boathouse apartment. I rolled onto my side, opened one eye, and looked at the clock sitting on the little table next to my bed. Who would be waking me up at seven-thirty in the morning?

I rolled out of bed with a groan, tugged on a hoodie over my tank top and boxers—getting it backwards first so needing to spin it around—and padded barefoot down the stairs to the yard. An older model Land Rover that looked like it had just driven out of the bush was sitting in my driveway. I had no idea who it was until the driver's door opened. Should've known. The vehicle fit Lupe perfectly.

"Sorry about the horn. I wasn't sure where on the property you'd be."

"So you decided to wake everyone?" I asked. "What are you doing here so early?" What was she doing here at all? I didn't realize she even knew where my house was. Although, just about anyone in town could point it out for her.

"I just came from the circus grounds. I figured you'd want to know before everyone else. It's Gianni. He's dead."

Chapter 22

"CREDENCE FOUND HIM THIS MORNING," Lupe said from her spot at my kitchenette table. "She was out for an early morning walk. I guess she likes to walk along that raised pathway by the animal enclosures. When she got to the tiger cage ..." Lupe shivered.

"Hang on, he was inside the enclosure?" I set a mug of coffee in front of Lupe. "With the tiger?"

"Why does that surprise you so much?"

"Because Gianni told me he rarely went inside the enclosures." I removed the used pod from the coffee maker, inserted a fresh one, and pressed the start button. "Maybe the tiger was having a problem. Does anyone have any idea what happened?"

"No one else was awake when I was there, just Credence." Lupe added lots of cream to her coffee. "Sounds like it was an accident."

"Sure," I agreed. "Just like it was an accident that Berlin became entangled in her silks. I can't even —"

"What?"

"Lily Grace, one of the fortune tellers, had a vision of some kind the last time I saw her. She was upset about the reading she had just given Tripp and I hugged her. A second later, she pushed away from me saying she saw body parts. Maybe this is what that was all about."

"No. Oh, geez, sorry. Gianni's death wasn't gory. Credence said she couldn't get into the cage, but she got close enough to see he wasn't torn apart or even attacked. She thought maybe he had a heart attack."

Questions tumbled in my brain like clothes in a dryer, and it took every ounce of willpower for me to not rush over to the circus and ask them. I made the decision last night, though, that I had to focus on the house. Wandering around pretending to still be a cop was satisfying, but it wouldn't keep me in Whispering Pines. Turning the house into a bed-and-breakfast was my best opportunity for that.

"What do you want to do?" Lupe asked.

I shook my head. "Nothing. I made a big stink about getting a new sheriff here. He's here now, I need to stay out of his way."

"You didn't stay out of Berlin's death."

I motioned for her to follow me outside. "That's because Sheriff Warren did nothing."

"What if he does nothing for Gianni?"

"I'm sure Credence will insist on a thorough investigation," I said as I sat on one of the sundeck chairs. "If the initial autopsy results come back suspicious and the sheriff still does nothing ..."

"Then you'll step in." Lupe sat across from me.

I put my hands in the air in a noncommittal shrug.

"Fine, but for the record, I think the fact that you dug into Berlin's death was really important. Maybe the powers that be around here didn't like it, but it was the right thing to do. Are you laughing at me?"

"Only because you sound like a longtime resident of Whispering Pines. Powers that be?"

"Please. I don't need to have lived here for ten years to know that something's going on."

I sipped my coffee and contemplated for the thousandth

time what exactly that meant. What *was* going on around here?

"Even if I went to the circus simply as a curious citizen," I said, "Sheriff Warren would kick me out before I got within visual distance of that tiger cage." I glanced across the yard at the house. "No, I have a closet and bathroom to pack up. That's my priority right now."

Lupe frowned and stared into her mug. "Gotta say, I'm a little bummed. I liked the thought of us working together."

Despite my insistence on a different priority, I knew the questions I had about Berlin and Gianni wouldn't leave me alone. "You can keep digging into this. After all, your job is to cover stories in Whispering Pines."

"That's true." She leaned toward me. "Tell me, officer, do you have any suggestions for an angle I might pursue?"

"For the record, my last title was detective." I laid my head back and looked at the puffy clouds floating past. A direction for her to start in … "Nearly everyone I talked to fingered Gianni as Berlin's killer. I didn't want to believe that, still don't, but it's possible he murdered Berlin and his death was in retaliation for that. In that case, who would want Gianni dead?"

"You mentioned a possible love triangle between Gianni, Abilene, and Dallas."

"That's as good a place as any to start."

Lupe drained her coffee mug and set it on the table. "Humans can screw up their lives so bad. You know?"

"Five years with the Madison PD and it never ceased to amaze me how often that's true." I pointed toward the village across the bay. "Go. Investigate. Good to know I've still got eyes and ears over there."

She stood at attention and gave me a sharp salute followed by a wink. "I'll report back later, boss."

After Lupe drove away, I took a quick shower and then called my mother. It went right to voicemail, which meant she was already in the thick of things at Melt Your Cares, her

168 | SHAWN MCGUIRE

day spa, or she was still on her way to the spa. She never answered her phone while driving; she treated her car as self-imposed solitary confinement where no one could talk to her.

"Hey, Mom, it's Jayne. Things are coming along nicely with the repairs. The wallpaper is off and Tripp is painting the downstairs this week. We'll start on renovations upstairs soon.

"I'm wondering if you located Dad and made a decision yet." Pushing her could backfire, she might fire back with a no, but we had to move forward one way or another. "Remember, the numbers I sent you are the low end of the earnings scale, so turning the place into a B&B makes more financial sense than selling it."

I paused, feeling myself getting emotional about having to leave and not wanting my voice to shake.

"I've thought a lot about this; it's what I want to do. And I meant what I said, you won't ever have to be involved. I need a little help getting started and will take full responsibility after that."

I hated how needy I sounded.

"Anyway, things are moving along quickly up here. It would be great if I could start advertising openings and taking bookings. Give me a call, please."

I hung up and stood there for a minute, staring at the phone as though expecting Mom would call back instantly. I knew better than that. Even if she had an answer for me right now, she was busy. The soonest I'd hear from her was after she got home tonight.

Meeka appeared in the doorway on the deck and gave a little bark, a little nudge that said *isn't there something you should be doing?*

"I know. I'm going to grab breakfast and finish Gran's room today."

Inside the house, I was happy to once again find Tripp in the kitchen making breakfast.

He handed me a mug of coffee. "Morning. Who was here earlier?"

"That was Lupe." I gave him a quick rundown of why she had come. The more I said, the deeper his frown became. When I finished, I put my left hand in the air, my right over my heart. "I solemnly swear that I am not getting involved with that investigation. Today I'm going to finish packing up Gran's bedroom and bathroom."

He turned an ear toward me and leaned in closer. "Sorry, not sure where the pause was between those statements. You're not getting involved with that investigation *today*? Or you're not getting involved with the investigation period?"

"I made my statement. It's up to the jury to interpret it."

We had a quick breakfast of blueberry muffins, soft-boiled eggs, sectioned oranges, and coffee. We chatted about our individual plans for the day, and then I went upstairs and he went to put another coat of paint on the dining room walls.

Once in Gran's bedroom, I didn't give myself a chance to freak out and just went straight to the closet. I started by sorting everything into piles. At least half of her clothes were in good condition and could be donated. A third of what remained was worn out and needed to get tossed. What was left after that needed some attention—laundering, buttons sewn back on, hems tacked back up—then could be donated.

There were a couple of things I wanted for myself. The sweater I borrowed that night, a couple of classic dresses that would fit me after a little tailoring, and a winter jacket that would be perfect during Northwoods winters. I left the items I wanted on her bed and then folded everything else and put them into separate boxes. I needed one entire box just for her shoes. Gran really loved shoes.

As I had expected, the closet turned out to be a big job. It took me nearly three hours to empty it. Once done, I ran downstairs to fill my water bottle and grab an apple and went right back up to do the bathroom. Now that I had started on this, I wanted to finish as quickly as possible.

The area beneath her sink was stocked with all the standard bathroom supplies—lotions, bath salts and oils, shampoo and conditioner—all things I could use, as long as I didn't tell my mother. She insisted I used only products from her salon. I had to admit, not one hair on my head had a split and my skin was nearly flawless. Not that any of that was a big deal to me. Mom would have to go to bed for the afternoon if she ever saw me with a blemish, however.

After separating everything under the sink into keep for myself or throw away boxes, I moved on to the linen closet. My final task. Once it was empty, there would be nothing left but furniture on the second floor of the house. The basement and attic, well, we'd get to those after all the renovations were done.

After assembling two larger packing boxes, I pulled winter blankets off the top shelf and dropped them into one box. Sheets, both flannel and lighter weight, from the second shelf went in next and filled that first box. The next two shelves held a large assortment of bath towels, hand towels, and washcloths. I pulled out a stack of bath towels and froze.

Chapter 23

AFTER DROPPING THE HANDFUL OF towels into the box next to me, I rushed out to the landing at the top of the stairs and hollered for Tripp to come up.

"Where are you?" he called.

"Gran's bathroom. I need you to see something."

Seconds later, he entered and I pointed to the back of the closet shelf at the small harlequin doll I had unearthed when I pulled out the bath towels.

"You found that there?" Tripp asked.

"Right there. Tucked in behind the towels." I reached in to grab the doll and then stopped. "I should take a picture. And bag it."

"Always a cop, aren't you? But I agree. Knowing where that thing likely came from, you should definitely handle this like a crime scene."

I looked over my shoulder at him with a smile. "Speaking of cops, I'm rubbing off on you, aren't I? You're turning into a regular old gumshoe."

My cell phone/camera was in the apartment. Tripp waited while I ran to get it and a plastic bag from the kitchen downstairs. After taking a couple of shots of the doll, both from the outside of the closet and close up, I wrapped the plastic bag around my hand and grabbed the doll, encasing it in the bag to preserve any fingerprints. Then I checked it over more closely through the bag.

"Who is this one supposed to be?" Tripp asked.

Donovan not only ran Quin's and instructed sculpting classes out of his home studio, he also claimed he could foretell death. He said he would go into a trance and create a harlequin doll when someone nearby was about to die. Even creepier than that, the dolls ended up looking very much like the person after they died. The doll Tripp and I had found in Yasmine Long's tent at the campground, for example, was emaciated and skeletal, almost identical to how severely dehydrated Yasmine looked when I found her body. That harlequin even had on red shoes that matched Yasmine's red Converse sneakers.

"This is my grandmother." I pointed out the tiny fingertips. "Blue nail polish. My grandmother always wore blue nail polish."

"Why does the body look like that?" He meant the parts of the doll not covered up by the blue and black tunic and leggings — the face, arms, and hands. They had a bloated and wrinkled appearance. The skin had a slight blue tint.

"I assume it's supposed to represent a waterlogged corpse." I pointed at the antique clawfoot bathtub a few feet away. "My grandmother drowned here."

Surprised, Tripp inhaled sharply. "Jayne, why didn't you tell me that? I would've taken care of this room for you."

I shook my head. "It's okay. Really. There's nothing in here that's traumatizing, except for this doll. Morgan told me that some of the village ladies came in and cleaned up after Sheriff Brighton was done with his investigation. The only reason I know it happened here is because I was told that it happened here."

He took hold of my shoulders and turned me toward him. "You know it's okay to ask me for help. I'm here for you. Just like you were for me when I found out the truth about my mom."

I gave him a grateful smile. "I know. Thanks."

I turned the doll, scrutinizing every bit of it the best I could through the clear plastic zip top bag.

"There's a bump here." I showed Tripp a small lump on the harlequin's forehead just above its left eye.

"What's that supposed to mean? Something to do with her death, I assume."

"You're probably right. Donovan is extremely precise with these dolls."

"What did the police report tell you about how she died?"

"We never saw the report. Sheriff Brighton sent us a letter explaining what was in it, that she was found face up in the—"

Wait. That couldn't be right. I moved to the bathroom doorway to take in the scene.

"What?" Tripp asked. "What's the matter?"

"His letter said she was found face up in the bathtub. It also stated that it appeared she had slipped or tripped, hit her head, and then fell into the tub."

I'm just about ready to get into my bath. I sprinkle lavender bath salts on top of the water as the tub fills. I light a trio of candles perched on the bathroom vanity. I take a sip of Chardonnay, set the glass on the window ledge next to the tub, and untie my bathrobe.

"Jayne? You checked out on me. Are you visualizing the scene?"

"My grandmother took a bath every night before going to bed. She would pour a glass of Chardonnay and bring it up here. While the tub filled, she would add bath salts or bubble bath or a scented oil of some kind." I pointed to the set of three candlesticks at the back of the vanity. "Then she would light candles, get in, and soak until the water cooled off. Sometimes, if she had a stressful day or was achy or whatever, she would let out some of the cold water and add more hot."

"Exactly that way?" Tripp asked, amused at my detailed recounting.

"Exactly that way. She told me one time. I think we were talking about routines. I told her about investigating a crime scene, and she told me about her nightly bath ritual. She said it comforted her and helped her sleep."

"Okay. Tell me what you were visualizing."

Grateful to walk through this with someone, I paraphrased the sheriff's words. "She slipped or tripped, hit her head hard enough to pass out, and fell into the tub."

I set down an imaginary wine glass on the windowsill and stood next to the tub in the approximate location Gran would stand to adjust the water. I turned as if lighting the candles, turned back to the tub, and mimed taking off my robe.

"She's ready to get in. Sheriff Brighton's theory was that she either got tangled in her bathrobe's belt, tripped on the bathmat, or slipped on a bit of water on the floor."

Tripp analyzed everything I'd done and said. "Right. I'm with you so far, but I don't understand what you're stuck on."

I took a half step toward the tub and then leaned forward as though falling. With my hands resting on the edge of the tub I explained, "If I slip and end up with a lump above my left eye, which is what Donovan's harlequin shows, that means I fell forward."

"Right."

"Gran loved this tub because it's an antique, like just about everything else in this house. She especially loved that it's short and narrow. She wouldn't float around in this one like she would in bigger tubs. Her only complaint was that she could only fill it about halfway because the overflow drain is set so low." I pointed out the round chrome cap on the tub below the faucet. "If she filled it further, the water would drain out when she got in. That meant the water wouldn't cover her completely unless she held her foot over the drain."

"Okay, still not seeing the problem."

"Everyone knows that it's possible to drown in just a couple inches of water, but—"

"But she was found face up," Tripp said, the pieces falling together for him now.

"Exactly. If she fell forward into this tub, she would either end up halfway in with her face in the water, or if she fell all the way in she could have easily lifted her head so it was out of the water."

"You said she probably hit her head hard enough to knock her unconscious. She wouldn't have been able to lift her head."

"Right." I stared at him and then the tub while analyzing further. "If that's the case, how did she end up face up?"

His turn to stare and analyze. "Maybe her body rotated after she fell in." He immediately dismissed his own comment. "There would have only been ten or twelve inches of water. That's not enough space for her body to turn over. That means it's highly unlikely she fell forward."

"See why I become obsessed with this stuff? Details matter."

"How about this, maybe she fell backward, and since she was unconscious her face went beneath the water, causing her to drown." He threw his hands in the air as though he'd just made a touchdown at the Super Bowl and then dropped them again. "Sorry. Didn't mean to celebrate something related to your grandmother's death."

"No offense taken," I said. "One problem with that theory. If she fell backward, how did she end up with a lump on the front of her head?"

He stood, silent for a minute, still deducing. "Something's not right about the letter?"

"Something's not right with that letter." With each word, I poked his surprisingly solid shoulder with my finger.

"You think your grandmother was murdered?" Tripp asked gently.

I stared at the clawfoot, the scene playing through my mind again. "Briar, Morgan's mom, seems to think so. Sheriff Brighton hinted at it. He didn't give me any details, only a comment about Flavia being determined to become high priestess of the Whispering Pines' coven. Briar held the role for many years and then suffered a stroke seven months ago. At that point, my grandmother stepped up. When Gran died, Morgan became the high priestess." I looked up at Tripp. "I've got to say, I'm a little concerned for Morgan's well-being.

"Becoming high priestess of a Wiccan coven, of a *religious* group, is reason for murder?"

"It might be in Flavia's eyes."

"That's disgusting."

"I'm not making any accusations, against Flavia or anyone. Not until I've seen my grandmother's case file. I need to get over to the sheriff's station. I need to see that file."

"I'll finish the linen closet."

"You're sure?"

"Positive. Go. Get the information you need."

***

I entered the sheriff's station to find Vera Warren sitting on top of what used to be Deputy Reed's desk in a full lotus meditation pose.

"Good afternoon," she said in a breathy voice. "What can I help you with on this beautiful day?"

"I'm Jayne O'Shea," I began.

"Merry meet, Jayne O'Shea."

Part hippie, part Wiccan. This should be interesting. "About four months ago my grandmother, Lucy O'Shea, died in a home accident."

Vera placed her hands over her heart and gasped. "I'm

so sorry. You poor, dear girl."

I gave her a smile of thanks. "I've got questions about a few of the details. I'd like to take a look at her file, please."

"Well, now, I can't give you the file. Not until I get Zeb's okay."

"I'll sit right here and look, if that helps. Won't even leave the building."

She stared at me, as though trying to come to a decision then slapped her hands to the desk, climbed down, and like a stereotypical used car salesman said, "Tell you what I can do for you. I'll get the file out and put it front and center on Zeb's desk. Give me your name and number and I'll give you a call just as soon as he gives his okie dokie. How does that sound?"

She was following the rules. I couldn't fault her for that. "That sounds great. Thank you, ma'am."

"Alrighty." She wandered into the sheriff's office muttering, "Lucy O'Shea. O'Shea, Lucy."

While she repeated Gran's name forward and backward, over and over, I did some meditative breathing of my own to try and ease my throbbing blood pressure.

"Sorry, hon," Vera called from the office and then drifted back into the main room. "No such file in the cabinet."

"What do you mean no file?" Stupidly, the first thought that entered my mind was that Gran hadn't really died. "There has to be a file."

"All I found was this placeholder card." She held up a piece of thin cardboard about the size of a standard sheet of paper. "Looks like someone checked it out."

I held my hand out to her. "May I take a look at that, please?"

Vera gave me a tickled pink smile. "Such good manners. Of course, you may."

The check-out info stated that in late February, the month Gran died, Sheriff Brighton had taken the Lucy O'Shea file.

Why would he do that? He mentioned that during the winter months he didn't spend a lot of time in the office. There were very few tourists in the winter, which meant very little crime, so he worked from home. That was probably it. Or maybe, as my paranoid brain supplied, he took it to keep evidence hidden. Only one way to find out. I needed to get over to the sheriff's house and pay Reeva a visit. Maybe she had come across that file while packing.

Chapter 24

SHERIFF BRIGHTON'S HOUSE SAT DIRECTLY north of the negativity well. There was no straight-line path to get there, so I had to cross the bridge over the highway, then the bridge that spanned the creek, then take a left at the dirt road that ran next to the creek. I came to the Barlow cottage first so paused to say hi to Briar who was busily but contently weeding and tending the plants.

"We never finished our conversation," she reminded me.

"I know. Trust me, a chat with you is high on my list. Right now, I'm on a mission." I explained to her that I was on my way to talk to Reeva and why.

"Oh, to be a mouse in your pocket during that conversation. You know where to find me." She gestured at the garden behind her.

I promised to come back soon then continued down the road. Three or four hundred yards later, I arrived at the little red Cape Cod where Sheriff Brighton used to live and rapped on the door using the brass knocker shaped like a fish.

The second Reeva appeared in the doorway, I could tell she was exhausted. I understood. As if it wasn't hard enough losing a loved one, packing up their belongings made it worse.

"Hi, Mrs. Brighton—"

"I go by Long, my maiden name. Have since Karl and I separated."

"Ms. Long. Yes, ma'am. I'm Jayne O'Shea."

"I remember. We met the other day, near the Pentacle Garden."

"We did. I'm sorry to bother you, but I'm looking for my grandmother's file. Sheriff Brighton checked it out of the station a number of months ago, and I think he brought it here. I was hoping that you could get it for me."

I knew she already knew about Gran's death, but she seemed neutral about it. Everyone else I'd met here either loved Gran or disliked her; no one was neutral about her.

Reeva did seem to lean toward the dislike side regarding me. It probably had to do with her husband's death. Even though I was there when he died, Karl Brighton's death wasn't my fault and not something I could've stopped. Somehow, I needed to make Reeva trust me if I wanted her help.

"Ms. Long, I have no proof, but I don't believe that my grandmother's death was an accident."

Her eyebrows arched. "And this file you're looking for is going to give you proof?"

"I don't know for sure, but I think it might get me closer to it. After she died, we received a letter from Sheriff Brighton with some of the details, but they're not adding up. I used to be a detective. I'd like to look through that file and see if I can put together the details for myself."

Reeva's lips pinched into a flat line that mimicked one of her sister's common expressions. "Karl was a by-the-book lawman. You sound as though you're accusing him of something."

"I know he served Whispering Pines for a long time, and I'm sure for most of that time he was indeed a 'by-the-book lawman.' I'm not accusing him of anything, but on the day I got here, a little over a month ago, I could tell that even the law is handled differently in Whispering Pines."

She frowned. Reeva hadn't lived in the village for more than twenty years. Did she know what had been going on during her absence? Was she someone who might help me?

"Regarding this letter he wrote you," Reeva said, "you think he was lying to your family?"

I chose my words carefully. "I think he told us as much of the truth as he could." I locked eyes with her. "Or was allowed to. I think someone here has been running the show for a while."

Clamped shut again, her lips twitched like she was stopping herself from saying something. Instead, she pushed her shoulders back and returned to the original subject.

"I'll keep an eye out for that file. I'm going through the house one room at a time, packing up some things, disposing of others. I'm sure you can appreciate what a slow process that is."

"I understand exactly. That's why I came here, to pack up my grandparent's house. At least, that was my original purpose."

"Your purpose has changed?"

"Kind of. I'm still packing up the house, it's just that this place has grown on me in the last month. I want to stay and convert it into a bed-and-breakfast or rental property. I'm trying to convince my parents to let me do that."

Her expression softened. "How is Dillon?"

"You know my father?" This took me completely by surprise, although it shouldn't have. They were about the same age and grew up in the village together. That was before it became such a tourist destination.

"I don't honestly know," I told her. "He's an archaeologist and spends most of the year in another country, digging around in the dirt."

Reeva laughed, a happy sound. "That doesn't surprise

me at all. He used to dig around in the dirt when he was little, too. Always claimed he was searching for lost treasure."

"I didn't know that." And just that fast, I missed my dad. "He's somewhere in Egypt right now. My mom is having a hard time finding him regarding the house."

"I hope he agrees to your plan," Reeva said, her demeanor much gentler now. "It's a great house and would make a wonderful bed-and-breakfast. Besides, it could be disastrous for Whispering Pines if your family left."

She was right. We owned the land. Did the village have the funds to buy it from us? What if new buyers didn't want to host a village?

I placed my palms together and thanked her. Channeling Morgan again. "If you don't mind me asking, what are you planning to do with this place? Will you sell it?"

"I'm not sure yet. I've only been here for a few days, but it's starting to feel like home for me again as well."

Holding her gaze, I said, "I understand you didn't leave under the best of circumstances."

A tight smile turned her lips and something that I can only describe as ominous crossed her face. I wanted so badly to ask questions about her sister, but now wasn't the time. I needed to gain her trust first, and the best way to do that was for me to walk away now.

"Thanks for your time, Ms. Long. If you have time to look for that file ..."

"I'll look for it," she promised. "I'll drop it off with the sheriff when I find it."

"Would you do me a favor?" She cocked her head in question. "Would you let me know before you do that? I want to make sure I actually get it."

She gave me a pen and pad of paper to write my phone number on and sent me on my way.

From Reeva's place, I traced my steps back through the

village. I ran into Lupe coming out of Treat Me Sweetly with a small bag. She reached in, pulled out a small handful of lemon drops, and handed them to me.

"Why not?" I popped one into my mouth, savoring the sugary coating and anticipating the sour punch that would strike in a minute. "You spoke to the carnies?"

"I did," she said as she unwrapped a Sugar Daddy candy bar and made me wait for more of an explanation while she enjoyed the flavor for a few seconds.

"Sure, give me sour while you get sweet."

"Figured the lemon drops matched your personality better." She gave a big cheesy grin. "Anyway, yes, I talked to the carnies. They were hesitant to say much about Gianni."

"Why?" The sour struck, making the back of my throat contract painfully. Like a brain freeze from too much ice cream too fast, all I could do was ride it out until my taste buds adjusted.

Lupe laughed, a satisfied sound. "If I had to guess, I'd say they're numb from all the negative stuff that's happened."

"Did you tell them you wanted to write a memorial piece about him?"

"Yeah, that helped. I couldn't ask them flat out about a love triangle. Instead, I asked if he had a girlfriend or someone special in his life. Most said he had no one, no family. A couple of them commented that he had a crush on Abilene."

"A crush? That's not how he made it sound to me." Without thinking, I popped two more lemon drops in my mouth. Brilliant.

"A few folks insinuated that Gianni might be slipping." Lupe tapped her temple, meaning Gianni's mind wasn't all there.

If that were the case, who knew what kinds of problems he'd been causing. Not good anytime, worse when dealing with wild animals.

"That brings up another question. Who's taking care of the animals now that he's gone?"

Lupe was busy with her Sugar Daddy again, so I had to wait for her to say, "Janessa is."

"Janessa?" The sour hit me again, this time making me clamp my hand to my jaw. I shoved the remaining drops back at her. "Take these. Janessa can do all that with her hands the way they are?"

"She's not doing the physical work. She found Gianni's contacts list and called a keeper at another zoo to get care instructions. This person is going to come up here and fill in until the circus can hire someone permanently. In the meantime, Janessa supervises as a couple of the groundskeepers do the feedings and stuff."

Found his contacts list? If Janessa had access to the files in Gianni's office, did she also have access to the Ketamine?

"What are you thinking?" Lupe asked.

"I'm thinking we need to keep a closer eye on Janessa."

"I'll see what I can dig up on her." She pondered this and an idea struck. "I know, I'll tell her I want to include mini bios on the carnies with my articles."

"That's a good idea. I mean, you'll really do that, right? They're an interesting group. Personally, I'd love to learn more about them."

"I will." She dug into her bag, pulled out another Sugar Daddy, and handed it to me as though presenting me with a rose. "Sorry for causing you pain."

The only thing I loved more than caramel was chocolate. All was now forgiven. "Thanks. I've got to go harass a man about a doll now." She gave me a confused look. "Tell you later."

A short distance down the Fairy Path, I came to Quin's clothing store. The little shop was packed, which wasn't a surprise. Donovan carried an eclectic collection of clothing that fit in perfectly with Whispering Pines' Renaissance feel. His was also the exact kind of thing people tended to buy while on vacation—flouncy blouses, pants in crazy colors, bags good for only the beach. How much of it was worn or used once they got home? How many purchases ended up in a donation box or shoved in a drawer only to be pulled out every now and then as a memory of their trip to the village?

I stood off to the side to observe for a couple of minutes while Donovan rushed from the register, to a fitting room to exchange a size for someone, to helping someone pick out the perfect bracelet to go with the dress she'd just chosen. For a big man, Donovan scurried like a squirrel.

"Jayne," he greeted tersely. "Something I can help you find?"

"Not here to shop. I found something while cleaning out my grandmother's bathroom today. It's a little disturbing, and I need to ask you about it."

"I'm busy right now, as you can clearly see. You'll have to come back later."

I removed the cloth bag hanging from my shoulder and held it open so Donovan could see the little Lucy O'Shea harlequin lying in the bottom. He paled slightly.

"You want to tell me what this is all about?" I asked.

"I'm sorry, I know they can be upsetting. I delivered that to your grandmother the day before she died." He strode on long legs back over to the register, probably thinking I wouldn't follow. Silly man.

"I'd like an answer," I said. "You can spare a couple of minutes. Surely, you have help during the tourist season?"

"Of course, I do." Donovan smiled at the elderly, elegant, and obviously wealthy woman standing across the counter from him. "Ivy is on a break right now."

"When will Ivy be back from break?" I asked as sweetly as possible.

"I'm not positive. Ten minutes or so."

"Tell you what, I'll wait on your front porch. Would you come out and chat with me as soon as Ivy gets back?"

"Thank you so much for stopping in, Mrs. Bamberg." He stepped around to the front of the counter and handed her two bags stuffed full of items. "I certainly hope we see you again soon."

The woman offered her cheek to Donovan, and he placed a chaste kiss on it.

"You know you will," Mrs. Bamberg crooned. "We love coming to Whispering Pines, and I love coming to Quin's. Your grandmother would be so proud of how you've maintained the shop."

Grandmother? I remembered Donovan saying she taught him how to make the dolls, but I didn't realize his family had a history in Whispering Pines. I made a mental note to ask Morgan or her mother about that.

Donovan walked Mrs. Bamberg to the front door and held it open for her. He jumped, startled, when he turned around to find me standing right behind him.

I pointed through the front window at the rocking chair. "Ten minutes."

Less than five minutes later, Donovan appeared next to me. He grabbed hold of my upper arm, his large hand almost completely encircling it, and led me behind the shop.

"This is unacceptable, Jayne," he demanded in a hushed voice. "What kind of a person comes into someone's place of business and does that?"

"What exactly did I do? All I wanted was to ask a question or two. If you would've talked to me right away, I'd already be gone." I looked down. "I suggest you release my arm."

He did and then tilted his head side to side, his neck cracking with each movement. "What's so urgent? I already explained this to you. When I make these dolls, I'm in a trance. I don't consciously think about the dolls' appearance as I make them."

I pulled the Lucy doll out of my sack, still in its plastic bag, and shoved it in his face.

"You really want me to believe that you had a vision, or whatever the hell you want to call it, about my grandmother's death? Then you stood there with a mound of clay in front of you, your hands twisting and turning and shaping, right down to her little blue fingernails and the lump on her head, and you had no control over them?"

"Believe it or don't, but that is what I'm telling you. Are we going to have to go through this every time you find — ?"

He stopped talking midsentence, realizing what he was about to say, just as I wondered how many of these things were out there.

"How did she react when you delivered it to her?"

"I didn't hand it to her," he said after a short hesitation. "I left it on her doorstep."

"Interesting that you remember that detail. Last time, when I found the Yasmine doll, you told me you delivered them while in a trance."

He didn't respond this time, just glowered down at me.

"Who's working your strings, Donovan? Who's telling you to make these dolls? Flavia?"

"We've already had this discussion." He released a bored sigh. "You ask anyone in town, they'll back me up. My gift is to foretell death."

Donovan stood nearly a foot taller than me and had well more than a hundred pounds on me. But right then, I was in full cop mode and there was nothing about the man that intimidated me.

I stepped closer and stared back at him. "I don't believe you. There is nothing paranormal or supernatural going on in this village. That's just an excuse you, and probably a couple of your buddies here, have conjured. Everything going on can be explained, including who murdered my grandmother and why. I think you were part of that, and as soon as I can prove it, trust me, I will take your ass down."

Chapter 25

MY ENTIRE BODY SHOOK WITH anger as I stormed away from Donovan and toward the village center. The arrogance and ego of that man. A couple of weeks ago, I asked him how long he had been in the village. He seemed so knowledgeable, so familiar with both the visitors and the villagers. I was surprised to find out he'd only been here six months, not that much longer than me. His familiarity with everyone and everything came from the fact that his grandmother was likely an Original.

I stopped dead in my tracks. Six months. He arrived shortly before Gran died. There were no coincidences. The two things had to be connected. Did his grandmother factor into this somehow?

"You look like you're in search of a puppy to kick."

I blinked and all thoughts of Donovan burst into a million pieces and blew out of my mind. I blinked again and saw Morgan standing before me, looking concerned.

"Meeka would never forgive me if I kicked a puppy."

"I'm not sure I would either. Violence is never the answer." Morgan smiled in that gentle way of hers. "What's got you so upset?"

"Right now, Donovan." I gave her a recap of the last

couple of hours, starting with finding the harlequin and ending with my discussion with Donovan. "His grandmother left him the clothing shop? When did she die? Shortly before Gran, I assume."

"Take a breath, Jayne." Morgan laughed, a sound meant to calm me.

I shook my head. "I need to know what really happened to Gran."

"I understand that, but as I've told you, unearthing secrets around here isn't easy. You may never know the truth, and you have to prepare for that." She stood there, looking me in the eye until I nodded. "Are you carrying the charm bag I made for you? The one for strength?"

Was that really all Morgan needed to keep her life in control? A tiny cloth bag filled with herbs and trinkets?

"No. Forgot to grab it."

"Remember that it will also help center you. You're highly emotional right now. A good dose of serenity would do you well."

I couldn't argue with that.

"Come inside with me." Morgan placed her hand on my back and steered me toward her shop. "I'll make you some tea."

"You have a tea that provides strength and protection?"

She smiled. "No, but I have one that will help to calm you down."

"It's too hot for tea."

"Then I'll make iced tea. Good Goddess, but you're snarly today. Jayne, please, I'm concerned about you. Come inside with me."

"Hang on, Morgan."

Sheriff Warren just came out of Ye Olde Bean Grinder with a cup in hand. I started toward him, calling his name. "I was looking for you earlier today. I'm trying to locate—"

"Your grandmother's file," he interrupted. "My mo—My deputy told me you stopped by the station."

"Good. It's important that I look at that file. I have some questions surrounding her death. I was hoping you'd go ahead and give your deputy the okay to release it to me once it's locat—"

"I'm a busy man," he said before I finished speaking. "I've got far more important things to worry about than looking for a lost file."

He wasn't listening to me. He wouldn't even look at me. I took a breath, prepared to try again, but Morgan spoke first.

"I'm sure that investigating Gianni Cordano's death must be taking a great deal of time. Have you been able to uncover any more details on that yet?" She crossed her arms tightly against her torso. "Another murder. It's so upsetting."

"Who said it was a murder?" Sheriff Warren looked between us. "I was at the scene for a good hour. I didn't find anything to indicate murder."

"An hour?" I blurted. "You can't do a proper investigation in an hour. You need to search the area, take pictures, talk to witnesses to see if anyone saw anything of importance."

He closed the gap between us in one large step. "I know how to conduct an investigation, Ms. O'Shea. I told you, there are other issues I need to focus on."

"More important than a man's death?" Morgan asked. "Nothing could be more important than that."

Zeb took a slow sip of whatever was in his cup then cleared his throat. "I stuck around the area until the coroner … What's his name?"

"You mean Dr. Bundy?" I asked. "He's the medical examiner."

"Right. I stayed until he got there. He didn't need me hanging around, getting in his way while he took care of the body. Once he sends me his report, if there's anything suspicious, I'll go back up there and talk to people."

The muscles in my neck got tighter with every passing second. "You have to talk to people while things are still fresh in their memory. If you wait—"

"I investigated," he snapped.

This was useless. It was a complete waste of my time to try and talk sense with this man. He would probably make a fine patrol officer. His name would be at the top of the leaderboard for the most number of citations issued each month. His captain would love him. But right now, he was in way over his head. It was time to do something about this; he'd been here long enough.

I explained again that Reeva was looking for the file. "She'll bring it to your office when she finds it. Since you're so busy, I'd appreciate if you'd sign off now on me looking at it. That way your deputy can hand it over to me once Ms. Long finds it. Unless, of course, there's something in it that someone doesn't want me to see."

Damn. I hadn't meant to say that last part out loud.

Zeb inhaled deeply, once again looking anywhere but at me. "I will take your request under consideration. In the meantime, I need to get back to work."

Shocked, Morgan stared as Zeb walked away. "I can't believe what I just witnessed. What could possibly be more important right now than Gianni's death?"

"The directives he's receiving from someone on the council." I put my hands over my face and let out a groan of frustration. "I shouldn't say that; I don't know it for a fact. There are plenty of people out there who feel a cop's only job is to bring in the bad guys. Good community relations aren't a priority. Maybe that's Zeb's mindset. Regardless, I'm glad you got to witness him first hand."

She nodded, watching Zeb wandering among the crowd in the Pentacle Garden. "Your instincts were right."

"They've always served me well. I knew I was right, but for the record, I didn't want to be this time."

"Come on inside with me," Morgan said. "I'll make tea.

I think we could both use some. We'll sit in the reading room and you can tell me what's going on."

"You just heard everything. I don't know what else is going on. I'm supposed to mind my own business, remember?"

She frowned at me. "Then come inside and sit quietly for a minute. This isn't negotiable. You need to relax."

A couple of minutes later, I was sitting in Shoppe Mystique's cozy little reading room. Currently, the lights were dim and the room was cool. After half a mug of Morgan's special "Chill Out" tea, I did feel calmer.

"Better?" Morgan peeked her head around the corner like she was afraid to come in for fear I might bite her head off again.

"I am. Thanks, Morgan."

She rounded the corner holding a silver tray loaded with cheese and crackers and fruit. She set it on the little square wooden table in front of me and sat at the other end of the loveseat.

"It's after seven. I just closed the shop. Willow is taking care of closing out the register, so I can sit here with you as long as you like."

I ate a cracker with a square of cheese and then assembled six more on a small plate and added a clump of black grapes.

"Thanks for this. I haven't had much to eat today."

"I can tell." She waited while I ate a few more crackers then said, "You're right about what's going on around here."

My heart lurched and I paused in my chewing. "What exactly do you mean? There are a lot of things going on around here."

"I was referring specifically to our new sheriff. We needed to hire someone, but I'm starting to think that anyone else would be better than this man."

"I'm glad we agree." Although, I'd hoped she was about to reveal a big bombshell about Flavia and whoever else was in cahoots with her. Or maybe a clue towards Gran's death.

"It's not that I disagreed with you before." Morgan picked some grapes from the cluster on the tray. "It's just that I always feel people should be given a chance to do the right thing. Too often we write folks off simply because we think they might do the wrong thing."

"Yeah, you need to work on that." I grinned and popped a piece of cheese in my mouth. "What are we going to do about this? In his desperate attempt to make Whispering Pines appear to be a utopia, Sheriff Warren is having the opposite effect. Yes, it needs to remain a family-friendly place, but people my age, mid to late twenties, make up a huge percentage of our visitors."

"I agree," Morgan said. "We need to have this discussion with the council. I'll send around a notice for another meeting."

"We shouldn't wait. He's not even willing to look further into Gianni's death. And I've never even heard him mention Berlin's. The carnies must feel abandoned."

She touched her fingertips to my knee. "Don't worry about this. I will take care of calling a meeting. We can't do it tonight; it's too late. Creed and Janessa won't be able to come. They just finished one performance and have another starting soon. We'll do it first thing in the morning. Go home, get some rest, and come back at seven o'clock."

"In the morning?" I groaned and then winked to let her know I was teasing. Kind of. I drained the rest of my tea, had two more crackers with cheese, and grabbed the remaining grapes. "I'm feeling better now. I think I will head home."

"Can I ask you to do one thing with me first?"

I gave her a sideways glance. "It's something witchy, isn't it?"

With a bright smile, she said, "It is. Stay right here." She left the reading room with the tray and came back a few minutes later, the tray reloaded, this time with dried plants, a couple of stones, and a small amulet.

"Another charm bag?" I asked.

"Not exactly. I want to cast a spell for Zeb. He's not ready to take on these kinds of responsibilities, we all see that, but he's clearly dedicated to his job. I want to cast a spell that will guide him successfully along his career path."

That Morgan, she was one good witch. "Great. Why do I need to be here?"

"Because you want him to succeed as well. As a fellow brother-in-blue, so to speak, your positive energy will infuse the spell."

I hated it when she got into my head. She was right about Zeb being dedicated to his job. The last thing I wanted was for someone that eager to fail.

"Okay, let's do this, then. I've been gone all afternoon. Tripp and Meeka are going to think I skipped town if I don't get home soon."

I paused at how much that made us sound like a family.

Morgan went to the built-in bookcases lining the wall in the reading room. She took hold of one of the cases and tugged. The section pulled forward, revealing Morgan's altar room hidden behind it. I assumed she had another at her cottage for her own personal worship, but this room was where she cast spells and created charm bags for her customers.

As she had the first time I'd been in the room, she asked me to stand just inside a circle that had been burned into the wood floor. She took her position on the far side of the small rectangular table covered with a green cloth. Last time I was here, there was a purple cloth.

As Morgan lit first a white and then a black candle placed at opposite corners of the table, I asked, "What's my job this time? I assume I'm supposed to think about something."

When she made my charm bag, she told me that the

only thing I needed to do was stand in this very spot and think about "love and protective energy."

She closed her eyes, looked skyward, and held her hands at her sides, palms up. "Strength, success, and fairness."

I considered her choices. "Those seem like good qualities for someone in law enforcement."

While Morgan added the ingredients from the silver tray into a small cast iron cauldron, softly chanting the whole time, I stood silently and repeated the three words in my mind. I had to admit, the more I thought about Zeb in connection with those words, the more I genuinely wanted him to succeed. The longer the ritual went on, the more I felt like the room was filling with positive energy for him. Living proof that a positive state of mind was a very strong tool.

After all the ingredients from the tray had been placed in the little cauldron, Morgan added a pinch of salt from a bowl sitting on the altar. I knew from past experiences with Morgan's *witchcraft* that salt was for purity. I liked that. The world couldn't have enough pure cops. Then she lit the contents on fire. I don't know how she did it, but it almost appeared that she pinched off a bit of the flame from one of the candles and dropped it into the cauldron. She might not be able to turn a toad into a teacup, but Morgan Barlow had serious skills with sleight-of-hand.

A few seconds later, the flame in the cauldron extinguished, and Morgan looked at me. "You felt that, didn't you? You felt the energy in this room."

"I felt something," I admitted. "I figured it was a power surge from all the air conditioning units running today."

Morgan made a disapproving face at me. "Go ahead, keep playing the skeptic, but I know you believe in some small way."

"Be exposed to woo-woo for too long and something's bound to rub off, I guess." I nodded at the cauldron. "Now what?"

"Once the cauldron has cooled, I will pour the contents into a small bag and bury it in the woods at midnight."

"Shouldn't he carry it with him?"

"Burying the charm bag," Morgan explained, "or emptying its contents into the lake is similar to sending intentions out into the universe. This should be quite effective for him."

I said goodnight to Willow as I walked past on my way to the front door. The tall, thin woman gave me a knowing smile, as though she knew Morgan and I had just worked some sort of hocus-pocus.

"Relax tonight, Jayne," Morgan said. "I'll see you first thing in the morning. Blessed be."

Chapter 26

TRIPP AND MEEKA JOINED ME on the sundeck minutes after I got home. Tripp didn't make one comment about how long I'd been gone, but Meeka was mad. She wouldn't look at me and stepped just out of reach every time I tried to scratch her ears in apology. She did accept the kibble I put in her dish, however.

"Did you have dinner?" Tripp asked. "I made chicken stir fry."

"That sounds good, but I had something with Morgan. I'll warm up some stir fry later. Cheese and crackers and grapes won't last long."

The sun was still up, but hanging low in the sky. We sat on the sundeck and watched as the boats and jet skis and paddleboarders started to slowly head to the Marina for the night. A few fishing boats stayed out there, waiting until the very end to get one more bite.

"Did you find the file?" Tripp asked.

"No, but I think I know where it is."

For the next half hour, Tripp sat patiently and listened to me go through the events of the afternoon. I told him everything, starting with finding Vera Warren sitting on top of the desk and ending with the ritual for Zeb in Morgan's

198 | SHAWN MCGUIRE

hidden altar room.

"There's a council meeting at seven o'clock in the morning," I said. "I know many of the business owners are upset with Zeb because the tourists are unhappy. Hopefully this meeting will be fast and effective. I know the guy means well, but Zeb Warren needs to hand in his badge."

"Let's go for a boat ride."

That came out of nowhere. Confused, I waited for him to say more, but he didn't. "You mean now or are you planning a Caribbean cruise?"

Tripp paused, considering this. "A cruise would be nice, wouldn't it? We should do that sometime. But I meant now." He swept a hand across the lake. "Just about everyone has gone in so there's almost no traffic. Let's go for a night ride."

He didn't have to ask me twice. It sounded like a great idea. My grandparents had both a fishing boat and a small sailboat. Considering there was no breeze, we opted for the fishing boat. I told Meeka, who was slowly forgiving me, to go pee before getting in the boat.

Tripp laughed. "She's just like having a kid, isn't she?"

"She's really good practice, I have to admit." And then I clamped my mouth shut. The last thing I wanted was for Tripp to think I wanted a baby. I wouldn't say never, but I would say not soon.

While I ran upstairs to get the key for the boat and a few bottles of beer, Tripp gathered lifejackets and grabbed a small cooler from a shelf in the boat garage.

Gramps had been an avid fisherman, one of the many reasons he agreed to buy the two thousand acres on the lake, and this was his dream boat. With its big outboard motor, cushy captain's chair, miniature captain's wheel instead of a standard steering wheel, and comfortable leather bench seats at both the bow and the stern, it was more of a speedboat but served his fishing needs just fine.

With Tripp's help, I figured out how the thing worked

and slowly backed it out of the boathouse. Once we were to the middle of the lake, I turned off the engine, left the lights on so we could be seen by any other night riders, and let the boat float. Then Tripp and I lay down on the floor up front and stared at the star-filled sky.

"What's behind your evil plan?" I asked. "Why the sudden need to bring me out on the water?"

"You're too stressed out. Seriously, you should hear your voice. We've both been working hard on the house, and you're getting involved with all these village problems. I figured we could use a little break."

"You sound like Morgan."

"I know it's none of my business," Tripp began, "but I'm a little worried about what will happen after this meeting in the morning. I mean, it sounds like getting rid of this Zeb guy is a good idea."

"But?" I sighed, wanting the whole Zeb issue to disappear.

"But you won't have anyone to replace him. Not right away, and maybe not for many days. I know you. You're going to want to step in and do the job."

"Someone has to."

"I know, but that someone doesn't have to be you." He turned his head to look at me. "Unless that's what you want, of course."

I didn't answer, just kept staring up at the sky.

"Do you want to?" He stopped me before I could respond. "I'm not looking for an answer. You should think about it, though. You're getting pulled in lots of directions and you're reacting rather than thinking things through. That's why you're so stressed. You have to figure out what you want." He looked back up at the sky. "Whatever that means."

He was right. I did feel like there were too many things, both self-imposed and otherwise, needing my time: Renovations on the house. My life in Madison on hold while

I was up here. Law enforcement, both the fact that I couldn't stay away and that I wasn't sure I should or could go back. Then there was the desire to stay here and turn the house into a B&B. And possibly most confusing of all, where did Tripp fit in all of this?

"You need to decide what you want to do," he repeated. "If you want to get back into law enforcement, that's fine. But you keep saying you want to run a bed-and-breakfast with me."

He made it sound like those two things had to be exclusive, one or the other. Was he asking me to choose? I could divide myself between both ventures.

"That's why I wanted to come out here. Not for you to choose, but for you to think about your choices." He pointed at the stars. "Look at where we are. We're not connected to anything right now. Not the house, not the village, not whatever happened to your grandmother, or what's going on with your parents. If each of those things were waiting on a different side of the lake, and you had to pick one thing to go to when you brought this boat into shore, which would it be? What calls to you the most?"

Good question. I closed my eyes and took in a deep breath of the lake and pine-scented air then let it out slowly. I felt myself relax, so did it again. My heart rate slowed; the pressure constantly pushing on the top of my head and at the base of my throat eased. I took another breath.

"Good," Tripp said. "No more talking. Just relax. I learned one important thing during my travels. If I didn't know what to do next, I'd get quiet and the answer would come."

The gentle rocking of the boat coupled with the sound of the water sloshing against the sides was very soothing. While I had no problem falling asleep, I hadn't slept well for the last couple of nights. Tripp was right, I felt pulled in too many directions.

As I lay there in the boat, watching meteors shoot across

the sky and listening to crickets, frogs, and a wolf far off in the distance, there was no doubt in my mind what I really wanted. Over the last month, the village, this lake in particular, had become very important to me. As much as my grandmother loved it, I did too. I didn't need to think very long. I knew I wanted to stay right here in Whispering Pines and turn the house into a bed-and-breakfast. I never dreamed I'd say that, but sometimes you don't know what you want until it's right there in front of you.

I must've drifted off because the next thing I knew, a flash of lightning lit up the sky and jolted me awake. A crack of thunder followed quickly. I hadn't noticed any storm clouds when it was still light outside, but something clearly had been brewing on the horizon.

"Hang on tight," I told Tripp. "And hang on to Meeka, would you? We have to get off the water."

We were almost to the boathouse when the rain started, lightly at first but quickly picking up in intensity. I pulled the boat into the boathouse, doing my best to not ram the wooden walkway inside that ran around the perimeter and between the two boats, but I did bump it softly. We jumped out of the boat and stood on the walkway, watching as the rain came down in sheets, sometimes straight down, other times sideways as a gust of wind changed its direction. Immense branches of lightning lit up the sky, followed almost instantly by cracks of thunder. Meeka huddled against my leg, her anger at me from earlier forgotten. I picked up my little dog and hugged her close.

"I suggest we wait it out here," I told Tripp. "Even if we rush up to the apartment, we'll be completely soaked by the time we get halfway up the stairs."

"Works for me."

He took down some folding chairs from pegs on the walls and set them on the walkway. Then he grabbed two beers from the little cooler, and we settled in to watch the show. Meeka was terrified by the storm, but as long as I held her, she'd be okay

"This came out of nowhere," Tripp said.

"It did."

"And I left the rain flaps on the popup unzipped. Good thing most everything inside is weatherproof."

I sat there, wide-eyed, feeling insignificant within the power of nature. I watched the pines whip back and forth, side to side, and seemingly in every direction at once, fearful that they'd snap in two from the force. Then I reminded myself that they'd been here for a long time. Long before Gran and Gramps bought the property, the trees were here watching over the lake and the land. They'd surely be here for a long time to come.

"This excites you, doesn't it?" Tripp asked, grinning at me. "Not in some weird, sexual way. Or does it?"

I swatted his shoulder with the back of my hand. "Freak. No, I'm not turned on. But this is exhilarating, isn't it? I can hardly wait to go through our first blizzard together up here."

Tripp opened his mouth to respond, but clamped it shut again and sat back with a small smile.

As usual, I didn't even realize what I'd said for a second. Maybe, like not knowing what you want until it's in front of you, the best way to figure out the truth is to just let it fall out of your mouth.

Chapter 27

THE STORM RAGED FOR A good forty-five minutes. It was so fierce at times, I was almost as jumpy as Meeka. Finally, when we were sure it was never going to let up, the downpour turned to a gentle, but steady rain. Taking advantage of the relative calm, I headed upstairs and told Tripp that he should sleep in the house. Regardless of its now soggy interior, his popup wasn't safe in a storm, and who knew if it would start raging again.

A few gentle rolls of thunder passed overhead during the night, but nothing like the cracks from earlier. Just like listening to water slosh against the sides of the boat, the distant thunder was soothing. I slept hard and well, but nowhere near long enough. I knew a council meeting as soon as possible was important, but seven in the morning?

Meeka looked at me like I was speaking a different language when I told her it was time to go. The storm had worn her to a furry frazzle, and she was still so tired when I opened the door, she didn't even run down the stairs like she usually did. In fact, she made me pick her up and put her in her crate in the back of the Cherokee.

"Like that storm was my fault," I said.

She responded by turning in three circles and dropping

to the floor of her crate, her back to me.

The only council member not half-asleep or crabby about a breakfast meeting was Violet. She opened the coffee shop by six o'clock every morning, so being up at this hour was normal for her. Fortunately, she knew us well and arrived with plenty of coffee. And Sugar brought breakfast.

"Thank the Goddess," Morgan said as she entered the meeting room. "Scones and coffee. I love you people."

"Rough night?" I asked her.

"That storm." She shook her head. "Because our plants are crucial to our livelihood, years ago, Mama and I constructed tarps on frames to put over the plants when inclement weather comes through. We've gotten pretty quick at setting them up, but that storm came out of nowhere."

"Did you suffer much damage?" Effie asked as she took two scones from the box.

"I was afraid to look this morning," Morgan said. "We were up half the night propping up a few especially tender plants that had gotten hit before we could get the tarps over them."

"If there's anything I can do to help," I said, "I'm happy to come over after the meeting."

"Bless you, Jayne. I think it's out of our hands now. It's up to the Goddess to save what she will."

I didn't point out that if it was up to the Goddess, they should have let the storm take its course and not worried about tarps and propping. Instead, I filled coffee cups for both of us, filled Meeka's travel bowl with water and set it in the corner, then took my seat at the table.

By quarter after seven, everyone had taken their seats. Flavia was the last one to sit, glaring at me and Morgan as she did so. Before we could even begin to discuss the problems with Zeb Warren, she opened her own issue.

"Until the loss of Karl Brighton," Flavia said, "we have always had a member of the Whispering Pines law enforcement staff on the council. I think we need to revisit that."

"We discussed this already, Flavia," Cybil said. "We voted to let Jayne have his seat."

"It wasn't a unanimous decision," Flavia said.

"The only unanimous decision I ever recall us coming to," Mr. Powell said, "was agreeing to give this Zeb boy a chance." He then proceeded to knock over his cup and dump hot coffee in his lap. I gasped, but he insisted he was okay. "Happens to me a lot. That's why I take my coffee with half cream. It's more warm than hot."

"Let's get to the reason we called this meeting," Morgan said.

"Agreed," Effie said.

"And what exactly is the topic?" Flavia asked.

She didn't know? "We need to discuss our new sheriff. I think we can agree that Zeb Warren isn't working out."

"I don't agree with that at all," Flavia said.

"Neither do I," Donovan added.

I noticed Donovan looked anywhere but at me since entering the room. Was he feeling bad about that granny harlequin? Or maybe he was afraid that I was going to make good on my promise and take him down.

For the next five minutes, the business owners discussed things they had been hearing from the tourists.

"Business here at The Inn hasn't suffered, yet." Laurel stood to refill her coffee. "That's because most of our guests are older and more subdued. I stay in touch with the guest cottage owners and managers. A lot of families and twenty-somethings rent there. They've had people leave early and even a few reservations get canceled altogether."

"And you think this is because of Zeb?" Donovan asked, annoyed.

"I know it is," Laurel said. "They actually said they heard we were having trouble with law enforcement and don't want to bring their kids here."

I took a scone from the box and tossed a bite to Meeka. "There's nothing wrong with enforcing rules. That's Zeb's job, but giving vacationers a little leeway to enjoy themselves is good customer service, as long as their actions won't hurt anyone. Issuing warnings is fine. Writing tickets for vandalism for picking a flower is over-the-top."

"What are you proposing we do about Zeb?" Donovan asked the council in general. "I don't understand this attack. She just said he's doing his job."

"He's doing part of his job." Creed stood, placed his long slender hands flat on the table, and leaned toward Donovan. "Two of my carnies have died in less than two weeks. Mr. Warren wasn't here when Berlin passed, but he was when Gianni did."

"And I understand," Donovan said, "that he did investigate Mr. Cordano's death."

"If you want to call it that," Janessa said. "He made an appearance and didn't even stay an hour."

"Tell us," I said, "what exactly happened up there that day?"

Creed took a shaky breath and paced the length of the table. "I was out for my early morning walk. I like to walk along that platform Gianni constructed so I can see the animals." He closed his eyes and put his hands to his face, clearly remembering what he found in the tiger cage. "I was the first at the scene. Except for approximately five minutes to ask Janessa to call 9-1-1, I didn't leave the area until they took Gianni's body away."

"How long did it take Zeb to get there?" Donovan asked.

"Not long," Creed said and Janessa nodded her agreement. "I'd say he was outside the animal enclosure in fifteen minutes, give or take."

"That's acceptable," I acknowledged. "How long did it take for the medical examiner to get there?"

"Sheriff Warren said he had called the medical examiner

before leaving his home. Dr. Bundy arrived about forty-five minutes after the sheriff got there."

"What did Sheriff Warren do while he waited for the medical examiner?" Maeve asked. "Did he go to Gianni at all?"

Good questions. Exactly what I was wondering.

"Not at first," Creed said. "The tiger was coming out of sedation by the time he got there, so—"

"Hang on," I said. "The tiger had been sedated? Who did that?"

"I have no idea," Creed said. "The animal was just coming out of sedation when the sheriff got there, but we were able to secure it so it couldn't attack when it came fully to."

"Who did that?" I asked, adding to my mental list of people who had worked with Gianni. If they knew how to properly secure the tiger, they may know about the Ketamine.

"Gianni kept a container of supplies by each enclosure," Creed explained. "We called over a few of the stronger carnies. In less than ten minutes they had a steel collar around the animal's neck which latched onto the enclosure's fencing."

"What are their names?" I asked.

Morgan cleared her throat and leveled a glare at me. I knew that look. It said *stop investigating*.

"After they subdued the tiger," Morgan began, "what did Mr. Warren do?"

"He entered the enclosure and went over to Gianni. He felt his neck, then announced that there was no pulse and that the medical examiner was on the way. After that, he wandered around inside the enclosure for a couple of minutes, staring at the ground. Then he did the same thing outside the enclosure, wandering and staring at the ground. That took maybe five minutes. For the rest of the time he was there, he just stood guard and waited for Dr. Bundy."

"What does a standard investigation involve, Jayne?" Sugar asked.

"Every crime scene is different," I said, "but it sounds like Zeb started the process properly. Making sure the tiger couldn't harm anyone was the obvious first step. Determining whether the victim needed medical attention or was deceased would be the next."

"And if you were doing the investigation," Laurel said, "what would you do while waiting for the medical examiner?"

"Why are we asking her these questions?" Flavia demanded. "She wasn't there. She can't know what would've needed to be done."

"But she's an experienced detective," Laurel said. "We are trying to determine if Zeb's skills are adequate for Whispering Pines' needs."

Murmurings of agreement rose from around the table.

"After determining the condition of the victim," I said, "I would start taking pictures. We take a lot of pictures—of the victim, of the area directly surrounding the victim, and further out as well. I would methodically scan the area around the victim for anything of importance, which is what Zeb seemed to be doing. I'd look for footprints, a dropped cigarette butt, anything we might be able to get DNA evidence off of. It's amazing what criminals leave behind at the scenes."

"How long does that usually take?" Laurel asked, clearly very interested in this process.

"Different factors come into play, of course," I said. "The number of victims, the size of the scene, the amount of clutter at the scene. Either way, we're generally talking hours, not minutes. After that, I'd start interviewing witnesses."

"Did Sheriff Warren do that?" Mr. Powell asked Creed. "Did he interview anyone?"

"He asked me who found the body," Creed said slowly,

recalling the event. "I said I did, and to my knowledge that was the last thing he said to anyone."

"I don't think we need to talk about this anymore," Effie said. "It seems pretty darn obvious that this young man hasn't been handling things right."

More murmurings of agreement from the group.

"We all agreed that Whispering Pines must have a sheriff on duty at all times," Flavia said. "You all seem to feel that Zeb isn't cutting it, so now who do you want?"

"Jayne," Violet said.

I spun her direction. "What? Me?"

"It's obvious from listening to you," Violet said. "You're the perfect person for the position. You were when Sheriff Brighton died, I don't know why we didn't appoint you then."

"I agree," Creed said. "You've got the experience, and it's obvious you care about this community. I nominate Jayne O'Shea as Sheriff of Whispering Pines."

Flavia opened her mouth, surely to object, but before she could, Violet seconded the nomination.

"All those in favor?" Morgan asked.

This time, Flavia slammed her hands down on the table hard enough to make all the coffee cups shake. "I run these meetings. Not that anyone could tell from the way today's has gotten so out of control. I will call for the vote."

"If that's what makes you feel better," Cybil said while poking around in the scone box. "Go ahead, call for the vote."

Flavia released a hiss through her teeth. "I would like for you all to remember what could happen with an O'Shea in a position of power."

"What's that supposed to mean?" I snapped as a few of the council members gasped.

She sniffed at me, her eyes never leaving mine. "All those in favor?"

Seven hands shot into the air—Laurel, Creed, Effie,

Cybil, Janessa, Violet, and Morgan.

"All those against?" Flavia said as she raised her own hand.

I didn't know Maeve or Mr. Powell all that well, and I fully expected Donovan to vote with Flavia, so their votes didn't really bother me. Honestly, it stung to see Sugar joining them.

"Jayne," Flavia was all business, "you didn't vote. Not that it seems to matter, you already have the majority. You do need to either vote or abstain, however."

Shocked by this turn of events, I stood and all eyes were on me. "The day Sheriff Brighton fired me from my deputy position, I was certain I had messed up so big I'd never get a job in law enforcement again. Since then, I've come to realize that he let me go not because I couldn't do the job, but because I wasn't doing the job the way some people in the village wanted me to."

I gazed around the table, lingering on those who voted against me. Had any of them been pulling Sheriff Brighton's strings? Had any of them been responsible for Gran's death? I skipped quickly past Sugar, but she wasn't looking at me anyway.

"There are two things I know for sure," I continued since I had the floor. "First, Whispering Pines is where I belong. I figured that out a couple of days after I arrived here and I don't plan to go anywhere. The other thing is, I will never be able to walk away from law enforcement. That's probably obvious to those of you who keep telling me to mind my own business. I don't know what that 'O'Shea in power' comment was all about, but rest assured, I don't take law enforcement lightly. I'll be fair and I'll make sure the truth, whatever that means, is always uncovered."

I focused across the table on Flavia and Donovan. He squirmed.

"My vote is a big hell yes."

A small cheer rose from the seven people who voted for me.

"For such a small village," I said, "there's a lot going on

here. I'm going to need to hire a deputy."

"Martin will be available soon," Flavia said.

My relationship with Martin Reed, the deputy on duty when I first came here, started out on rocky ground, but eventually we came to an understanding. Still, I wasn't sure it would be a good idea for me to bring Flavia's son into my workplace. I'd have to see where his mind was when he was ready to return.

"He's on the list. If any of you know anyone else who would be suitable for the position, please let me know."

Had my ex-captain in Madison sent that list yet? Maybe someone from it would be suitable as a deputy. I needed to check my email.

Acting as though I was now the one in charge, everyone stood and scattered. Janessa and Violet came at me from both sides and hugged me. Laurel shook my hand. Meeka barked at all the excitement. Cybil nodded and smiled from across the room.

"Please," Creed said desperately, holding both of my hands, "tell me the first thing you'll do is take care of these deaths."

Janessa stood at his side looking equally anxious.

"It's at the top of my list," I assured them. "I'll be up there as quickly as I can. It's probably obvious I have a lot of questions regarding Gianni's death."

"We'll help in any way we can," he said and they left the room.

"I have not closed this meeting yet," Flavia called out.

"Give it a rest, Flavia. There's no need for all this formality." Effie placed her hands on either side of my face and squeezed. "Oh, my girl. Lucy would be so very proud of you right now."

I blinked, my eyes stinging. I was too choked up to speak, so smiled and nodded my thanks. A second later, my emotions turned colder as Sugar walked up to me.

Chapter 28

SUGAR TOOK MY ARM AND pulled me over to a corner. She spoke quickly, as though worried someone might overhear her.

"This is not a vote against you. I have no issues with you being sheriff. The thing is, the longer you're in Whispering Pines, you'll see that it's not the perfect place it appears to be." She swallowed as though choked up. "I'm not sure it ever has been."

"I've already started to figure that out." I mimicked her low voice. "What the hell is going on around here?"

She shook her head. "This isn't the time or place for me to answer questions. I just wanted you to know that I have no doubts regarding your ability to be our sheriff. I just didn't want you to get messed up in the muck."

She gave me a quick hug and hurried out of the room, cutting in front of Maeve who stayed close to Mr. Powell, probably to be sure the world's klutziest man made it out of the building without hurting himself or anyone else.

Flavia and Donovan were the only ones left sitting at the table. She looked furious while he appeared shattered.

"Let's go grab a table in the restaurant," Morgan said, leading me through The Inn's lobby. "We need to celebrate."

I wanted to get right over to the sheriff's station and let Zeb know about the vote. I wanted to get to work on figuring out what really happened to Berlin and Gianni. I was still a little too much in shock over what had just happened at the meeting, though, and food more substantial than the wonderful cinnamon chip scone I had seemed like a good idea. Besides, I now had a million new questions for Morgan bouncing around in my brain.

It was early enough that The Inn's restaurant was still quiet. We had barely taken our seats, Meeka tucked beneath the table, when Laurel arrived next to Sylvie, our server.

"This hasn't been formally announced yet," Laurel told Sylvie, "but Jayne has just been voted in as our new sheriff."

Sylvie's smile couldn't have been any bigger. "That is the best news I've heard in weeks. There's been a lot of grumbling around the village about that boy wearing the badge."

"Anything they want" — Laurel nodded at Morgan and me — "it's on the house."

Morgan ordered the fruit platter, a strawberry-orange muffin, and hot tea. I felt a long, involved day coming so I ordered the skillet scramble.

"Coffee too, please, Sylvie," I said. "Lots of it."

"I'll bring you a carafe," she promised and hurried off to the kitchen.

"Did you plan this?" I asked Morgan.

"Breakfast? While I always tend to have it about this time of day, I had not planned to eat with you. This is a happy surprise."

I gave her a strained smile. "Funny. You're a funny, funny witch. I mean, did you have anything to do with me being named sheriff?"

Oh my god, I was the sheriff. The shock was starting to wear off and reality settling in.

Morgan smoothed her napkin over her lap. "All I did was tell everyone the topic of the meeting. Well, everyone

214 | SHAWN MCGUIRE

except Flavia and Donovan. I may have forgotten to tell them."

I bit back a laugh. "You're a wicked witch, too."

Sylvie appeared with a carafe of coffee for me and pot of tea for Morgan.

Morgan filled my cup and then prepared her tea.

"Although I'm thrilled with the outcome, I did not suggest to anyone that you should be Zeb's replacement." She looked at me over her teacup as she took a sip, her expression too innocent to be believable. "Okay, fine. I might have cast a spell for you last night."

Well, that surely sealed the deal. As I added cream to my coffee, I pondered the vote.

"What did Flavia's comment about an O'Shea in power mean?" I asked. "I know not everybody loved my grandmother, but the longer I'm here, the more it seems she had a pretty big group of haters."

"I don't think anyone hated Lucy. Some may have hated some of her decisions, especially those regarding who could live here and who couldn't. No doubt about it, Lucy's word was law. Rightly so, it was her land, but now that she's gone, someone else needs to take over the top spot. It's human nature for there to be an alpha. I think that question—who is now in charge—is where a lot of tension is coming from."

"That would explain why Flavia is so against me being the sheriff. It's no secret that she wants the alpha to be herself. That's why she runs the council meetings and wants to take that high priestess rank from you."

Morgan laughed softly. "I can assure you that while being named high priestess is an honor, I have no more power in the coven than anyone else. Like running a council meeting, I mostly guide our gatherings."

"Oh, come on. The Wiccans rule the village, and you sit highest among them. You don't let it go to your head, though." I took a long sip of coffee, pondering the hierarchy in the village. "You told me once that Flavia considers herself to be the village's self-appointed mayor. Power can corrupt someone in a village the size of Whispering Pines as easily as it can in a metropolis the size of New York City. Flavia is power hungry."

Morgan nodded toward the kitchen. "Our food is coming."

"Before you tell me I brought the wrong muffin," Sylvie said as she set a plate in front of Morgan, "Wesley has been playing around with his recipes. He swapped out the powdered sugar and orange juice icing for streusel. So far, folks favor the streusel."

Morgan smiled down at her plate. "I can hardly wait to taste it."

"Thought you might want to try one as well, Sheriff."

Along with my own orange streusel muffin, Sylvie placed a dinner plate sized cast-iron skillet on a small wood plank in front of me. The skillet was heaped with scrambled eggs, potato chunks, red pepper pieces, diced onions, hunks of ham, and a healthy sprinkling of Cheddar cheese.

"I'll never eat all of this," I told her. "Would you bring a box, please. I'll save half for later."

"You bet. I'll throw in another muffin, too." She handed me a small waxed paper bag. "This is for our very well-behaved guest hiding beneath the table."

I looked in the bag and found it stuffed full of dog biscuits for Meeka. I held two beneath the tablecloth and in seconds felt a wet nose press against my hand, and then the biscuits disappeared from my fingers.

The first couple of bites of my scramble were heavenly. Not for the first time, I wondered if the kitchen witches in this village cast a spell over the food. I had yet to have a bad or even average meal.

"Before he died," I said after Sylvie walked away, "Sheriff Brighton warned me to watch out for a few people in the coven."

Morgan looked surprised, but not as much as I'd

expected she would. Was her reaction because there really was someone to watch out for, or that the sheriff told me about it?

"Who did he tell you to be wary of?"

"He never gave names but did say that if anyone could catch *her*, I could. He also told me to make sure that you and your mother protect me."

Morgan smiled as though touched by the directive. "Of course, we'll protect you. Haven't I been doing that since you got here?"

"You have." It was sweet, but I didn't need witchcraft to keep me safe. "I assume the warning was against Flavia."

"I can't say with certainty that you're right, but I also can't say that you're wrong."

"Do you think she was involved with the destruction of my house?"

"Involved is a good word," Morgan said. "I don't think she did it herself, but I think she may have asked someone to. I don't have any proof yet, but I'm starting to suspect that's the case."

"She must've drawn the graffiti though."

"Also, a good possibility. As I told you, sigils hold power. If she was involved, the most likely scenario is that she had someone tear up the place while she drew the sigils. That way she could infuse her intent into them as she drew them."

Woo-woo. I think the only thing Flavia wanted to do was scare my family off by breaking in and trashing the house.

"I know you don't believe, Jayne, but Flavia is a powerful traditional witch."

"What's a traditional witch?"

"One who prefers to follow the old ways more so than contemporary ones. Flavia works closely with the moon and planetary cycles. She favors symbology, meaning runes and ancient alphabets."

"Which explains the sigils embroidered on her robes." During the new moon ceremony a few weeks ago, I couldn't help but notice that the embroidery on Flavia's robes was nearly identical to the graffiti on my walls.

"Right. Also, she claims to not do it anymore, but I know she has performed dark magic in the past. Repelling spells in particular."

I blinked at Morgan. "I think you just described my vandal."

Her shoulders dropped slightly and she looked disappointed. "When put together that way, it does seem so, doesn't it?"

I stirred cream into a fresh cup of coffee, staring as the light brown and ivory liquids swirled together in the cup. People formed opinions about each other the moment they first met. That opinion could either be favorable, in that they wanted to get to know each other better, or neutral, in that they treated each other as strangers passing on the street. The only reason for an initial opinion to be one of instant malice, like Flavia's was of me, was because there was a history of some kind. Something must have happened between Flavia and my grandparents.

Reeva popped into my mind then. Specifically, the way she asked about my dad. Reeva, Flavia, my dad, and many other villagers were all about the same age. All Originals. Had something happened between them? That would explain why Dad was so eager to sell the house and be done with the village.

"As much as I want to dig into all the negativity going on around here," I said, as much to myself as Morgan, "other things have to take priority. Now that I'm sheriff ..." I paused as that sunk in and looked at Morgan. "I'm the sheriff."

She grinned. "I heard."

I sat straight and pushed my shoulders back. "Now that I'm the sheriff, Dr. Bundy and I can talk openly about his findings and feelings regarding Berlin's and Gianni's deaths."

"This also means," Morgan's voice was cautionary, "that you can't share information with me anymore. Or Tripp."

Leave it to Morgan, always making sure I stayed balanced.

"True," I said, "but for five years I managed to discuss my work with Jonah without giving away any crucial details. I'm not worried."

The bigger problem was, I told Tripp last night that I was going to put all my efforts into turning the house into a bed-and-breakfast. Not even twelve hours later, I was divided in two again.

Chapter 29

MEEKA AND I WALKED WITH Morgan around the Pentacle Garden to the start of the Fairy Path. Morgan blessed me and went left toward Shoppe Mystique while I was about to take a right toward my new office. If Zeb and Vera were still there, it meant no one else had told them about the changing of the guard, and I would have to tell them that they had to leave.

"Jayne!"

I turned to see Lupe running my way from the direction of the Bean Grinder.

"Congratulations, Sheriff O'Shea."

"How did you find out so quickly? It hasn't even been an hour since the vote was cast."

"What kind of reporter would I be if I didn't know the breaking news first?"

Violet. Not to discount Lupe's abilities, but Violet had to be spreading the word to all who entered the coffee shop. On the other hand, Lupe was a good reporter and could be valuable to me with my new position. If I could trust that she would work with me and not just dig for "breaking news" to get the story. Maybe I should just deputize her. Problem solved.

"This is so exciting." Lupe held up her camera. "How about a picture? I'll post a little blurb right away this morning about you taking over. I'll do a longer interview later. Maybe I'll follow you around, do a day-in-the-life kind of piece."

"A blurb sounds like a great idea, but don't say anything negative about Zeb. This wasn't totally his fault. He shouldn't have accepted a position he wasn't ready for, but Donovan never should've suggested him."

"Whatever you say, boss."

"Let me put my uniform on first, then you can take pictures." I pointed down the Fairy Path. "I was on my way to the station. Hopefully, the shirts I wore for the three days I was a deputy are still there."

When we got to the spot where the Fairy Path split north and south, with the sheriff's station dead ahead, I asked Lupe to wait.

"Let me go in and talk with Zeb and Vera first. No sense having an audience for his dismissal."

Once inside, the first thing I noticed was that both jail cells were full of millennials in swimsuits looking cold, angry, and tired. They started calling for me to help them. I held up a hand to them, indicating I'd deal with them in a few minutes.

Both Zeb and Vera were there, waiting for me. By the looks on their faces, and the fact that Zeb was dressed in khakis and a polo shirt instead of a uniform, I assumed they had already received the news.

"Congratulations, Sheriff." He wouldn't look at me as he handed me the station keys. He seriously needed to work on maintaining eye contact.

"I want you to know," I said, "I think you have a great deal of potential. You just need a few more years on your resume. I'm sorry that Donovan put you in this position."

"My boy has oodles of talent," Vera defended. "Whispering Pines just isn't right for him."

"You know, Ms. Warren, I think you're right. This village requires a certain kind of person." One who isn't afraid to say no to Flavia. I turned to Zeb. "I see a ton of passion and dedication in you. I think being a patrol officer would be a perfect fit for you. If you're interested, I'm happy to recommend you to my captain in Madison."

"You know what?" Zeb replied with all the arrogance he had from the moment he stepped foot in the village. "I don't need help finding a job."

Fine. I tried to be nice.

"I assume you left everything in my office," I said, trying and failing to leave the emphasis off *my*. "Your uniform, belt, service weapon, badge ..."

I stepped into the room to verify as he assured me everything was there. Without another word, the Warrens left the building. Approximately three seconds later, Lupe walked in.

"How'd he take it?" she asked.

"Hard to tell. He wasn't emotional and wouldn't accept my help to find something new."

"Everyone's been giving him a hard time. He probably wasn't surprised. Did you find your uniform?" She started snapping pictures around the building. "Why are all those people locked up?"

"Yeah," one of them called. "Thought you were going to help us."

I'd forgotten about my hardened prisoners. I had a good idea why they'd been locked up. They looked like the attendees at just about every UW campus party I'd busted.

"Let me guess," I said as I inserted a key in the first cell door but didn't unlock it, "you were all drinking down at the beach and maybe dropped an f-bomb or two."

Random comments drifted out of the cells.

"We were partying on the beach," said a guy in a multi-colored Speedo. "We had a cooler, but none of us were drunk."

"It was just beer."

"Helen has the sewer mouth."

"Dude said our music was too loud."

"That woman ... deputy ... whoever she was told us we needed to sit here and think about what we'd done."

"Did you?" I asked and they all nodded.

"What else did we have to do in a jail cell?" a pink bikini-clad woman asked.

"Other than sleep," a guy in yellow board shorts added, "nothing. They separated us by sex."

A few of them snickered at that.

"Like that mattered to Clark and Jason."

More snickering as two guys in the back started to object.

I had to raise my voice to be heard over the mumbling. "Okay, listen to me. The beach is a public area. There are signs all over the place stating that alcoholic beverages are not to be consumed there. Jail time is over the top unless any of you are underage."

A chorus of protests, everyone insisting they were legal, floated out of the cells.

"We can show you our IDs."

I held up my hands for silence. "All right, I believe you. Where are you all staying?"

"We rented a few of the guest cottages on the east side," said the apparent leader, a tall guy with broad shoulders, no shirt, and impressive pecs.

"How about you keep the beer, or whatever you're drinking, at the cottages? And the noise under control? There's also a great pub on the far side of the Pentacle Garden called Grapes, Grains, and Grub. The folks over there would be happy to serve you."

They all agreed.

"Consider this your official warning." I unlocked the cells. "I'll write tickets if you do it again."

Once the station was empty, I went into my office and

flipped through the keyring until I found the key for the credenza. The cabinet reinforced with steel plates was where Sheriff Brighton kept the weapons, ammo, and other tools. Inside, I found my shirts, neatly folded on the bottom shelf.

"Success," I announced and held one up to Lupe. "Give me a minute to change, and you can take your pictures."

I stepped into the small bathroom between the office and the interview room and pulled off my tunic shirt. First, I slipped on a black T-shirt then a uniform shirt over it. The emotion I felt putting on that shirt as Sheriff of Whispering Pines was unexpected. The only time I'd felt more professional pride was the day I graduated from the police academy. The day I was named detective a close third. With the shirt on, the only thing I was missing was my belt and a badge. And my tactical pants. The roomy cargo pockets made them much more practical than jeans. I'd have to have Mom or Rosalyn send up the pairs I left in Madison.

As for the badge, the council had issued Zeb a generic "Sheriff" star. For now, I'd be happy to wear the temporary insignia, but they might as well go ahead and order that shiny gold badge with "O'Shea" at the bottom. I wasn't going anywhere.

Lupe let out a long, low whistle when I stepped out of the bathroom. Reacting to the whistle, Meeka appeared from beneath the deputy's desk, sat in front of me, and looked up, barking and wagging her tail. She knew what the shirt with all the patches meant. I could tell already, she was excited to be a K-9 again.

"Looking pretty hot in that uniform, Ms. O'Shea," Lupe teased.

I laughed. That was basically what Tripp had said the first time he saw me wearing it.

She took a bunch of candid shots of me followed by a few serious ones. "Do you want to choose which one I post?"

"No, I trust you. If I don't look good, you don't look

good, right?"

Lupe followed me into my office and watched as I sorted through the equipment Zeb had left on my desk. Then I loaded a belt with handcuffs and keys, a flashlight, baton, pepper spray ... While I slid bullets into the magazine of my department-issued Glock, I thought about how Deputy Reed had laughed when I asked about a Taser. A Glock in Whispering Pines just didn't seem necessary. Then again, considering there was a killer on the loose, better to err on the side of caution.

"What can you tell me about Gianni's death?" Lupe said casually and out of nowhere, taking the chair across from my desk.

"Nothing."

"What? I thought we were working together on this." Lupe was instantly defensive, her accent intensifying as her emotions flared.

I held up my hands for her to calm down. "I told you before that I was going to stay away from the circus. I can't tell you anything new because you probably know more than I do at this point. I plan to get up there soon; I promised Creed that Berlin's and Gianni's deaths were my top priority. So how about you tell me what you know?"

She deflated a little. "Sorry. You can't shut me out, though."

"I thought you were here to write happy stories about a quirky village. Your questions sound more investigative than touristy."

She gave me a blank stare. "Two murders in ten days? Three in the last two months? The public has the right to know if there's something going on here. Not just so they can decide if they want to bring their families here for vacation, but also so they can be on guard if there's a murderer running around Wisconsin."

We studied each other across my desk. Honestly, I needed another set of eyes and ears and again considered hiring her as a reserve deputy.

"Here's the deal." I took a seat in my chair. "You're gathering a lot of information. If you share what you know with me, I promise I will tell you whatever I can. You know there's going to be certain things that shouldn't be revealed right away."

"If you only tell me and news gets out, you know who the leak is. I wouldn't risk the opportunity at exclusive info."

I couldn't argue with that. Fine. Until she gave me a reason not to, I would trust her. "All right. We work together."

"And you'll tell me everything right away? Don't know if you've noticed, but there are a lot of chatty residents around here. And the tourists are kind of like kids; they see a lot and whether they understand it or not, they tell their friends or they start tweeting and posting pictures. And they'll tweet stuff wrong."

I put my right hand in the air. "I promise, I will give you information as soon as I know it's accurate. If I ask you to hold details for a while, you'll hold them. Deal?"

She put her hand in the air, mirroring me. "Deal."

"Nifty." I leaned back in my rather comfy leather chair. "Tell me what's been going on at the circus. Have you been able to find out anything new?"

"I've been asking more questions about Gianni." Lupe pulled out her reporter's notebook and flipped through the pages. "My memorial to Berlin ran today. They must've seen it and approved of it because they're starting to open up. They're saying that Gianni was obsessively careful about safety for himself, other people, and the animals. No one believed he would've accidentally ended up in the tiger cage that way. It's weird."

I didn't believe it either.

"More suspicious than weird. I witnessed his obsession with safety myself. That day I followed him during feeding time, he insisted I keep Meeka under tight control even though we were on a sixteen-foot platform and the animals were behind twelve-foot fences. He didn't want her getting excited and jumping down next to the enclosures, and he didn't want the animals getting worked up about there being a dog in the area."

How did he end up in the enclosure? Did someone lure him? Was there something wrong with the tiger and he went in to check on it? Did he have a heart attack like Credence originally thought? Too many questions, not enough answers.

More thinking out loud than sharing info with Lupe, I said, "Gianni insisted he was the only one who had access to those animals. I don't believe that. Maybe he could handle the normal, day-to-day care and feeding of them by himself, but what if he got sick? If he was so obsessive about them, he'd have a backup plan. What if one of them did attack? I don't care how careful he was, they are wild animals. I said it before, there has to be at least one other person on the grounds with access to the Ketamine and the knowledge to use it."

"Janessa?" Lupe asked.

I nodded. "She's first on my list."

Lupe closed her notebook and stuck it in a thigh pocket. "I didn't get to interview her yet for the bio. I'll go back and try to catch her."

"Okay, but Lupe, be careful. I don't think we're looking for two killers. I think whoever killed Berlin also killed Gianni, and he or she is still out there, maybe still in the village. They might get nervous if they know you're poking around."

She gave me a little salute. "No worries. I've interviewed plenty of dangerous dudes. I know how to ask the right questions and when to back off."

Lupe left for the circus, and I needed to get to work as well. Creed had looked understandably haggard this morning. The deaths of his two carnies were weighing heavily on him. I pulled out Gianni Cordano's file and read through Zeb's scant notes regarding what he observed in the tiger enclosure. He confirmed what Credence had said, there was no gore so the tiger hadn't attacked. There were no pictures in the folder, but there was a hand-drawn map indicating where Gianni's body was found — near the front gate — and where the tiger had been when he got there — at the back of the enclosure. There were no other details, so the map was all but useless.

If Gianni wasn't the killer, and my gut told me he wasn't, who was next on my list? On a single sheet of paper, I recreated the suspect board that was on my wall at home. To me, Dallas was the next most likely. There was one quick way to figure out how much time I should spend on him. He said he'd been with Abilene at The Inn the night Berlin died. If I would have thought to verify that when I was there this morning, I wouldn't have to go back now.

"Let's go, girl," I called out to Meeka.

She had slid between the bars of one of the jail cells and was lying under the cot bolted to the wall. She crawled forward a few inches, so I could see her face in the shadows, but seemed happy in her new hidey-hole and not interested in going anywhere. I really needed a more dependable deputy.

"Working," I commanded.

That did it. She crawled out from beneath the cot, squeezed back between the bars, and was by the front door in a matter of seconds. I attached her leash, and we were out the door.

During the approximate half-mile walk from the station to The Inn, no fewer than twenty people congratulated me on my new position. Some were villagers, but most were tourists. That made sense. Not only were there more tourists than residents in the village right now, Zeb had spent a lot of time wandering around talking to, a.k.a. harassing, the tourists. Those who'd had a run-in with him were happy to see someone else wearing the uniform.

We were almost to The Inn when a nun on a bicycle whizzed past us. The woman was literally wearing a habit.

"Blessed be, Sheriff O'Shea," the nun called out. "Whispering Pines just became a happier place."

I'd never seen her before. Was she a villager I hadn't met yet or a tourist looking for attention? My money was on tourist. No way I wouldn't have noticed a nun on a bike. Still, I needed to wander the village more.

Inside The Inn, I asked Emery at the front desk if Laurel was around.

"She's on the second floor," he said, his voice cracking. "She's checking on damage to a room. Up the stairs, take a right, all the way to the end of the hall."

I thanked him and started up the narrow, slightly crooked stairway immediately to the left of the reception desk. Every step creaked and popped as we made our way past the first floor and onto the second.

"What happened?" I asked from the doorway of a room that looked like last night's storm had gone through it.

"I've had rock stars stay here who didn't do this kind of damage." Laurel shook her head. "This was the work of one person. A teenage boy who met his *soulmate* at the beach yesterday and had a bit of a meltdown when his parents said they were going home today."

A wooden chair now resembled a pile of sticks. Pillows had been sliced open. Mattresses tossed and sheets ripped. Curtains and their rods pulled off the windows. Impressive work for one kid.

"Does this happen often?" I asked. "Do you want to press charges?"

"Thank the Goddess, no. This doesn't happen often. His parents were horrified and said they would pay for everything. They even signed a form stating I could charge their credit card. Otherwise, I probably would press charges this time."

"I assume you have new guests coming. Will the room be ready for them?"

"That's the great thing about the people here," Laurel said with a big smile. "They come to the rescue. I called Mr. Powell not even an hour ago, and he just called back saying he had a team on the way to fix it up. Like I said, it doesn't happen often, but repairs need to be made often enough that I have a supply of carpeting, paint, and bedding in a locker at Mr. P's warehouse."

"I'm not sure if that makes me feel happy or sorry for you."

She shrugged. "Part of being in the hospitality business. Anyway, did you need something?"

"Yes, I'm wondering if you can tell me if a specific guest stayed here recently?"

"Sure, I can. Let's go down to my office, and I'll bring up the records. Who is it?"

"Dallas Brickman. He tells me that he and Abilene were here the night Berlin died. I just wanted to verify that."

"I don't have to bring up records to check on that. They were here. It was her birthday. They have a standing reservation every year on her birthday."

"I'd ask if you're positive, but it sounds like you are."

"No doubt in my mind."

"Any chance they left in the middle of the night?" They could have gone back to the grounds, did the deed, and come back to The Inn.

"I'm pretty sure Emery was working that night. He's been taking on all the shifts he can get lately. He's saving up to build a little cottage for himself and his cats. Let's go ask him."

Back downstairs, I asked Emery if he remembered that night.

Without hesitating, he answered, "Sure, I remember."

"Why?" I asked. "Any reason that night stood out?"

He blushed a brilliant cherry red.

"Emery?" Laurel pushed with a cocked eyebrow.

"Abilene came in," he said, as though that answered everything.

It did. He had a crush on her, too. Popular lady. I could picture poor, awkward Emery tripping over his own tongue as she stood before him.

"Do you know if they stayed all night," I asked, "or if either of them left at any point?"

"They didn't leave," he assured without hesitation.

"How can you be so sure?" I asked.

"I didn't leave the desk all night," he said.

"Not even to go to the bathroom?" Laurel joked.

He shook his head and in all seriousness replied, "I've got a bladder of steel."

That presented an interesting image.

"Besides, there's only one way out of the building," he continued and pointed at the stairway to the left of the desk. "You've heard the noise those stairs make. You can't miss people going up or coming down them. So unless they rappelled out of a window ..."

Guess that was possible but highly unlikely. With that, I mentally crossed Dallas and Abilene off my list. Great. I was fresh out of suspects.

Chapter 30

I FELT LIKE I WAS all the way back at the starting line with this case. If I was going to figure out what had happened to Gianni, I needed to investigate the scene of the crime. Fortunately, it was still early enough in the day when we got to the circus that the performers weren't prepping for the afternoon show yet. That gave me time to track down Dallas and have a little chat with him before investigating the tiger enclosure.

Both Dallas and Abilene were hanging out in the food tent, where the mood was decidedly subdued. Understandable, the carnies had lost two co-workers, two friends, in less than two weeks. They were even more than friends. These people lived together. Berlin and Gianni had been members of their family.

Abilene saw me coming and her eyes went wide. She sat up straight and then scooted to the edge of her chair.

"Ms. O'Shea," she said. "We heard a rumor that you were the new sheriff. Congratulations."

Her hands fidgeted in her lap. Her eyes darted everywhere. Why was she so nervous? Was she hiding something? While I'd been in her presence before, this was the first I'd spoken directly to her. Maybe she was a naturally nervous person.

"Thanks. Sorry to interrupt your lunch, but I need to speak with Mr. Brickman alone if you don't mind."

"Mr. Brickman." Dallas winked at Abilene. "So formal. That can't be good."

Abilene shot to her feet. "I don't mind. Of course, I don't mind. I hope everything's okay. Well, obviously things aren't okay. Two people have died."

"Abilene," Dallas said in a gentle voice, "why don't you go for a little walk? I'll come find you when I'm done talking with Sheriff O'Shea."

She nodded while playing with the ends of her long coppery ponytail. "Okay. I'll go over to the big top and check that everything is set up for our act."

Dallas watched until Abilene had gone fifty yards or so, and then turned to me.

"The deaths have really upset her. She's not always this twitchy." He chuckled. "Of course, her job is to have sharp objects thrown at her. If anyone has the right to be twitchy, it's Abilene."

"You've got a point there. No pun intended." I held a hand out to the chair Abilene had just vacated. "Mind if I sit?"

"Please do."

"On second thought" —I looked around the tent—"I want to talk with you about the deaths. Maybe we should go somewhere a little more private?"

"All right." He pointed to the far corner of the food tent. "Why don't we move back there?"

I walked ahead of him, choosing a chair that allowed me to see the entire tent at once. Meeka lay with her body inside the tent and her head poking out beneath the canvas.

"What's up?" Dallas asked as he sat.

"I'm narrowing down my suspect list in the murders."

"Murders? That's how they're being classified? Not accidental deaths?"

"There hasn't been an official ruling yet," I admitted, "but my belief is that neither death was accidental. I heard from a lot of folks that you and Berlin used to argue quite a bit. That didn't seem like much of a motive to me, so I verified your statement about being with Abilene at The Inn the night Berlin died. I'm happy to tell you that you're off that suspect list."

He ran a hand over his mouth. "I'd act more relieved, but I'm surprised to learn we were on the suspect list to begin with." He leaned forward slightly, gripping the arms of his white plastic chair. "You said off *that* list. Is there another one?"

I didn't believe there were two killers, but I couldn't dismiss the possibility outright.

"I believe that neither of you killed Berlin. Where were you the night Gianni died?"

"Gianni?" He laughed. "You need to broaden your suspect list, Sheriff. While I can't say I'm surprised he's dead, I didn't kill Gianni either."

"What about Abilene?"

Dallas sat straight, nostrils flaring. Getting angry now. "Now you just sound desperate. What possible reason could she have to hurt him?"

I didn't have proof. All I had was testimony from a few carnies, filtered through Lupe, that Gianni had a crush on Abilene. Even though he was much older, Abilene could have shared his feelings. I'd seen stranger relationships.

"Dallas, did you know that Abilene and Gianni had been seeing each other?"

His shoulders slumped and his head dropped forward. "What makes you think that?"

"Because Gianni told me they'd been seeing each other for months. I'm sorry if this is upsetting news for you, I really am. Sadly, keeping secret relationships quiet, or getting revenge for discovering them, is a very common reason for murder."

Dallas' light-blue eyes flashed with white-hot fire. Did I reveal something he hadn't known? Did I open a topic he had known about but was trying to keep secret? Or had he killed Gianni and I was getting too close for comfort?

"She was with me the night Gianni died, as she is every night."

"Will she corroborate that claim?"

"What, am I back on the list now? You don't think I killed Berlin but that I might've killed Gianni? Why? To get revenge for an affair?"

I waited, silently, for him to answer my question.

"Of course, she'll say the same thing. Abilene and Gianni were not seeing each other. Unless, of course, you mean in the literal sense, as in seeing each other around the circus grounds." Before I could ask what he meant, he continued, "He was obsessed with her and asked her out constantly. Sometimes multiple times per day. No matter how many times she said no, he kept asking, telling her how beautiful she was and how good he would be to her. I had to step in and tell him to quit harassing her. Maybe he forgot, or maybe he was a jerk, I don't know. Either way, he upset Abilene. The senile old fart belonged in a nursing home, not here caring for wild animals."

Senile? Another carney who felt Gianni's mind was slipping. I hadn't noticed senility the day I followed him around as he fed the animals. If it was true, maybe that was the reason he insisted only he had access to the Ketamine. Maybe he truly did believe he was the only one.

"I'm not saying that I don't believe you," I said, "but you and Abilene are now each other's alibi for two suspicious deaths. Is there anyone who can verify that the two of you were together the night Gianni died?"

He glared at me. "You just gonna skip over the part where you accused the woman I love of having an affair and me of killing her supposed lover? Fine. Yes, Creed saw us together the night Gianni died. Why don't you go talk to him? Now, if you're done upsetting my world, I'd like to go find Abilene."

I held my hand out in the direction Abilene had gone. "By all means. I am sorry to have upset you, but my job is to cover all the bases. If you know anything about baseball, you know how hard that would be for one person to do."

After Dallas took off after Abilene, I glanced down to see Meeka looking up at me. She had that look on her face, the scolding one that said I'd done something wrong.

"I did not," I said as I rose from the chair. "I'm just doing my job. Sometimes that means upsetting people." Meeka yawned and looked away. "Fine, let's go check out the tiger enclosure."

***

Yellow "Police Line Do Not Cross" tape was strung across the front of the tiger's cage. Someone, animal control most likely, took the tiger away. Even though it didn't seem that the animal had harmed Gianni, they'd hold her until we knew for sure. I really hoped she hadn't hurt him because if she had, she'd be put down. That would be a real blow to Gianni's memory after he'd done so much to save her.

Meeka lay in front of the tiger's enclosure, her chin resting on her paws. Like the other animals all asleep in their cages, she knew something bad had happened in there. What did happen? I thought of the diagram Zeb had drawn and stared at the spot on the ground where Gianni's body was found.

"You were near the door. Were you trying to get out? Did you somehow get locked in and were, perhaps, calling for someone to let you out?"

I enter the cage because ...

After waiting a full minute for more to come to me, I couldn't complete the sentence. I couldn't visualize what had happened. Maybe because I hadn't worked the scene. I

236 | SHAWN MCGUIRE

hadn't seen Gianni's body or watched the tiger coming out of sedation. I hadn't scanned the area for evidence. Connecting with the victim was what made it possible for me to put myself in the victim's, and sometimes the criminal's, shoes. Now that the enclosure was empty, there was nothing for me to latch onto.

The one thing I could "see" was the tiger laying at the back of the enclosure. Why had she been sedated? The only reason I could think of was if Gianni needed to treat her. But why would he do that in the middle of the night? No, not the middle of the night. Early in the morning. That's when Credence went for a walk.

Gianni said that Ketamine kept an animal sedated for about an hour. If the tiger was just coming out of it around the time Zeb Warren got here, Credence must've just missed witnessing Gianni's death.

Meeka was staring at me, tail still. Poor dog. She didn't like it here right now.

"Okay, girl, let's go find Credence. Maybe she can provide some details."

Meeka got to her feet and shot off ahead of me. She really wanted to get away from the enclosures. Since the grounds were almost empty right now, I let the leash extend as far as it would go.

About halfway down the midway, tucked into a small clearing in the pines behind the water gun target game, I spotted a contortionist. The woman was currently folded into a circle, with her chest and chin on the ground and her legs wrapped up and over so the tops of her feet were also resting on the ground. I asked if she knew where I could find Creed, and she lifted her right leg and pointed toward the food tent.

"Last I knew," she said, "he was in his trailer. Follow the path behind the tent through the woods but be on the lookout for the trailer or you'll miss it."

I pointed at a two-foot-tall birdcage sitting near her.

"Let me guess, you can fit inside the cage?"

"Yep, want to see?"

Curiosity got the better of me and I watched in open-mouthed fascination as she slowly pulled her entire body inside.

Meeka barked as I applauded. "Bravo. That's amazing. You can get out again if I walk away, right?"

"Oh sure," came her voice from inside the tangle. "No problem."

"Great. Thanks for your help."

She stuck a foot between the bars to shake my hand. "Pleasure."

We'd gone a hundred yards or so down the path behind the food tent when I understood why the contortionist told me to pay attention. A forty-foot fifth wheel trailer, tucked into a thick cluster of pines and painted to look like more trees, was so well camouflaged I almost didn't see it. Other smaller trailers and a number of cottages were tucked in among the trees as well. This must be where the carnies lived when the weather turned frigid.

I climbed the metal trailer stairs, knocked, and was momentarily surprised when Janessa opened the door.

"Hey, there, Sheriff," she said, slightly subdued. "What can I do for you?"

"I'm looking for Creed ... or Credence. Is he, or she, around?"

"Yep, Creed just got home. Have a seat." She indicated a pair of comfortable lawn chairs set up at the far end of the trailer. "I'll go find him. I'd invite you in, but the place is a disaster."

Confused, I thanked her and went to have a seat. I thought this was Creed's home. Maybe it was the business office, too? Did Janessa also live here?

Meeka ruffed at me as though to say, *Duh.*

"I didn't realize they were together," I told her.

A minute later, as I was contemplating Janessa's

possible involvement in Gianni's death and wondering if Lupe had interviewed her yet, Creed walked out and handed me a glass of lemonade.

I took a long sip. "Just what I needed. Thanks."

"Glad to see you here. I'm sure just knowing that you're walking around the grounds will ease minds. What can I help you with?"

"I have questions." I took out my phone and opened my notetaking app. "Tell me again what you saw at the enclosure that morning."

Creed repeated everything he'd said at the council meeting. Then he went through what he, or rather Credence, had seen inside the enclosure, which wasn't much more than Zeb had reported—Gianni lying near the door, the tiger lying toward the back, no indication of what might have happened.

"Sorry," Creed said. "That's not much. Wish I could tell you more."

I wasn't surprised. Credence would've been very emotional at that time and not likely to be paying attention to details.

"That's okay," I assured. "I wish Zeb would've taken pictures. Tell me more about Gianni. Specifically, who helped him care for the animals?"

"No one. He was very protective of them and was happiest when the rest of us just left him alone."

"Taking care of all of those animals had to be hard work. You're saying he was the only one who had contact with them."

"No, Leah had contact with them, but she wasn't responsible for their care. In fact, her only contact was when she practiced her acts with them." Creed laughed. "What a fight that was. At first, Gianni didn't want them to perform, not even sit on those giant stool things. He just wanted her to bring them into the ring and educate the public about them."

"Sounds more like a zoo," I said.

"That's exactly what we told him. A circus crowd expects more than just animals in cages. Finally, he agreed to let Leah perform with them as long as she didn't make them do unnatural things, like jump through burning hoops."

"Did anyone else have access? Even just to throw food in at them?"

Creed shook his head. "He wanted everyone to stay away from *his* animals. It wasn't that bad at first, just a stern request. Recently, though, he became paranoid that someone was going to hurt them or take them away." Creed tapped his head, indicating as Dallas had that Gianni's mind might have been slipping.

"What about the medications?" I asked and took another sip of lemonade. "He told me no one else had access to the Ketamine he used in the tranquilizer darts."

"Oh no, we have access to the Ketamine," Creed said. "A controlled substance like that? We checked the inventory daily."

"Then why did he say no one else could get at it?"

"Because he didn't know." Creed's voice broke and he held a finger to his lips while he composed himself. "He didn't realize, but we checked up on him a lot, not just with the sedative. Janessa would wait until he was away from his office, then she'd grab the key and go do a count and make sure he was giving her all the bills for the things he ordered."

"Janessa did?"

"That was easiest. She'd run over there during a performance when Gianni and the rest of us were in the big top."

Janessa did have access to the Ketamine. With her disabled arms and hands, it would be difficult for her to fire the larger dart gun. The pistol-style shouldn't be a problem, though.

"Is there anyone else?" I asked. "Anyone who has, or

has ever had, access to the keys? Or even knew where the keys are kept? Specifically, the one for the Ketamine?"

Creed leaned back in his chair and held the icy glass of lemonade to his neck while he considered this. "There is one other person who knows where the keys are. She did a count for us once. Then I told Janessa it was too important and we needed to be in control of that."

"Who?"

"Tilda. She helps out here in the business office when Janessa gets swamped."

"Tilda Nelson?"

I instantly thought of the day she brought that group over to the circus wagons so Joss could teach them about the animals. I remembered Gianni telling me how she would bring Joss over to the enclosures so he could ask questions. At some point, a curious little boy like Joss must've asked about the tranquilizer gun on Gianni's hip. Probably told his mom all about it, too.

"What reason would Tilda have for killing either of them?" I asked, myself more than Creed.

"That's what I was just wondering. Tilda and Berlin were as close as sisters. That meant sometimes they fought like sisters, but it was only squabbling. I never got the feeling that there was any true animosity between them."

"Tell me what you know about Tilda."

"Not a lot," Creed said with a shrug. "She's kind of a loner. She loves to perform, but when not doing her act she prefers to be by herself."

"What about her background? What did she do before she came here? Before the accident?"

"I'm not sure. I'll run inside and get her file."

While Creed went back inside the trailer, I absently watched Meeka chase a chipmunk around a tree and went through the common reasons for murder in my mind. Financial problems, domestic violence, revenge, religious differences, self-defense, being under the influence of drugs or alcohol, concealing another crime …

Was one of those the reason? Did she owe Berlin and/or Gianni money? Was she looking to get revenge of some kind on one or both of them? Was she trying to cover something up?

"Just before the accident," Creed said as he exited the trailer, a file folder in hand, "she was a stay-at-home mom in New York. Upstate."

"She came all the way here from New York? Seems like a long way to go with a little boy to get a job with a small circus, don't you think?"

"We attract people from all over the world, Jayne." He sat back in the lawn chair. "Tilda is very talented, but with her disability, she'd have a hard time getting a spot with any of the bigger operations. This is a perfect place for her. Her physical limitations only add to the excitement of her act, and she fits in well with the other performers."

"That's true. Anything else there?" I nodded at the file. "Any mention of family?"

Creed studied the page. "Says here that her husband is Percy Nelson."

"You mean her late-husband?"

"Late-husband?" Creed checked the file again and shook his head. "Nothing here about him being deceased. I thought she was divorced. Or separated."

"Tilda told me he died in the accident."

"I honestly have no idea. I only know what's in her file." He looked at the pages again, squinting and bringing the folder in closer. "She listed Percy Nelson in New York as Joss' emergency contact. She scratched it out, but I can still read it."

Scratched it out? Maybe she wrote it out of habit then remembered he had passed? I jotted down the name. "Percy Nelson. I took her word for it that Joss' father was dead. She was never on my suspect list, so I had no reason to question what she was telling me. I'll see what I can find on this Percy guy."

"Why would she lie about him?"

"Let's think about that." I set my phone in my lap. "A talented aerial artist comes all the way to northern Wisconsin from New York with her little boy. Sure, she has a disability, but why come all this way and stay for a job doing sideshow acts? There had to be something else she could do closer to home."

"Like the rest of us," Creed's voice took on a defensive tone, "she stayed because she's accepted here."

"Or she wanted to get away from someone."

His expression turned to surprise. "You're thinking that she ran with Joss?"

"It's possible." I pointed at the file in Creed's hand. "What did she do before staying home with Joss? Anything about where she grew up?"

"We don't go back that far with our questions." He scanned the pages and then paused, eyebrows arching with interest. "Says that she was in the Olympics a number of years back. And before you ask, she didn't list her sport."

A husband who may or may not be dead, a possible kidnapping, and an Olympian who didn't declare her sport? Time to dig in further. I stood, drank down the last of my lemonade, and placed the glass in the drink holder in the arm of the lawn chair. I whistled for Meeka. "Thanks for the information, Creed."

"Where are you going? What are you thinking?"

"I'm thinking that I need to go do some research on Ms. Nelson. Listen, don't say anything to anyone about this. Not even Janessa."

"Do you think Tilda could've done this? Murdered both Berlin and Gianni, I mean?" Creed put a hand over his mouth and shook his head.

"I know that look. You hired her, you thought you knew her, but you can only know what a person reveals. Don't beat yourself up over this. You're not in any way responsible."

Without warning, Creed wrapped me in a hug. It was more for his sake than mine, so I let him.

"Don't you have a performance to get ready for?" I finally asked.

Startled, Creed stepped back. "I almost forgot. This is the first time I have ever forgotten a performance. Yes, I most definitely have to prepare."

Creed's voice softened, as did his features and gestures. I had a feeling Credence would be the ringmaster this afternoon. She seemed to come out when a more nurturing persona was necessary.

"Don't let this upset your performance today. Like I said, you're not responsible. If we were capable of spotting killers before they killed, my job would basically involve investigating petty crimes."

"If only." Creed pushed his shoulders back and held his head high. "Don't concern yourself with my performance. I'm a professional, darling. I'll give my audience what they expect."

Chapter 31

I WANTED TO GO STRAIGHT home, log onto the internet, and find out all I could about Tilda Nelson. During the short drive from the circus, I remembered that Zeb's contact information was still posted on the station door, so I went back to quickly take care of that first. I had no sooner opened the back of the Cherokee to let Meeka out of her crate when a group of ten or so tourists walked past, congratulating me on my new position.

That reminded me that for now, I was a department of one. That meant I was responsible for more than just investigating the murders. I needed to spend some time trying to fix some of the damage Zeb had done. Research would have to wait a little longer.

It was hot and humid again today, resulting in a ridiculously long line outside of Treat Me Sweetly. Everyone wanted ice cream when the temperature rose. I decided an iced something-or-other from Ye Olde Bean Grinder would have a similar effect.

"Your usual?" Violet asked when I walked inside the coffee shop.

"What's your Drink of the Day today?"

She broke out in a big smile. "Iced coconut-macadamia

latte."

"That sounds summery and wonderful. I'll try one." My eyes drifted to the covered dish on the counter next to me. "And a scone."

"You got it."

Violet kept glancing over at me while she made my latte. The normally bubbly, chatty barista was unusually subdued. Although, I noticed she was bouncing on the balls of her feet. Which meant only one thing.

"Go ahead and ask whatever it is you want to ask me, Violet," I said as I chose a coconut-chocolate chip scone.

"It's just," she sighed dramatically, "I'm used to you being plain old Jayne. Not that you're plain, mind you. Or old. I don't know ... How am I supposed to act with you now that you're the sheriff?"

I worried this might happen. "Listen, the only difference between the me you knew yesterday and the me now is this shirt." I flicked the collar of my uniform. "Unless you had planned to tell me about illegal activity you partake in when not here at the shop, you can act exactly as you did before. And I wish you would."

"Well, that's a relief." She handed me my drink and then leaned across the counter on her elbows. "In that case, what's going on up at the circus? Any leads on who the killer might be?"

If Violet ever decided to close the coffee shop, she'd make an excellent gossip columnist. No one in town knew more about the goings on than her.

"I might have a lead," I admitted. "Let's keep that between you and me, though. Okay?"

A secret with the sheriff. She liked that.

"My lips are sealed." Instead of pretending to zip her lips shut, Violet wiggled her fingers in front of her mouth.

"Is that some sort of Wiccan thing for keeping secrets locked inside?" I asked.

She winked and handed me a biscuit for Meeka.

I stuck ten dollars in the tip jar and waved goodbye as Meeka and I left to visit with more people. For the next three hours, we wandered around the Pentacle Garden greeting new tourists and assuring those who had been around for a few days that they could relax. The days of over-the-top tourist scrutiny were over.

As I chatted with a group of relaxed retired couples and a few fatigued young parents, the nun on a bicycle rode past on the path next to the lake. As though she wasn't entertaining enough, the guy in the Speedo I'd just let out of the jail cell followed her on a unicycle while playing a violin. The crowd cheered and waved as they went by. Glad to see things getting back to normal around here.

***

It was only four-thirty when we returned to the station, but I decided it was time to head home. I had research to do on Tilda, which I could have done at the station, but I also wanted to tell Tripp about my new job before someone else spilled the news first.

Halfway home, I realized I was still wearing my uniform shirt. That was not the way I wanted him to find out. Quietly as I could, I rolled down the driveway to my spot in front of the garage and pushed the door shut instead of slamming it. As soon as I let Meeka out of the back, she tore around the house barking her furry little head off.

"Meeka! Hush!" I whisper-yelled.

She paused twenty feet away, stared at me, let out a taunting bark, and then raced down the pier and made a flying leap into the water. Great. No way Tripp missed that show.

I raced up to my apartment and had just changed out of my uniform when, sure enough, Tripp called for me from the sundeck.

"When did you get home?" he asked.

"About a minute ago. If you would've gotten here fifteen seconds sooner, you would've seen me changing clothes."

He stared, one eyebrow arched, apparently visualizing me without a shirt. "I need to work on my timing."

"I've got something to tell you about. Let me know when you're at a good stopping point. We can fire up the grill and make some brats."

"Sounds perfect, I'm starving. Give me about an hour."

I gave him a thumbs-up. "Bring the brats when you come back. And the potato salad. And whatever else you want to eat."

He returned my thumbs up and stood there studying me.

"What?" I asked.

"I don't know. You seem anxious. Want to tell me your news now?"

"What makes you think I have news? I don't … I mean … it's nothing. Nothing urgent. It can wait an hour."

Was it possible for a person to sound any more brilliant? He gave me a last, suspicious squint then returned to the house. Meeka followed him through the yard, yapping the whole way. Traitor. Good thing Tripp didn't speak Westie.

I popped the top off a Summer Shandy, powered up my laptop, and prepared to do research on Tilda and Percy Nelson until Tripp came back. I opened the browser and waited. And waited. Nothing happened. There was no connection. I reset my modem and tried again, still nothing. I powered down the machine, turned it back on, and opened the browser again. Still no connection. I dug around in the drawer of the side table in the living area, found the business card for my internet company, and called the twenty-four-hour service line.

"What do you mean it's my modem?" I asked the customer service representative. "It's barely a month old."

"There's a problem with that entire shipment of

modems," he explained in a soothing, keep-the-customer-calm voice. "We'll replace it at no charge to you, of course, but there's nothing I can do about it tonight."

"If you knew about this, why did you wait for it to fail?"

"We sent you an email."

Seriously? "Which I couldn't retrieve because my modem failed."

"We anticipated you'd receive it on your cell phone as most people do."

I didn't bother trying to explain the lack of coverage here.

"I'll make sure someone gets a new unit to you as quickly as possible tomorrow."

Wasn't his fault. All I could do was thank him and emphasized the importance of me being able to connect. He reminded me that it was important for all their customers to connect and repeated that someone would get a new unit to me as fast as possible.

Unfortunately, that meant I couldn't do my research tonight. Unless I went back to the station. The thought had no sooner occurred to me when Tripp appeared at the door, food in hand.

"I finished faster than I thought," he called to me as he set the food on a deck table and lit the grill. "Besides, I'm dying to know what you wanted to talk to me about."

Oh, I got it. He thought I had news about the bed-and-breakfast. I joined them on the deck and opened the package of brats.

"You were gone all day," Tripp said. "Did the council agree with you? Are you going to replace Zeb?"

I stood with my hand on the grill's cover, waiting for it to heat up. "It wasn't unanimous, it's never unanimous, but the majority agreed that he wasn't working out. In fact, we already replaced him."

"Already? That's great. Someone else one of the members knows?"

"It's someone we all know, actually. Someone who used to work for the Madison PD."

I looked over my shoulder at him to judge how many hints I'd have to give.

"Someone we know who used to work in Madison, hey?" He spoke quietly as he busied himself taking the lid off the potato salad. "I assume I should say congratulations, Sheriff O'Shea?"

The dam burst and I told him everything about the day, starting with the council meeting this morning. Had it really only been this morning? A lot had happened and it hadn't even been twelve hours.

Out of habit, I started to tell him what Dallas and Creed had told me when I interviewed them but stopped myself. I had to stop telling him *everything*. First, he may not want to know every detail about my life. Second, for his own safety, I needed to zip my lips. The less he knew about some things, the better. Not that there were mobsters or big-time criminals wandering the pathways of Whispering Pines, but I couldn't be sure. Instead, I told him that I was pretty sure I had a good, solid lead on the killer after speaking with some people at the circus and left it at that.

Tripp sat silently as I grilled our bratwurst and rambled on about my excitement and concerns with the new position. When I finally stopped talking long enough to take a bite of my sausage, he took the opportunity to respond.

"I'm not quite sure what to think about this," he said. "I'm a little nervous for you because law enforcement can be dangerous. But we are in Whispering Pines where things are relatively safe, except for the two murders."

With my mouth full of baby carrots, I held up three fingers.

"Right, three murders."

I chewed and swallowed. "Those numbers are high, especially when you factor in how small the community is. Honestly, I don't believe that anyone here, myself included, is in danger. Yasmine was killed for personal reasons. I mean, it's not like if she wouldn't have been killed someone else would have been. I'm not sure yet why Berlin and Gianni were killed, but I don't believe that it's someone randomly targeting villagers. In other words, I think we're all as safe here as we would be anywhere else. Safer, even."

He considered this. "That makes me feel better, I guess. I know this is what you love. If you have to go back to law enforcement, at least you're doing it here. Which means you can stay."

He looked out of the corner of his eye at me and let that comment hang out there. I knew what he was thinking. Now that I had a job, and a little pull in the village, maybe I could help him get a job.

"You want to be my deputy?"

"Sounds like a proposal," he said with a wink that made me blush. "If that's my only option, I'll take it."

"No, you'd be miserable. I know you. You're fine with small groups, but you're a solitary guy."

He shrugged and gave a little caveman grunt of agreement.

"The bed-and-breakfast thing is still a thing," I reminded him. "I called Mom again. She hasn't called back with a no, so I'm still hopeful."

We sat there until the sun was long since set, sometimes chatting and sometimes not, then Tripp said he was tired and headed to bed. Meeka trotted after him, accompanying him halfway to his popup, and then made three laps around the backyard before racing back up the stairs, into the apartment, and flopping down on her cushion. She was asleep in seconds.

I thought again about going back to the station to use the internet, but I was suddenly wiped out, too. It had been a long, eventful day. I'd learn everything I could about Tilda Nelson first thing in the morning.

With the screen doors and windows wide open, I got

into bed and let the trees whisper me to sleep.

Five hours later, I was wide-awake. Meeka wasn't at all interested when I told her it was time to get up and go into the office. She stood up on her dog bone-embroidered cushion, turned in a circle, and lay back down with her back toward me. I let her sleep while I took a shower, but as soon as I was out, I filled her bowl with kibble. That at least got her off the cushion.

She eyed me while I put the uniform shirt on for a second day in a row, probably still skeptical after our short three-day stint as deputies. She'd see, we'd be doing this for a long time. Just not at five in the morning every day.

"Working," I commanded as I stood by the door with her leash in hand. Her tail started wagging, a little, and she trotted off ahead of me. Since she'd be hanging out at the station with me every day, maybe I should get her a second cushion. Of course, she seemed content beneath that cot.

Tripp was sitting outside his popup, taking in the quiet morning, as I approached the Cherokee.

"You must be anxious to get to work. Not even going to take time for breakfast?"

I explained the problem with the modem last night and how I needed to get this research done. "Plus, I've got leftover skillet scramble from The Inn in the station fridge."

"Sounds much better than the oatmeal I plan to make. See you two later."

Yeah, but I'm sure his oatmeal would be some gourmet wonder, not the gloppy, sticky instant stuff out of a packet I created. After a quick stop to grab a mocha from Violet, we got right to work. The first thing I did was set up my email account. Then, I sent a quick message to Dr. Bundy, letting him know that I was now his contact at the Whispering Pines Sheriff Station and asking that he send me everything he had regarding Berlin's and Gianni's deaths. A quick internet search brought up an article about Tilda and the sport that earned her a spot in the Olympics.

"Sheriff Jayne?" Lupe appeared in the doorway of my office just as I was nearing the end of the article. "I've got some interesting news. Did you know that Tilda competed in the Olympics as a—"

"Biathlete?" I pointed at the computer screen. "I'm just finishing an article about it."

Her face fell like I'd popped her balloon. "How did you even know to search for such a thing?"

"Creed mentioned that she was in the Olympics, but he didn't know for which sport. You realize what this means, don't you?"

"That the woman is an expert in cross-country skiing and, more importantly, rifle shooting." She flipped open her notebook and placed a finger on something. "Do you suppose a woman who can fire an Anschutz Model 1827F Fortner with ninety-seven percent accuracy could also fire a tranquilizer dart gun with equal accuracy?"

My phone rang three times before I realized I was the one who was supposed to answer it.

"Thank God," a panicked man at the other end said. "I've been calling all night. Don't you people have an answering service? I need to talk with whoever is in charge around there."

"I'm Sheriff O'Shea. How can I help you?"

"This is Percy Nelson."

I almost dropped the phone. Tilda's husband … or ex-husband … or late-husband, well, no not that, obviously. The man I was planning to investigate next.

"I saw a picture of my wife and son in an article about your village. I've been searching for them for nearly two years. Her name is Tilda, Matilda Nelson. His is Joss. You'd know them if you saw them. She's in a wheelchair, he's missing most of his left arm. Please, are they still there?"

The guy sounded frantic.

"It's ironic that you called me, Mr. Nelson," I said. "I was actually going to try and track you down today. Yes, both Tilda and Joss are here."

He let out a huge sigh of relief. "I'm in Chicago on business. The only reason I even know about Whispering Pines is because one of the people I'm working with here keeps talking about it. He went on and on about what a great little tourist destination it is. I finally got curious and looked it up. Their picture popped up first thing. Listen, I'm on my way; I'll be there in a couple of hours. Do me a favor, don't let Tilda know I'm coming. Please. If you do, she'll just run again."

Run *again*? I'd been around enough marital disputes to not simply take his word for it. I'd do a little research first, see if anything came up on Percy or Matilda Nelson. Maybe she kidnapped her son. Maybe she was an abused spouse. Maybe this was someone pretending to be her husband. Whatever the truth, my biggest concern was Joss.

"Travel safely, Mr. Nelson. Once you get to the village, come to the sheriff's station. Just ask, pretty much anyone can give you directions."

I returned the phone to its cradle and looked up to see Lupe staring at me.

"Sorry," I said, hoping she'd ignore everything she just heard. Fat chance. "What were you saying about guns?"

She looked up from jotting something in her notebook. "I was wondering if skill in shooting one weapon meant skill in shooting another."

"I don't know about equal accuracy, but I'm guessing it wouldn't be too difficult for her to hit a person with a tranquilizer dart from twenty-five yards. If that's what you mean."

The phone rang again. Was it always this busy around here?

"Whispering Pines Sheriff's Station. Sheriff O'Shea speaking. How may I help you?"

If this was a 9-1-1 call, the person at the other end would have bled out by now. I'd have to shorten that greeting.

"Sheriff O'Shea, this is Dr. Bundy. Congratulations. Glad to hear you're the one in the big chair now."

"Thanks, Dr. Bundy. I assume you got my email?"

"I did. I'll send everything right over. I wanted to let you know about something that could be urgent, though."

"Yeah?" I opened the top desk drawer and dug around for a pad of paper and pen. Then made a mental note to organize my messy desk. "What have you got for me?"

"You remember that tranquilizer dart found during the Berlin investigation?"

"Sure do. What about it?"

"Deputy Atkins from the County Sheriff was just in here talking with me about another case. Apparently, Sheriff Warren had told him in no uncertain terms that his help was no longer needed, so the deputy didn't pass this information on to him. I'll tell him to send everything he has to you as well, but I thought I'd let you know about this right away."

"Dr. Bundy, you're killing me with suspense here. What is it that you're trying to say?"

"They lifted a print off that dart. It came back as a match to Matilda Nelson."

Chapter 32

I REMEMBERED THE GENERAL LOCATION of the carnies' living tents, but it had been dark the night Tripp and I caught Lupe eavesdropping outside Tilda and Berlin's tent. There was no way I'd be able to identify it among the dozens of miniature big tops.

"Which tent is Tilda Nelson's?" I asked the first person I came to on the circus grounds. That happened to be a troupe of tumblers, all of them little people.

"Follow us," one of the tumblers said.

Meeka and I, with Lupe about twenty feet behind us, followed the group of five men and three women as they somersaulted and cartwheeled down the midway. They took a left at the food tent and kept going.

"You could just tell me," I called out.

"What's going on?" Credence asked, rising from a table in the food tent.

"Join the parade," I responded with a resigned sigh. "You'll find out in a minute."

The moment I saw the octagonal, deep red canvas tent with black fringe along the top, I remembered it.

"Okay, thanks for the escort," I said. "I've got it from here. You can go back to whatever you were doing."

The band of tumblers intertwined their legs and locked elbows, forming a four-foot-tall wall of protest, silently letting me know they wanted answers to the murders and weren't going anywhere. Behind me, even more carnies had joined the group. It was a public place, I couldn't force them to go.

"Look, this is an official call. At least step back with the rest, okay?"

In the blink of an eye, the wall became a ball of little people. As a single compact unit, they rolled back by Credence and the others. I dropped my head forward, biting back a laugh, then asked the group to give me space and not come any closer. I should have specified that they not come closer to the tent, because the group matched me step-for-step as I approached Tilda's home. Instead, I held out a hand and gave a warning look.

Since there was no door to knock on, I called out, "Matilda Nelson? It's Sheriff O'Shea. I need to speak with you."

Shuffling and whispering sounds came from inside the tent.

"Ms. Nelson," I spoke with more authority. "Come out now, please."

The canvas doorway parted and Tilda in her wheelchair appeared. She had a smile plastered on her face, but I could see the nervousness in her eyes.

"Hi, Sheriff. What's going on?" Because her chair held the canvas flaps open, I could see that she was in the middle of packing up her tent.

"I want to see the doggie!" Joss hollered from inside.

"Is someone inside with your son, Ms. Nelson?" I asked. "Is he all right?"

"Joss?" She blew out a breath, blowing off my concern. "Of course, he's all right."

"Let me go!" Joss demanded and burst out between the doorway and Tilda's wheelchair. "Meeka! I knew it was you."

Meeka's tail wagged furiously. I let the leash extend fully so the two friends could play off to the side. As my gaze shifted from the little boy with only one arm to the woman with only one fully-working leg, Lily Grace's vision came to me. Body parts. Her visions didn't have to be literal to be accurate. It hadn't meant that I was going to come across a literal pile of bloody body parts. It was telling me to pay attention to Tilda and Joss. Or at least that's how I was going to interpret it.

"Can't help but notice that you've got a lot of boxes in there," I said, nodding at the tent. "Are you going somewhere?"

She glanced casually over her shoulder then rolled her chair all the way out, letting the flaps swing closed again. "Yeah. Joss and I are going to hit the road."

Percy Nelson's plea sounded in my ears. *Don't let Tilda know I'm on the way. If you do, she'll just run again.* Did she know Percy was coming? Or was this a pattern and it was simply time to go again?

I took a step closer. "That seems sudden."

Her gaze shifted to her son and my dog. "It's just too much, you know?"

"What's too much?"

"First Berlin, now Gianni."

"It is upsetting." I lowered my voice. "That's why I'm here. I need to talk with you about their deaths. Why don't we go down to the station? I'm sure you'd be more comfortable, and it would certainly be more private."

She glanced at the group behind me and put on a confused expression. "Okay, sure. Can Joss play with the dog for a while first? Unless you want to leave her here, of course."

I laughed out loud. "I'm not leaving my dog. They can have a couple minutes. Do you need anything before we go?"

"That depends." Tilda shifted in her chair. "How long will I be gone?"

If things went the way I expected, a very long time.

"Colette," I called toward the tent. "Would you come on out here, please?"

A moment later, the tent flaps moved and Colette's head poked out. I motioned for her to step to the side with me.

"What's going on?" I motioned toward the tent.

"Beats me. Tilda asked me to come over and help her with Joss for a little while. I got here to find her packing up their stuff. I have no idea what's going on."

I couldn't say for sure that she was lying, but I wasn't sure I believed her either. "Would you watch Joss while Tilda comes with me?"

"Of course." Colette pulled me further aside and in a low voice asked, "What's going on? Did she do something?"

"Just keep an eye on the boy for me, okay?"

I motioned Credence over to me next.

"I don't want to know." She put her hands in front of her face as a shield. "Whatever this is, I'll find out soon enough."

"No problem," I said, "I wasn't going to tell you. Tilda is going to have to come to the station with me. I'm going to leave Joss in Colette's care; he's used to being with her. Would you keep an eye on them? Make sure they stay here?"

She lowered her hands. "You think Colette would run with Joss?"

"I'm preparing for any possibility." I called Meeka, letting her leash reel in as she trotted over. To Tilda, I asked, "Ready?" To Lupe, I said, "Sorry, you'll need to find another way back to the village."

"That's fine, I can walk," Lupe said. "But I'll have questions for you later."

The Strong Man, a beast of a guy who looked like he could bench-press The Incredible Hulk, stayed with Tilda while I drove my SUV down the horse wagon path from the parking lot to the circus entrance. He lifted Tilda into the vehicle, folded her chair, and put it into the back seat while I put Meeka in her crate. When we got to the station, I reversed the process myself, offering to help Tilda out of the vehicle and into her chair. Other than getting the chair out of the back of the Cherokee, she didn't want my help.

She didn't seem curious about why I brought her in. She didn't seem concerned that she might be in trouble. She did, however, seem angry that I had disrupted her packing.

"Is this gonna take long? Joss and I are almost ready to leave."

Without answering, I directed her into the small interview room. Employing an interview technique I learned from my captain in Madison, I pushed the simple wood table against a wall. With no barriers between us and no means of escape, Tilda would be fully exposed to me. I placed my chair in the middle of the room, facing the door and pointed to a spot across from it where I wanted Tilda to position her wheelchair, her back to the door. Finally, I started the recording app on my phone and set the phone on the table.

"Can I get you anything before we start?" I indicated the watercooler in the corner. "Water?"

Her gaze darted around the room, landing anywhere but on me. "No, I'm good."

Just that fast, my nerves set in. It had been a good eight or nine months since I'd conducted a formal interview. As I sat and scooted my chair a couple of inches closer to her, she leaned back in her wheelchair, uncomfortable. That small crack in her otherwise rock-solid exterior was all I needed. I was in charge here. I could do this.

"How is Joss handling all this? The deaths of Berlin and Gianni, I mean."

"He's confused." Tilda stared at a spot on the wall behind me. "He knows Berlin is gone but doesn't understand where she went. He misses her a lot. I haven't even tried to explain Gianni yet. I told him that he had to go away on a trip."

"Is that why you're leaving? Because it's too hard for Joss?"

She looked like I'd insulted her parenting skills. "He's five years old. First, he loses Berlin, who was like a second mom to him. Now a man who was the closest thing he had to a dad dies, too. Poor kid deserves to be happy."

"That's right, you claim Joss' dad died in the accident."

"Claim?" She pushed herself upright in her chair. "I told you before, he's dead."

I hadn't planning to bring this up so quickly, but since she opened the topic …

"That's strange. Who do you suppose called me this morning claiming to be Percy Nelson?"

Her eyes went wide and wild. "He called *here*? You didn't say anything about us, did you?" She turned her chair toward the door, trying to leave. "We have to go. He can't find us."

I stood to block her way. "We're not done here. The sooner you talk to me, the sooner you can leave."

Reluctantly, she returned her chair to its previous position, and I moved my chair even closer to her, making it almost impossible for her to move again. Off center now, she said nothing for a minute. Her hands fluttered from her lap to her throat to the armrests of her chair. Her breathing became rapid and shallow. Hyperventilating, she gulped in a long, deep breath and blew it out. Then she did it again. Every action was controlled and purposeful, not panicked or spastic. This must've been a tactic she used as a biathlete to slow her breathing and steady her nerves so she could shoot after skiing. Within seconds, her breathing was steady again.

I tapped the back of my hand to her knee to regain her attention. "Why don't you tell me what's going on with your husband."

Her expression … no, her entire body softened a bit.

Relieved to be able to tell someone the truth?

"We had to get away from him." She stared blankly, remembering something, then shook her head as though dismissing the memory. Then, for the first time since getting out of the Cherokee, she looked directly at me. "If he had a bad day, if things didn't go well at work, Percy would come home and fly into a rage. Same thing if I tried to talk about my job. He hated my job."

"I thought you were a stay-at-home mom. An Olympic biathlete before that."

She blinked, surprised. "Who told you that?"

Once a cop, always a cop, Lupe had told me a few days earlier. "I am a detective. Which job did he hate? Surely, not that you were a mom."

"No, he liked me being at home ... where I belonged." She rolled her eyes and acid tinged her voice. "I was a spokeswoman for a few biathlon equipment companies. My biggest contract was with a rifle manufacturer."

I tried to recall my notes since I forgot to grab the files before sitting down. "For your preferred rifle? Fortner Model 18-something?"

"Wow, you really did dig into my background. Model 1827F." She smiled, almost nostalgically. "Percy told me it was a stupid way to make money. He was just jealous."

A little part of me always broke when I learned a person could feel that way about their spouse. The fairy tales taught us that spouses supported each other's dreams unconditionally and were happy for each other's successes. I guess the keywords there were *fairy tales*. Sometimes, I felt like my mom was jealous of my dad. He got to travel the world, pursuing his passion while she was stuck in Madison with two girls. Had she expected the fairy tale? Was that why she could be so cold and angry at times?

I pulled myself back to the present. "Why would he be jealous?"

"Percy is a bicyclist. He rides a minimum of twenty

miles a day. His dream has always been to get into the Tour de France and the Olympics. Problem is, he's such a jerk, no Tour team wanted him. When I made it onto an Olympic relay team, that was the first time I saw his anger. He never made the Olympics either. After, with each contract I got, his anger flared hotter."

I could empathize with her. Jonah hated that I was a cop, didn't matter to him that it was my passion. When I became a detective, he started pushing me to get an office job.

"I needed the money, though," Tilda continued without me having to prompt her. "I made sure that every penny I made went into a bank account Percy couldn't touch. Finally, there was enough that I could make a decent life for Joss and me. One morning about three years ago after Percy left for work, I packed our clothes and we took off."

"Let me guess," I said, "that was the day of your accident."

She nodded, tears slowly trickling down her cheeks. "I was scared he was going to find us. I kept checking the rearview mirror to be sure he wasn't following. Plain and simple, I wasn't paying attention. My car got T-boned. Yes, it was mostly my fault, but the other guy was going way too fast. If he would've been going the speed limit, or even ten miles slower, our injuries would have been minor. For sure, Joss wouldn't have lost his arm."

Body parts. Miscellaneous bloody arms and legs. What the hell was that?

Tilda broke down then, crying with her hands over her face, her shoulders shaking. I grabbed a box of tissues from a cabinet in the corner and held it out to her. Once she had composed herself, I returned to my questions.

"I'm sorry for what happened to you, but I still need to talk to you about Berlin's and Gianni's deaths. What do you know about them?"

"Nothing." She dabbed her eyes. "Why would I?"

I told her to wait while I grabbed Berlin's and Gianni's file folders from my desk. I pulled a picture out of one of them and held it up to her. "Do you know what this is?"

She examined the image. "Looks like a tranquilizer dart."

"You've seen them before?"

"Yeah, Gianni carried them around for the animals."

"Right." I tapped the picture. "We tested this dart. It had traces of Ketamine in it."

She waited for me to say more and when I didn't asked, "So? That's no surprise. It's the medication Gianni used."

"How do you know that?"

Tilda's face remained neutral, but her hands absently played with the hem of her shorts. "I don't know. He must've mentioned it to me or Joss at one point. You know how Joss loves those animals."

"I do. Between Gianni and you teaching him, he knows more than most adults."

She smiled. Proud mom.

"Gianni's darts were color-coded," I said. "Do you know why?"

"No idea."

She answered too quickly. I was getting to her. My heart rate kicked up a notch.

"Really? Gianni didn't hesitate to brag to me about his system. He didn't tell Joss?"

"Oh, you mean the pre-filled darts." She nodded, smoothed her shorts. "Sure, he told everyone about the different colored stabilizers. He carried them in that black pouch on his belt. Each loaded with a different amount of the medication."

"Because different-sized animals need different amounts of Ketamine."

"Exactly." Tilda sat taller, suddenly a virtual encyclopedia of tranquilizer dart knowledge.

I tapped the picture again. "You know then that the

orange darts were for the tiger."

She hesitated before answering. "I guess."

"That would be more than enough to knock out a woman of say 118 pounds." I checked a page in Berlin's folder. "Right, one-eighteen. Actually, that's three times the amount necessary to kill a woman that size."

Tilda paled.

I held a new picture in front of her, one Dr. Bundy had taken of Berlin's body.

"Any guess at what this might be?" I pointed out the puncture wound on Berlin's upper left hip.

Tilda examined the picture for all of a second before looking away. "No clue."

"This picture was taken during Berlin's autopsy. It's a wound made by a tranquilizer dart."

She chewed her lip and shifted positions. "That's kind of specific, isn't it? How can you know it was caused by a dart?"

"Call it deductive reasoning." I held up the dart picture again. "This dart was found on the ground in the big top. There was Ketamine in it and in Berlin's system. The wound matches perfectly with the dart. To confirm this assumption, the medical examiner is testing the dart for Berlin's DNA."

"Is that how she died?" she asked, curious in almost an excited way. "From Ketamine?"

"No, she strangled to death after her silks became wrapped around her neck." My vision tunneled and I became laser focused on Tilda. "You knew Berlin's practice schedule, didn't you? I think you were either waiting for her in the big top that morning or entered after she had started practicing. You wheeled your chair next to the fencing that she and Gianni fought about so often. You took a deep breath, steadying your nerves much like you did here a few minutes ago, then shot Berlin with that dart."

"Ridiculous. Where would I have gotten a dart gun?"

Really? That was her concern?

"Sporting goods store. Internet. Garage sale. Anyone can buy a dart gun. Of course, you knew that Gianni had two. The rifle style he used during performances because it was bigger and offered a greater level of comfort to the audience. Also, a smaller pistol-style gun that he used the rest of the time because it was easier to carry around. It would have been easy enough for you to grab one or the other."

Tilda shrugged.

"Getting access to the Ketamine was a little trickier, wasn't it? Gianni locked up his medications."

"Triple locked." Her tone was one of frustration. Gianni hadn't made it easy for her to kill her friend.

"How do you know about the triple locks?"

She cleared her throat. "I told you, we talked with him about his animals all the time. You said it; he liked to brag about his system."

I waited, silent, long enough that she started fidgeting. "Tell me the truth, Tilda. You shot Berlin with this dart. Didn't you?"

"I've never seen that dart before."

Exactly what I expected she'd say. I wanted to blurt out my next question, but forced myself to pause and arrange my face into a confused expression, before asking, "Then how did your fingerprint get on it?"

A bead of sweat dribbled down the left side of her face. I could see her mind scrambling for a response. "Gianni showed one to Joss one time. He let me see it, too. That must've been the one."

Time for me to keep my mouth shut. My silence and her increasing discomfort would do far more than any question at this point.

"Even if I got a gun and a dart," she finally blurted, "how would I get the Ketamine? He never took off that pouch. Or his keyring. It's not like I have a set of keys."

Adrenaline flooded my system. Being back in the game,

slowly riding out an interview until everything fell together, was like a high.

"But Janessa has keys," I said. "Ketamine is a controlled substance, so Creed keeps close track of it. He told me that Janessa slips into Gianni's office during performances to do counts. He also told me that you did a count once."

Tilda pressed her lips tightly together.

"Here's what happened." I leaned closer, elbows resting on my knees. "You acquired a dart gun, either bought your own or *borrowed* one of Gianni's. You got Janessa's keys, took a Ketamine-filled dart from Gianni's supply, and then shot Berlin while she was practicing. You lost track of that dart, though, didn't you? You knew someone would find it during the investigation and that eventually Gianni would be questioned about it. I'm not clear on why, but for some reason you had to silence him to keep him from exposing you as Berlin's killer. Am I right so far?"

After nearly five full minutes, staring at her hands in her lap, Tilda let out a heavy sigh.

"Fine. You're right. Spot on. You figured it all out. Are you proud? Yes, I killed Berlin. Just the way you said it. While she was practicing."

She grimaced, pain clear on her face. Why? Remorse over killing a friend or because she got caught?

"How did you get the Ketamine?"

"Creed and Janessa never lock that trailer. I waited until they were asleep. My right leg gives me problems, but I can get around with crutches. The chair is just easier."

"So, you snuck into their trailer in the middle of the night, stole the keys, stole the dart, then returned the keys?"

She responded with a smug shrug.

"How did you kill Gianni?"

"I didn't—"

"Tilda, come on. I know you did."

She appeared to wrestle with what to say. "We were talking guns one day last year. One thing led to another and

I stupidly bragged about my shooting abilities. I couldn't risk him exposing me. I knocked out the tiger first, and just as I knew he would, Gianni panicked and went into the enclosure to find out what was wrong with her. When he did, I shot him with a dart as well. I was able to retrieve both of those darts." She shook her head, disgusted. "Should've searched longer for that first one. Or worn gloves."

Her attitude chilled me. That was her only regret? That she left behind a fingerprint?

"Are you telling me that you waited outside the enclosure until Gianni was unconscious?"

She looked away, refusing to answer the question.

After administration, it can take as long as three to four minutes for an animal to be rendered sedated, Gianni had told me.

Tilda shot the tiger and hid in the shadows until Gianni came along and found it. Did she sit there and watch for four minutes until Gianni passed out? Did he realize she was the one who had shot him? What happened to the body as it died slowly from Ketamine? I didn't want to know.

"You killed Gianni to keep him quiet. Why did you kill Berlin?"

She turned her head slightly to the right, as though sighting in her shot, and stared me dead in the eye. "To keep her quiet, too. I made the mistake of trusting her. I told her that Joss and I ran away from Percy. That, yes, I kidnapped my son to protect him. Percy never laid a hand on him, but I was sure it was just a matter of time before he did. I wasn't going to stay and wait for that to happen."

"It feels like there's a piece missing. The two of you were so close. I understand she loved Joss as much as if he were her own son. What made you think she wouldn't help you protect him?"

"Talk about irony." Tilda laughed, a truly wicked sound. "Berlin's mother had done the same thing with her when Berlin was a child. She ran with her four children to get them away from a bad situation at home. When she told me that, I thought for sure she'd understand."

"But she didn't?" Movement in the main room caught my attention. Probably Lupe coming to eavesdrop at the door.

"She never forgave her mother for taking her away from her father. Said every child deserved to be with their dad. For nearly a year, Berlin kept my secret. But as tensions started to rise around the circus—her frustrations with Gianni and that fence, me putting pressure on Creed to have a larger role, me offering to do that new act with Dallas— Berlin's temper got shorter. That night before she died, she accused me of trying to steal her spotlight. I told her I just wanted to ease her load and build more of a name for myself. She said if I didn't back off, she'd contact Percy and let him know we were here."

Tilda's expression went blank then, as though her mind had just snapped. Honestly, it scared me.

"What choice did I have?" Tilda asked, as though all of this was Berlin's fault. "I don't know if she would've followed through with the threat, but I couldn't take the chance."

"To keep her from contacting your husband, you killed her. You were really that scared of him?"

I almost felt sorry for her.

"And still, I found you." A man had entered the station, not Lupe, and he was now standing in the interview room doorway with a gun pointed squarely at Tilda's head.

Chapter 33

I SAW HIM APPROACHING THE doorway and was about to tell him I'd be with him shortly when I saw the gun. Without even realizing I'd done it, I was on my feet with my service weapon drawn and aimed at the man. Had I remembered to load a bullet into the chamber?

At the same time, Tilda had turned to face him and immediately went pale. In a voice so breathy I almost didn't hear her, she said, "Percy."

Great.

"Lower your weapon!" I gave him one second. "Mr. Nelson, don't make me shoot. Lower your weapon and let's talk about whatever it is that's going on here."

Tilda turned to me, rage replacing her look of shock. "You told him we were here."

"You think I need someone else's help to find you?" He took a step closer to her. "I've been looking for you for *two years*. I searched everywhere I could think that you might go. I contacted everyone I could think of who knows you. Finally, I saw your picture on a travel website yesterday."

Tilda looked confused. Lupe must not have told her she'd taken her picture.

Percy still had the gun pointed at Tilda's head, his

knuckles turning white he was gripping it so hard. As I stood there, my gun pointed at the center of his chest, index finger ready to squeeze the trigger if it came to it, memories of a day about eight months ago flashed in my head. The day my partner aimed his gun at our informant, Frisky Fox. I tried to talk him down, not for one second believing that he'd shoot Frisky. That memory blurred to a day not even a month ago when I had this very weapon in my hand and didn't shoot. Every single day since, I wondered if I had fired, even a warning shot into the pine trees, would Karl Brighton still be alive?

"This is the last time I'm going to say it, Mr. Nelson. Put your gun down or I will shoot you."

I meant the words, but I felt a drizzle of sweat run down the center of my back. Could I follow through?

"Do it!" Tilda demanded of me. "I told you what he did to me, what he most likely will do to Joss. If anything happens to either of us, that's going to be on you. Shoot him!"

"What *I* did? Years of emotional abuse. Your only concern was yourself, your contracts, and your precious biathlons. Threatening me with divorce and that you'd take my son if I didn't agree to let you have everything you wanted whenever you wanted it."

With the gun firmly in his right hand, he pulled papers from his back pocket with his left and held them up to me.

"Court documents. The top page is an order giving me full custody of Joss." He dropped the pages to the floor as he advanced, taking one long stride toward his wife while cupping his free hand around the one holding the gun and lining up squarely with her temple. At that moment, Meeka burst into the room. Snarling and barking, she locked onto Percy's calf with her sharp little teeth.

The sound of gunshot in the small cinder block room was deafening. My ears rang with the reverberation. Meeka yelped. Tilda's eyes locked onto mine with a look of shock mixed with horror. Percy slumped to the ground as a bright red stain spread slowly across the upper left quadrant of his white polo shirt.

It had been drilled into me time and again to aim for the center of the largest mass. That's what I had done, I had taken dead aim at the center of Percy Nelson's chest. From this distance, it should have been a kill shot. Whether he moved at the last second, or I did, or it was something with this gun, I couldn't know. A few weeks ago, when Sheriff Brighton deputized me and gave me a service weapon, that was the first time I had held a gun in six months. Just now, was the first time I had discharged a weapon in more than eight.

"Is he dead?" Tilda asked.

"No. I shot him in the shoulder."

"In the shoulder?" Tilda complained, disgusted with me. "I would've shot him in the head."

"And I'm sure you wouldn't have missed," I returned, equally disgusted.

Lupe burst into the station then. "What happened? I heard gunfi—" She saw Percy lying on the floor then.

"Contact medical services," I ordered. "Call the healing center first, but he's going to need to go to the hospital. Numbers are by the phone on the desk out there."

Lupe didn't hesitate and went straight to the phone.

After retrieving Percy's weapon and returning mine to the holster on my belt, I stepped into the bathroom next door, grabbed a stack of paper towels, and applied pressure to Percy's shoulder. Once the call was made, Lupe took over, keeping pressure on Percy's shoulder until someone from the healing center, just up the Fairy Path from the station, arrived.

"Do you need to use the restroom?" I asked Tilda.

"What?" She looked at me like I'd lost my mind.

I retrieved the court papers from the floor and gave them a quick scan.

"Percy was granted full custody of Joss three years ago. I'm guessing shortly before that day you left with Joss. You were granted supervised visitation only." I pointed to the far side of the building. "I'll be locking you in one of the jail cells over there until someone from the County Sheriff's Department can come get you. If you need to use the restroom, I suggest you do it now."

Five minutes later, Tilda was in one of my cells, complaining about how she was the wronged party. She seemed to have forgotten the fact that she had killed two people.

"You can't let her take Joss," Percy said weakly while one of the healers from the center tended to him as we waited for the ambulance.

"He can't take him either," Tilda called from the cell.

"I have a court order," Percy said. "You can't have any contact with him."

I leaned against the desk in the main room, shaking my head at the two of them. "Hate to tell you this, but neither of you will be seeing Joss for a while. Tilda, you killed two people. You're going to prison. Percy, you came into a sheriff's station with a gun and threatened to shoot your wife. You won't be going home anytime soon either."

"What's going to happen to Joss?" Tilda asked. "He likes Colette. She'll take care of him."

"I know he does," I said. "Unfortunately, someone from social services will decide where Joss goes. They'll most likely place him with a foster family. Colette will have to go through the process of becoming a foster parent if she wants him. That could take a while."

Broke my heart. Poor kid. His life was a disaster because his parents couldn't get along.

Even though Percy seemed to be weak from blood loss and in a lot of pain, I had no doubt that he'd be fine because he had no problem arguing with Tilda the whole time we waited for the hour it took the ambulance to get there.

Around the same time, Deputy Atkins arrived. I wasn't equipped to deal with processing this kind of crime from my little station. The County Sheriff would handle that.

"Somehow, I knew I'd be hearing from you again," Evan said. "What have you got for me this time?"

I played the recording of Tilda's interview and then relayed to him everything I had learned from talking with people about the deaths. He formally charged Tilda with the murders of Berlin and Gianni Cordano and then took her to his vehicle. Before leaving, he poked his head back in the door.

"Congratulations on your placement, by the way," he said. "I suggest you get help around here sooner than later. For such a small place, Whispering Pines has a lot going on."

"You don't need to tell me that," I said. "Getting help is at the top of my to-do list."

Followed closely by getting to a gun range to get comfortable with the Glock on my hip. Maybe carrying a gun, at least during the tourist season, wasn't such a bad idea.

Hours later, after first answering about a hundred questions from Lupe, I was nearly done writing up my reports on the deaths when the front door opened and Reeva Long walked in. Since I was currently the only one working in this office, it made more sense for me to sit at the desk out in the main area instead of in my office. That way, no one could sneak up on me again.

"Ms. Long. I'm surprised to see you here. Do you need help?"

"I found it." She held a thin file folder out to me. "It was on the top shelf in the closet in the bedroom Karl used as an office."

I took the folder from her, flipped it open to see "Lucy O'Shea" printed in bold handwriting on the top page, and closed it again.

"I didn't look at any of it, in case you're wondering."

Reeva stood there, clearly wanting to say something more, so I waited. "It's none of my business, you certainly don't need to say anything to me, but I'm curious. What about your grandmother's case are you questioning?"

Could I trust her? She and Flavia were at odds, but they were still sisters.

"I'm not sure that her death truly was an accident." I didn't care if she told Flavia. That might help speed things along. "Things aren't lining up for me, and I'm hoping there might be something in this file that will supply missing answers."

Reeva nodded, seeming to understand what I meant. Then she echoed Sugar's words from yesterday. "Whispering Pines appears to be a little piece of perfection, doesn't it? Don't get me wrong, I lived for the last twenty years in the Milwaukee area. I know that in comparison to many places, this village is a far cry better. But like anywhere else, not everyone here gets along."

I laughed. "Sorry. I'm not under any misconception that everyone here loves each other. In the month since I arrived, there have been three murders." I set my hand on top of Gran's file on the desk in front of me. "I have a strange feeling I'm about to uncover a fourth."

Reeva stood back, arms folded, and studied me. She seemed to be trying to get a read on me as much as I was her. Which side of the line that divided this village did she stand on?

She flicked a slender finger at the folder. "If you want to know the truth, you're going to have to go back fifty years. I can't tell you if Lucy was killed or not, but I do know that there were times when she regretted letting people come here."

"Some people more than others?"

"Of course. Your grandmother was a caring, loving woman. She knew that if someone was a bully, it was likely because they were fighting back against things in their own world."

Interesting choice of words.

"So far, I've only met one person in the village who I would truly consider to be a bully." Reeva squirmed like she was getting ready to turn and leave. No time for beating around the bush. "Has Flavia always been this way?"

Reeva pushed her shoulders back and raised her chin. "Don't ask me to talk about my sister."

"I'm not accusing her of anything. Just wondering what might've happened to make her so angry."

After a short pause, "No. She wasn't always this way. I already told you, if you want to know the truth you need to dig into the past. Not an easy task. Secrets are buried deep around here and lips sealed up tight."

With that, Reeva left the building.

That was basically the same thing Morgan said, that village secrets wouldn't be easy to unearth.

Hard as it was, I finished my reports on Tilda and Percy before letting myself open Gran's folder again. When I did, Reeva's and Morgan's warnings about secrets came to life. The one thing I really hoped to find in the folder wasn't there. Disappointed, but somehow not surprised, I opened an email to Dr. Bundy and requested Gran's autopsy report.

Chapter 34

MY FIRST FULL DAY AS sheriff ended on a satisfying note in that I closed Berlin's and Gianni's cases. Better still, the carnies would be able to sleep well knowing that there was no longer a killer prowling their grounds. I walked out of the station, intending to go home, but I couldn't quiet the niggling questions about Gran's death. Reeva told me to go back fifty years, to Whispering Pines' inception. How was I supposed to do that? Time travel? Transcendental meditation? Ask Morgan to conjure a portal in the pines?

I'd never get to sleep with these questions rolling around in my head. The easiest way to learn what happened fifty years ago was to ask someone who'd been here. I'd gotten all I'd get out of Reeva, for now at least. Once I had specific questions she'd say more. Flavia was an obvious option, but not now. I wanted to build my case more before talking to her. Effie or Cybil? Yes, but not tonight. Sugar, Honey, Mr. Powell? Laurel or Maeve? How many of the older folks here now were here at the start? That was a good place to begin.

If I wanted questions answered tonight, there was only one person to talk to. After tucking Meeka into her crate in the back of the Cherokee, I drove straight to Morgan and

Briar's cottage.

"Briar?" I stood outside the hedge surrounding their yard. "Are you in there?"

"Of course," came a voice a second later. Briar appeared at a gap in the foliage. "Well, Jayne. Look at you in your spiffy new shirt."

I smiled, knowing Gran would've said the same thing.

"You look tired," I said, noting her slumped shoulders and heavy eyes. "Have you been in the garden all day?"

She nodded. "Still tending the flock after that storm."

"I won't bother you then. I'll come back another time."

"Jayne." Her voice held a stern, maternal note. "You came all this way. What do you need?"

She made it sound like I'd driven across the country instead of less than a mile from down in the village.

"I spoke with Reeva Long about a half hour ago. I know she grew up in the village so I asked her about my grandmother's death. She told me if I wanted to learn the truth, I'd have to go back to when Gran let everyone into Whispering Pines."

Briar's head bobbed up and down. "She's right. To fully understand a problem, it's often best to start at the beginning."

Her words were slurring. This was not the time to interview her.

"I'll come back another time and we can talk about it then."

"We can do that, but I would only be telling you my interpretation of the events. No one person can tell you all that you need to know the truth. You have to talk to everyone who was here at the time. Somewhere among all those interpretations, you'll find the truth."

Talk to everyone who was here fifty years ago and weave the stories into the truth? This wouldn't be an easy task, but I was good at getting people to talk.

"Once I've gathered all my stories ..."

"I will help you make the pieces make sense."

That's all I could ask for. I encouraged Briar to go rest and said goodnight. When I finally got back to the house, I found Tripp waiting for me on the sundeck in one of the lounge chairs with an icy ale in hand. A pizza, covered in plastic wrap and ready for the grill, sat on the table in front of him.

"Long day at the office?" he asked, glancing over his shoulder.

"You waited to have dinner with me?"

"Sure did. Much nicer to eat dinner with a companion. Are you ready? I can throw this on."

How nice was that? "Go ahead. I'm going to take a quick shower while it's baking."

On the way home, all I could think about was digging into the village's past. I was positive Flavia was the source of the negativity going on around here, from Gran's death to the trashing of my house to whatever she and Donovan were currently colluding over. How could I break through that? Everyone was so tightlipped about her. It was almost like she had something on each one of them, like she was the keeper of the secrets, and they were all afraid she'd let them all spill out if anyone went against her.

"This won't happen quickly," I reminded the Jayne staring at me from the mirror. "Not only will gathering all those *interpretations* take time, you've got a house to finish renovating and law and order to maintain."

Funny, a little over a month ago I had absolutely nothing to do. I'd ended things with Jonah, quit my job at MPD, and moved into my parents' house. Other than taking Meeka for a few walks a day, cleaning the house, and going to therapy appointments with Dr. Maddox, my schedule was blank. Now, bored was about the last thing I felt.

I dried off, hung my towel on the hook on the back of the bathroom door, and pulled on cutoffs and a tank top. I'd just opened a beer when I realized the light on my answering machine was blinking, indicating two missed calls. I press the button and heard my mother's voice.

"Are you there?" A ten-second pause indicated she expected I was and was waiting for me to pick up. Then she sighed like my absence inconvenienced her. "I have something to discuss with you. I'll call again."

The time stamp was from 8:27 yesterday morning. I knew I'd forget to check the answering machine. If I moved it next to my bed there was no way I'd miss that blinking light. The second call came three hours later.

"You're still not there? I assume that means you're working on the house. Good. Naturally, I would prefer to tell you this in person. Meaning not in a voicemail. Not that I intend to drive up to that place. This will have to do. I'm a busy person, you know. I don't have time to keep trying to track you down. I was finally able to speak with your father. He received the email I sent him, and I'm shocked to say that he agreed."

The beer bottle slid from my hand and landed flat on the counter, causing the beer to foam up all over the place, run down the side of the cabinet, and onto the floor.

"Of course, we'll have to make this legal at some point," Mom continued as I started wiping up spilled beer, "but here is the gist of it. Since you have insisted, repeatedly, that you can handle this on your own, that's what we're going to let you do. The success or failure of this venture lies entirely on your shoulders. We will pay for the renovations, but your father says you're not to do anything to the house that would make it difficult to sell should this fail. You have one year, through the end of the next summer season, to at least break even. With the numbers you forecast, that should be doable. If you are successful, we will allow you to continue. If not, you are to put the house up for sale, no questions asked."

I had no doubt that the B&B would be a success. If I had the means, I'd buy them out today. As it was, I couldn't do that, so I'd need to deal with them wanting regular reports and updates. I guess that was only fair, considering they'd be taking all the financial risk for the next year.

"As I mentioned," Mom continued, "we'll discuss the legalities later. For now, I suggest you and your friend kick it into high gear and get the place rented. The clock, as they say, is ticking."

My hands shook as I wiped up the beer on the floor. This is what we'd been hoping and striving for. I had to tell Tripp.

Out on the deck, the mosquitoes were in full attack mode. I turned on the bug zappers at both ends and within seconds, the little vampires were being obliterated.

"Pizza's ready," Tripp said, "are you?"

I popped the top off a fresh beer and fell into one of the lounge chairs. Meeka stood before me with a look on her furry little face that said *hang on, you forgot the dog*.

"I'm ready, serve it up." I went back inside, got a dish of food for Meeka, and presented it to her little highness. She gave me a snort as though to say, *don't do that again*.

"What happened today that you were at the station so long?" Tripp asked as he handed me a plate with a big slice of rustic pizza.

"Caught a killer."

"That's great," he said, enthused.

I waved my hand dismissively while relishing the gooey cheesy pizza goodness. "You don't want to hear about it. I don't want to talk about it. Tell me what's going on with the house."

"I'll be done painting the walls on the first floor tomorrow. Then I'll move upstairs—"

I couldn't wait another second so blurted, "Do you still want to be a bed-and-breakfast manager?"

Confused, he answered, "You already know that's my first choice."

I said nothing, just stared at him while I took another bite of my pizza. When he caught on to my pointed look, his eyes went wide.

"You're not just asking, are you? What exactly are you saying?"

I stood, plate with pizza slice in hand, and motioned for him to follow me inside. I hit the replay button on the answering machine and watched as he listened to my mom's message. Around the midpoint, he'd stopped blinking.

"Should I play it again?" I offered when it was done. "Do you need to hear one more time to be sure you believe it?"

He took my plate from me, set it on the counter, then picked me up and spun me around. Meeka thought this was great fun and joined in with some excited yips and tail-chasing. Then, Tripp planted a kiss firmly on my mouth.

I couldn't say who was more shocked. He set me down and backed away.

"Sorry," he said. "I didn't mean—"

"Don't worry about it. It was just a reaction."

"No, that was really inappropriate."

"Well, considering I'm now your boss ..." I laughed at his horrified expression, trying to break the tension, and led him back out on the sundeck. "Seriously, it's already forgotten. I'm glad that you're as excited about this as I am."

I was such a liar. The feeling of being in his arms. His soft, full lips against mine. The way his three-day beard left a prickly sensation around my mouth. Yeah, I wouldn't forget that anytime soon.

We sat in silence, eating our pizza and letting this new reality sink in. By the time he finished his first slice, Tripp's embarrassment had turned back into excitement. For the first time, we seriously discussed the plans we'd been tossing around for the last month. We talked about so many things, I had to run inside and get paper and pen so we could write them all down. It was after midnight when our thoughts finally slowed.

"I should let you go to bed," Tripp said. "You have a job

to get to in the morning."

He seemed happier than I'd seen him in weeks, but there was an edge in his voice that was slightly off.

"What's the matter?" I asked. "Something's bothering you."

"It's just, I'm obviously happy that we get to do the B&B. I thought we were going to do it together, though. Now that you're the sheriff—"

"Don't worry, we're still doing this together. Yes, I'll be sheriff full-time, but I'm going to have help at the station. I want the B&B to succeed as badly as you do. Maybe more so. If it fails, I'll never hear the end of it from my parents."

"Okay. Good." He slumped back into his chair and stared up at the trees. "We're really going to do this?"

"We're really going to do this."

"Now that we're on a deadline, it might be a good idea for me to bring in a crew. I can paint fast, but seven bedrooms will take time. Renovating those bathrooms will take months if I do that by myself."

"I agree completely. Talk to Mr. Powell tomorrow, tell him what you need. I'm sure he'll round up some people for you."

"One other thing. We need a name." A slow smile turned his mouth. "I have an idea."

"You do?" I leaned forward. "Tell me."

"What do you think of calling it Pine Time?"

His term for things moving at their own pace in the village. Gooseflesh instantly covered my body.

"It's perfect." I held my beer up for a toast. "To Pine Time, may it be as successful as we know it can be."

"To Pine Time." His eyes softened and his voice grew husky. "The perfect venture with the perfect partner. Here's to many, *many* happy years together."

Sometimes it was hard for me to believe that it only took a month for Tripp Bennett to become such a huge part of my life. If I believed in Morgan's "the universe knows what you want" woo-woo, I'd have to say destiny brought us together. I mean, it was a purely accidental meeting. I needed help with a dead body, and he was paddling by in a kayak. Then I found out he needed a job just as I needed help with the house. And now, we were running a B&B together.

I still wasn't ready for us to be *together* in his perfect partner, many years way. However, just like Whispering Pines feeling more and more like my home the longer I stayed, the more I was around Tripp, the more I wanted to be around him. What was next for us? Who knew, but I sure was ready to find out.

Acknowledgments

I could never release my books without the help of a team of fabulous people behind me.

To Rachael Dahl, my first reader, thanks for helping me figure out when things aren't working.

To Maria Rosera, my editor, for making my sentences shine.

To Steven Novak, for the great covers and for being extraordinarily patient when I say, "not quite yet," too many times.

To my ARC Team, for letting me know about those straggling, pesky typos. Special thanks to Erin Finigan, Bonny Thompson, Carol Edholm, and Michelle Curtis.

As always, to Paul, because I love you so very much.

Suspense and fantasy author Shawn McGuire loves creating characters and places her fans want to return to again and again. She started writing after seeing the first Star Wars movie (that's episode IV) as a kid. She couldn't wait for the next installment to come out so wrote her own. Sadly, those notebooks are long lost, but her desire to tell a tale is as strong now as it was then. She lives in Wisconsin near the beautiful Mississippi River and when not writing or reading, she might be baking, crafting, going for a long walk, or nibbling really dark chocolate.

CPSIA information can be obtained
at www.ICGtesting.com
Printed in the USA
LVHW110151160822
726063LV00006B/129